THE
STOLEN
GIRLS

An absolutely gripping crime mystery with a massive twist

JEZ PINFOLD

DCI Bec Pope Series Book 2

Joffe Books, London
www.joffebooks.com

First published in Great Britain in 2024

Cover art by Nebojša Zorić

ISBN: 978-1-83526-487-4

This is dedicated to Nik, Livi and Martha,
who I couldn't do all this without.
Much love!

CHAPTER ONE

Present day

She stood in the brilliant rectangle of the doorway. Silhouetted against the fierce sunlight, arms outstretched as if preparing for a crucifixion. She was quite still, her body only wavering slightly, as if she were carrying an almost unbearable weight. Unable to escape from the coagulated blood that covered her plain, pale yellow dress, her arms, legs, hair.

DCI Bec Pope and DI James Brody walked down the stairs at Charing Cross Police Station, each holding a file, on their way to a team meeting. Both had their sleeves rolled up, sweltering in the heat of an exceptional London summer — the hottest since '76, when the whole country was scorched for weeks. As they neared the bottom of the stairs, they both saw her at the same time and stopped dead.

Pope's eyes widened. The woman looked young, nineteen or twenty. Her blonde hair was unkempt, her frame slight. The blood that covered her screamed danger, and Pope instinctively rushed forwards. But the young woman looked terrified and Pope stopped, not sure exactly what to do.

Brody was not far behind, equally cautious. Pope decided something needed to happen. She took the final step and slowly brought her right hand up, put it on the girl's shoulder, found a small patch without a covering of blood. As she touched her, the girl faltered and Pope reached further around. At this the young woman collapsed, placed all her weight on to Pope. Brody saw what was about to happen and attempted to reach out, but Pope was caught off guard and the women tumbled to the ground, limbs entangled in a twisted mess.

With the two locked at an uncomfortable angle, the young woman stared into Pope's eyes, close and intense, and said only two words.

'Help me.'

CHAPTER TWO

Eight years ago

'Come on. Breakfast. You're going to be late for school.'

Did it have to be a battle every day? Emma Lowrie continued her part of the morning ritual. At least that would be carried out with efficiency and relatively good humour. As she reached up to the cupboard for plates and bowls, her husband, Mike, shuffled into the kitchen and gave her a kiss on the cheek.

'I slept so badly last night,' he complained. 'We need a new mattress, that one's hopeless. Let's go out this weekend and buy a new one. What do you think?'

What Emma thought was that if Mike didn't stay up so late marking books, grading papers and planning lessons, he might actually be able to relax properly before he went to bed and that might help him get some decent sleep. It would also be a great deal less expensive than a new mattress. That, however, is not what she said.

'Good idea. Let's have a look online this evening and get a sense of prices.'

Mike sat down with a satisfied smile, poured himself a bowl of cereal and reached for the milk.

'How does your day look?' she asked.

'*Macbeth* with Year Ten, followed by poetry with Year Seven, and then a fabulous afternoon of the difference between the definite and indefinite articles with Year Eight.'

'Sounds exciting,' she replied. He raised an eyebrow, then began devouring his breakfast.

Emma marched out of the kitchen to the bottom of the stairs. 'Are you on your way down?'

'I'm coming,' she heard from somewhere upstairs. The sense of irritation behind the words was palpable. The joys of waking a thirteen-year-old girl. She returned to the kitchen.

'Are you going to be late home tonight?' Emma asked.

'No, shouldn't be. I've got a meeting at four, but that won't last more than an hour.'

At that point the relative calm of the kitchen evaporated as the third occupant of the house walked in, a casual glance at the clock. She looked carefully coiffed and made-up, her uniform immaculately pressed, her school tie perfectly knotted. Emma could remember what it was like to be thirteen, parading in front of your peers all day for the sole purpose of being judged — your hair, your clothes, your make-up. She considered commenting on the length of the skirt but thought better of it. *Choose your battles*, her mother would say.

Emma asked what the day had in store for her daughter, who listed her lessons without enthusiasm. Maths, science and French. Emma commented that it sounded like an interesting day. The parent's job was to supply unflappable optimism in the face of relentless negativity, right?

Emma looked on as her daughter prepared a rushed, simple breakfast. Something didn't feel quite right. Her daughter seemed . . . edgy. Was that it? She couldn't quite put her finger on it. 'Everything OK, sweetheart? You don't quite seem yourself this morning.'

'Yeah, just tired.'

Emma felt a pinch somewhere inside her. Should she push?

'I'll be late home today. I'm trying out for the drama club.'

Emma's shoulders relaxed a little. 'Wow, that sounds great. Do you think you've got a good chance?'

'I dunno. There's a lot of kids going for it, and some of them are really good.'

'I'm sure you'll be brilliant. What time do you think you'll be home?' Despite the developing independence, it was still difficult to let go. Force of habit.

'I should be home by five thirty.'

Mike got up and picked up his briefcase. He said goodbye and went out to the hall.

Emma followed him out, watched as he put on his overcoat.

'What are your plans for the day?' he asked.

'I'm meeting Jo for coffee later this morning. Then we're going to try to find a present for Mum.'

'Oh, yeah. Her sixtieth.'

'Yup, next Thursday.'

'Do you have any idea what you're going to get?'

'Absolutely none whatsoever! That's why I'm enlisting Jo's help. I'm hoping she can give me some inspiration.'

'Good luck.'

They kissed, and Mike went out to the car. She watched him pull out of the driveway.

There was no reason for Emma to notice the dark blue Volvo parked across the road, some way further down. Or the figure sitting behind the wheel.

'OK, time's getting on.' The roll of the eyes that greeted this reminder was predictable. But, again, old habits die hard, and she felt the justification of the righteous parent as her daughter rushed upstairs.

Emma waited patiently for a couple of minutes. Should she call up? Then her daughter was down, putting on her jacket — impractical but fashionable — and opening the front door. They said goodbye and Emma watched her turn left out of the drive. No more school runs for her. She noticed the large bag on her daughter's shoulder and considered how much she had to carry for one day's studying. More than usual today.

She closed the door. Now the rest of the family were taken care of and packed off to work and school, it was time to organize herself for the day. She texted Jo to confirm their trip, looking forward to meeting her friend. She made herself a cup of coffee and went upstairs to get ready. It was 8.45 a.m. She was in good time.

As she prepared herself for the day ahead, thinking about her mother's birthday present and her daughter's ambitions for the school drama club, Emma Lowrie was blissfully unaware that very soon none of these things would be of concern to her. She was also unaware that a short distance down the road the driver's side door of the dark blue estate was slowly opening, and the occupant was getting out. She had not seen her daughter quickly change direction as soon as her mother went back inside the house, and she certainly did not see her climb into the passenger side of the car, followed by the man getting back into the driver's side and quietly closing the door.

CHAPTER THREE

Present day

'Help me.'

Pope looked back into the young woman's eyes and saw the look. The look that all victims get when they are unable to comprehend what has just happened to them. Unable to understand the depths to which some human beings will go in order to cause damage and misery to others. It was unmistakable.

Pope looked up, decisive. 'Call an ambulance. Tell them to hurry.'

Brody pulled his phone from his pocket, dialled the number. Pope meanwhile sought to extricate herself from the tangle on the floor and then lifted the woman up, leading her the few steps to a seating area, where she slumped on to the nearest chair. Brody stepped back, talking on the phone. Pope went to join him, but the woman held her hand suddenly very tightly. Pope jolted backwards and was about to pull her hand free, when the woman again locked eyes with her.

'Stay with me.'

Pope hesitated, then nodded and sat down. She caught Brody's warning look.

'I'm just going to talk to my colleague,' said Pope, but the woman's hands remained firm.

'Please. Don't go.'

Pope understood. The blood, the shock, the need for security and reassurance. She needed to find out what had happened to this woman. And where the blood had come from.

'What's your name?' Pope's voice was gentle.

The woman looked blankly at her, seemed to be trying to recollect something, to articulate her thoughts. Brody finished the call and came close to listen.

'What's your name?' she repeated.

Again, a pause. Then, 'I don't know.'

'You don't know your name?' Pope tried not to react.

'I don't remember.'

'OK. Where have you come from today? Where were you before you came here?'

A vacant look. 'I don't know.'

Pope glanced at Brody, who raised his eyebrows. She really wanted to ask whose blood was all over her but she'd likely get the same answer and might upset this young woman even further.

'OK. An ambulance is on the way now. They'll take you to hospital and we'll get you checked out.'

The woman looked terrified. 'Will you come with me?'

Pope faltered but knew then she was in this for the long haul. 'Yes, I'll be with you all the way and get you settled in. Then we can see if you remember anything once the doctors have checked you over.'

The paramedics arrived quickly, and the woman held tighter to Pope's hand. Both were male and Pope wondered if this was the problem. She explained to them that it might be better to get her to the hospital first and that she would ride in the ambulance with them. The paramedics led the two women out, followed by Brody.

'Follow us in the car.'

'Will do,' replied Brody. He helped them into the ambulance and one of the paramedics closed the door behind them.

Pope caught Brody's eye through the window. Whatever he was thinking, he kept it to himself.

* * *

The drive to St Thomas' Hospital was quick, the flashing lights carving smoothly through the morning traffic of central London. The inside of the ambulance was stifling, the air outside already at an uncomfortable temperature. As they passed the Houses of Parliament and crossed Westminster Bridge, the Thames attempted to sparkle in the sunlight and gave the appearance, if not the reality, of cooling down the city. The paramedic in the back with them made attempts to talk to his patient but received nothing in return except wary glances. The woman moved away from him and even closer to Pope. She shook her head and they rode the rest of the trip in silence.

As they pulled up to the entrance to accident and emergency, Pope was reminded of the last time she was in a hospital. On a previous case, the death of a witness in protective custody, and at the same time, the diagnosis of a family member that would prove to have far-reaching consequences. She was surprised at the strength of her feelings, the rawness of the guilt and the grief, and reminded herself that it was almost a year ago. But the emotions were still raw, the repercussions ongoing. She wondered if her reaction to this woman was due in part to her inability to save the witness last year. But she banished the thought as the back doors of the ambulance were thrown open outside the hospital and reality took over.

Brody had pulled up behind them and got out of the car. They helped the young woman into a wheelchair brought out by a nurse, who pushed her in through the entrance. Pope walked alongside, Brody a few steps behind. The nurse took her straight to a curtained-off area, reserved for the most serious cases where privacy is vital. She was helped into a bed and the wheelchair removed, the nurse promising to return in a few minutes to triage the patient.

Pope and Brody pulled up chairs and sat down against the wall. It seemed relatively civilized for an NHS accident and emergency department. No one spoke until the doctor arrived. He was tall, broad, and Pope guessed he played rugby. He looked young, perhaps fifteen years younger than her. As he walked towards his patient, she flinched, then drew her knees up to her chest, shivering.

Pope went swiftly over to her, placed a hand on her arm. The doctor, not long out of medical school, was taken aback.

Turning away from the young woman, Pope reduced her voice to a whisper. 'Is there any chance of a female doctor? I think that might be more successful.'

He nodded, looking slightly offended.

As soon as he left the room the woman became calmer, seemed to relax. Pope was becoming more certain of her diagnosis. She sat down again and leaned back in the chair. Just then, the door opened and a different doctor and a nurse, both female, entered the room. Again, the woman tensed, but less so this time. The doctor introduced herself to the woman and nodded to Pope and Brody to indicate she had been apprised of the situation. She sat on the side of the bed and ran through what tests they were going to do. The young woman seemed to accept this and the two set about checking blood pressure, temperature, heart rate and other vital signs. Pope was glad to be able to take a back seat for a few minutes. She sat next to Brody.

'What do you think?' she asked under her breath.

'Where has that blood come from? It's clearly not hers.'

Pope nodded. 'I think we need to get her moved. She needs someone outside the door, and to be away from the bustle of A & E.' She didn't need to spell it out: the woman had either discovered whoever's blood this was or caused it. If the latter, she could be dangerous and needed to be isolated.

'Call the station and organize a couple of officers here ASAP. I'll talk to the doctor about moving her.'

Brody got up and left the room.

When they had finished the examination, the doctor spoke briefly to her patient, then came over to Pope.

'All her vitals are in good shape, although her blood pressure seems a little high for someone of her age, but I guess that's to be expected in her current situation. I'd like to run some additional tests to check for trauma to the head and neck, bearing in mind the apparent amnesia.'

'Is there likely to be a physical cause, or could it be psychological?' asked Pope.

'Either. Amnesia can be psychologically induced but our initial position would always be to check for physical damage.'

'Is it possible to move her to another room, where we can have some security outside?'

The doctor said that she would arrange that now and for an orderly to take her there. Pope thanked her and she left just as Brody was returning.

'Officers on the way.'

'Great. They're going to see about moving her.'

After a seemingly interminable twenty minutes in the pervasive heat, an orderly arrived with another wheelchair and the young woman was taken to the fifth floor, Pope and Brody following. Once she was settled in her new bed, exhaustion set in and she dozed off. Pope and Brody went outside and closed the door. They moved down the corridor, a few yards away from the room.

'Well, this is odd.' Brody's face wore a half-smile.

'Indeed. She can't even tell me her name. She seems to have total amnesia.'

'Yes. *Seems* to have.'

'What? You don't believe her?'

'I have no idea. It's a convenient way to avoid difficult questions. She wouldn't be the first to try it on. You feel she's telling us the truth?'

Pope was quiet for a moment. 'Yes . . . I know you're right. But . . . I don't know. There's something about her.' She struggled to finish the thought appropriately. 'She seems pretty genuine to me. Faking that level of distress takes a lot of doing.'

'It does,' agreed Brody. 'But it's not impossible.'

'Her reaction to men seems quite extreme. She was shaking when that first doctor came in.'

'Yeah, I noticed that. Do you think she's been abused?'

'From her reactions and appearance, it certainly wouldn't surprise me. I wonder if it's gone even further than that, though,' said Pope.

'What do you mean?'

'The way she presents, the fear. Maybe trafficking.'

'Hopefully we can identify her and find out if that's the case.'

'We'll keep an open mind. Can you give the station a call and see if they've got anything useful? And get Forensics down here. We need to get that blood to the lab. Tell them to send a female tech.'

Brody took off down the corridor, tapping his phone. Pope paused to glance at hers, sighed upon seeing an urgent message from Superintendent Fletcher, then silently returned to the room. Lying in bed with her eyes closed, the young woman appeared serene. She wondered what was going on below the surface, in her dreams, if she was sleeping deeply enough to dream. Pope looked around, noticed the lacklustre decoration of the room, in need of serious renovation. The drab and faded furnishings were not conducive to mental and physical recovery. She wondered who designed the interiors of British hospitals and if other countries suffered from the same decorative affliction.

As Pope took in her surroundings, her eyes landed back on the woman. She was slight, angular, almost malnourished. But there was also strength there, a stubborn tenacity. She got the feeling that she wouldn't want to cross her and wondered if someone else had made that mistake.

Pope stopped, suddenly aware of something. She leaned forward, studied the woman in front of her. Pope realized that she had the strong sense that she knew her. She tried to shake the thought, which hadn't materialized until now. But it was there, strong and resilient. Pope couldn't work it out, couldn't find the context. But she was pretty sure that their mystery woman was someone she had met before.

CHAPTER FOUR

Pope decided that she would keep her suspicion that she knew this woman to herself for the time being. She couldn't work out if she really knew her, or if it was her memory playing tricks. Either way, it would serve no purpose to discuss it with Brody at this point. She was feeling wrong-footed, too caught up in the case, and knew that this was the easiest way to compromise her objectivity and clarity of thought. It had not escaped her attention that this young woman, all of nineteen or twenty, was a little younger than Tina Waterson would have been if she had lived. Yet again, this past case, her first as a homicide detective eight years ago, encroached on her thinking. She would need to ensure it didn't work its way into her mind the way it had last year. She couldn't let that happen again.

Her thinking was interrupted by Brody's return.

'How did you get on?' asked Pope.

'Forensics are on the way to collect the clothes and process her, should be here within the hour. Nothing interesting yet, although Thompson and Miller are working to sort CCTV and checking missing persons. They'll update us as soon as they find anything. Two officers will be here in the next thirty minutes. And Fletcher wants to see you as soon as we've finished here. Miller said he was quite insistent.'

'He's texted me already. Wants to know what to say to the media.' Superintendent Richard Fletcher was always on the lookout for an angle in media interviews. The public face of the police often seemed to be his primary concern.

They turned their attention to the woman lying in the bed in front of them. They'd been talking quietly, but it had woken her anyway, and she lifted herself slightly, so that she was more sitting than lying. It looked uncomfortable. Brody went to help her, but the woman recoiled and he stepped back, offered a quiet apology.

Pope indicated with her head for Brody to take a seat and made a writing motion with her hand. He nodded and withdrew his notebook and a pen from his jacket pocket. She then pulled up the other chair next to the bed and sat down. The woman looked at her, unflinching. Pope held her gaze for a moment, but then looked down at the floor and rearranged herself, finding the intensity of the woman's eyes uncomfortable.

'I'd like to ask you a few questions, if you feel up to it?'

The woman just looked at her, said nothing.

'There are a few things we need to know, and it would be great to get that out of the way now, so you can get some proper rest.'

The woman looked at her for another few seconds, then nodded slowly, as if she was having to think very hard. Pope smiled and turned to check that Brody was ready to take notes.

'Can I ask you again for your name? Do you remember?'

The woman again seemed to be trying to think, to search far back in her mind for the one thing that everyone knows, that everyone *has* to know. She shook her head slowly. 'I don't know what my name is.'

Pope didn't say anything for a moment. She was giving her a bit of time, but also trying to gauge the response, trying to assess if she was telling the truth. Pope knew that Brody would be doing exactly the same thing.

'OK. Don't worry. Can you tell us why you came to the police station at Charing Cross? Were you close by? Had you been there before?'

Again, she looked to be thinking hard, trying desperately to remember something. 'I don't know.'

Long-term and short-term memory both seemed equally absent. This struck Pope as unusual, although she wasn't an expert on memory.

'Did you recognize the building when you walked in? At the police station?'

Before each answer there was a lengthy pause. 'No, I don't think so. I can't remember.' A tear appeared in her eye and she looked away from Pope for the first time. She brought up her hand and wiped it away with the sleeve of her hospital gown. Pope saw she was struggling with the loss of identity, the loss of self.

Pope put her hand on the woman's arm. 'Don't worry. It's fine. We can come back to it later. But maybe asking you the questions will jog something in your memory, however slight.'

The woman nodded, sniffed, composed herself and lifted her head. She was ready to try at least. Pope noted the stubbornness, the tenacity she thought she had seen in her earlier.

'Do you have any family? Parents? Brothers or sisters?'

Again, the answer came after a pause, and again it was the same. 'I don't know.'

It was beginning to look like a waste of time, and Pope worried that it would even be counterproductive, that it would be so frustrating that the woman might withdraw further and be unable, or unwilling, to answer any questions.

'I think we'll take a break, let you get some rest.'

The woman nodded, then suddenly started and, with a reflex movement, pulled the covers further up to her chin. Pope looked back over her shoulder and saw that two police officers had arrived outside and were looking in, trying to signal to her and Brody that they were there. She gave them a thumbs up and they moved out of view. The woman relaxed a little.

Pope didn't know what to think. On one hand she seemed genuine. That level of vulnerability was very difficult to fake. She appeared terrified of any male figure and of the officers outside the door. This certainly reinforced her suspicion of abuse and possible abduction, being held against her will. And there was a decidedly distant, dislocated quality to the way the woman presented. She was vacant, no memories to help her construct a personality, no context. Pope was reminded of *Invasion of the Body Snatchers*, but maybe she was being uncharitable.

It was also possible that she was playing a part. She came in covered in blood, and claiming to remember nothing would be one way to dodge difficult questions. If that was the case, however, why turn up at the station? That didn't make any sense. Pope would need to consult someone more expert in matters of memory than herself.

Just then there was a knock and a nurse opened the door. She was holding a tray of food and came in soundlessly, closing the door behind her. She took the tray over to the bed and placed it in front of the young woman with an encouraging smile.

'Shepherd's pie.'

Nobody said anything.

'Right. I'll leave that with you and I'll be back a bit later to collect your stuff.' She left Pope watching the woman, who was gazing at the food, unmoving.

'I'd eat something if I were you,' said Pope. 'It probably won't be great, but it will make you feel a lot better.' She nodded at the tray and smiled. Slowly the woman picked up a fork, gingerly started to pick at the contents of the plate in front of her. It was as if she had been waiting for permission to eat. She was clearly starving, however, as she soon began to tuck in and quickly devoured the meal. With her bedraggled hair and slight frame, she appeared almost feral. Pope turned away to allow her some dignity. The woman seemed to notice and, embarrassed, used her sleeve to wipe her mouth. Pope felt incredibly sorry for her and at that moment was utterly convinced that she was telling the truth.

When she had finished eating, Pope moved the tray down to the bottom of the bed just as the door opened.

The forensic team, two female officers, had arrived. Pope explained that this might help them identify her and get her back to her family. She tried to gauge her reaction, but the woman seemed to accept it and Pope told her that she would be outside if needed.

While the forensic technicians got to work, Pope and Brody left the room and walked to the far end of the corridor, out of earshot of the two officers on guard outside.

Pope spoke first. 'Is it usual to suffer complete memory loss? As in, short-term, long-term, the whole lot?'

'I don't think so. It's called global memory loss. But it's pretty rare. Everything goes. Often a response to some type of trauma.'

'So, a sort of PTSD?'

'Pretty much. It would be helpful to talk to someone who knows a bit more about it.'

'We'll sort that when we get back to the station. Let's wait until Forensics have finished, then we'll go in and let her know we're going off for a while.'

Brody eyed his boss. 'Do you still believe her?'

'Nothing's changed since you last asked me that question.'

'I know. It's just . . . it all seems pretty convenient. Too easy. Total memory loss.'

'You just said yourself, it does happen.'

'I did. But I also said it's pretty unusual.'

'Well, we're not going to find out standing here playing yes-or-no games. Can you see if you can find us a cold drink?'

'Good idea. I'm boiling in here.' Brody called the elevator and took off in search of refreshment.

Pope sat down on a chair just next to where they had been talking. She ran a hand around the back of her neck. She'd been waking up with a painful neck for weeks now — that is, on the occasions when she'd been getting anything you could call meaningful sleep. She leaned her head back and rolled it left to right and back again, the universal and generally unsuccessful method to relieve neck pain. The heat didn't help. London was not equipped for hot weather like this and on the rare occasions when it hit, it could be unbearable. She looked around to see if there were any signs of air conditioning in the corridor but didn't see anything. When she'd lived in New York for a year she remembered all public buildings having very effective air con. She was suddenly struck by melancholy — it was almost twenty years ago. She was sure that Brody would be able to furnish her with scientific or philosophical reasons for the rapid passing of time.

Pope's musings on time and public infrastructure were interrupted by the techs coming out of the young woman's room. They closed the door quietly behind them. They seemed to be handling the situation with the appropriate sensitivity.

The one in charge approached Pope. 'All done. We've got all we need. She seems pretty jumpy. Scared of her own shadow.'

'We don't know what she's been through yet. There may be a very good reason for that.'

'There may,' she replied. Their job was not really to consider the context.

'I need the results ASAP.'

'Doesn't everybody?'

Pope stiffened at the woman's flippant tone. 'She's covered in someone's blood, we don't know whose, and she can't remember what happened, can't even remember her own name. You'll need to prioritize this.' This came out sharper than Pope had intended, but it seemed to do the trick.

The tech looked slightly sheepish. 'OK. We'll get this to the front of the queue.'

'Good. Let me know the moment you have anything.' With this, Pope walked past the two technicians and into the woman's room. They walked towards the elevator, muttering conspiratorially. Pope assumed they were complaining at the way she had spoken to them. She didn't care.

She padded over to the bed and smiled. 'I'm going back to the station now. I need to try to work out who on earth you are,' she said. The woman looked unsure. 'It'll be fine. There are two guards outside, but they won't come in unless you call them. They're just there to make sure everything's OK and to get you anything you need. The nurses and doctors will also be around. You can call them if you need anything by pulling this.' She indicated the orange cord by the side of the bed. She had no idea if the woman knew what this was or remembered why you use it. She assumed under normal circumstances every adult in the country knew what it was for. But these were not normal circumstances.

'I'll see you later or first thing tomorrow.'

As she turned to leave, she felt a light hand on her arm.

'If you find anything out . . . I mean, my name, or anything . . .'

'Of course. As soon as I know anything, I'll be back. In the meantime, I promise you we're going to keep you safe.'

The woman leaned back and closed her eyes. Pope studied her face for a while before leaving. She knew exactly what she was looking for. She didn't find it.

Pope told the officers outside to contact her if there were any problems, then met Brody coming out of the elevator and directed him straight back in, pushing the button to take them to the ground floor. The elevator was even hotter than the other parts of the hospital. Luckily Brody had found water and Pope took a bottle, finishing it in one long swig.

Once they'd found the car, Brody drove, taking them away from the hospital entrance and back over the Thames. He was guiding them around Parliament Square and past the Houses of Parliament before either of them spoke.

'This is ridiculous,' he finally said. 'We have an unidentified woman, who could be perpetrator or victim, covered in blood from an as yet unidentified source. We don't know where she came from or how she got to the station. We don't know if she's telling us the truth or spinning us an elaborate lie and, at the moment, we have no way of finding out.'

'That pretty much sums it up,' replied Pope.

'So, what's our next move?'

Pope considered this. 'We need the forensics back, then we can get to work on trying to identify her and maybe find out where the blood came from. We'll hopefully have CCTV of her arriving at the station and that might help us trace her movements. Or at least figure out how she got there.'

'Do you think it's worth putting out her picture to try to help with identification?' asked Brody.

'Not yet. I want to see if we can find out before the circus comes to town. Once the media get a hold of this story we'll have journalists and photographers swarming into the hospital and that's the last thing she needs. I'm going to try to convince Fletcher to keep this quiet for as long as possible. At least until we know what we're dealing with.'

'He won't be happy with that.'

'No, well, his relationship with the media is not our main concern at the moment.'

'Just bear in mind that we could have two very different situations here.'

'I know.'

She looked out of the window as Brody guided them past Trafalgar Square. Pope could see a small group of protesters with placards. She couldn't read what they said, but the protesters were mainly young women, most around the same age as the woman lying in the hospital bed, and they all looked happy to be there, pleased to be able to make their voices heard for a common cause. She leaned back in the seat, closed her eyes and prepared for the investigation ahead.

CHAPTER FIVE

There was no air conditioning in the common areas of Charing Cross Police Station and today it felt like an oven. Just walking the two storeys up from the underground car park brought Pope out in a sweat. The past couple of months had been far from a usual London summer. At least they had the fans out in the office. They were up to combatting a bit of heat, but they offered little resistance to the stifling temperature today. Pope walked right up to one and stood in front of it, enjoying the brief respite.

DS Adam Miller looked up to see who was blocking his cool air. 'Hey, what are you doing?'

'Pulling rank,' replied Pope, turning around to get the cool air on her back. She nodded at Stephen Thompson, the Tech Support officer, who was engrossed in something on his computer screen. 'Let's see what we've got.'

Pope left the solace of the fan and she and Brody sat down around the larger table in the open-plan room. Thompson and Miller joined them.

'OK. Where are we? Miller, do you want to start us off?'

Just then the door opened and a tall man in a smart navy blue suit marched in. His shoes were buffed to a mirror-like shine and his tie had been knotted with extraordinary precision. His hair was combed with equal care. Superintendent Richard Fletcher wanted people to take him very seriously.

'Bec, James, how's she doing?'

'She's not in great shape. We were just about to have a catch-up,' replied Pope.

Fletcher looked at his watch. Expensive. He looked like he had somewhere else he would rather be, but took a chair and moved it slightly backwards, so that he was a little removed from the rest of the team. He folded his arms and waited.

'Miller?' Pope tried to pick up where they'd left off.

'I've been looking at missing persons, but no luck so far. There're lots of close matches. I mean, there's a lot of missing young women, but none that match her yet. I'm still working on it.'

'How far back have you gone?' asked Pope.

'Six months at the moment, but if I don't find her, I'll widen the time frame. The problem will be the number of hits.'

'How old do we think she is?' asked Fletcher.

Pope answered. 'She looks to be around nineteen or twenty. But she can't even remember her name, let alone how old she is.'

'So her memory loss is total?' asked Fletcher.

'Yes. Nothing there at all.'

'OK.' Fletcher gave the signal to carry on.

'Thompson, any luck with CCTV?' asked Pope.

'Well, we have some, but it doesn't help us much.'

Pope nodded to encourage him to continue.

'We've found her arriving at the station. She walks up Agar Street from the direction of the Strand, but no car as yet. I'm still tracking back from there. I hope to have something for you soon.'

'Anything from Forensics?' Fletcher asked Pope.

'They've only just left the hospital, so they won't have anything just yet. But I've asked them to prioritize this and hopefully they'll do the blood comparison first. We need to know who the blood came from and to confirm it didn't come from her. We can't do much until we know who she is, whose blood it is and where she came from. We might get something from her clothes or under her fingernails if she was attacked.'

Fletcher looked at Brody. 'James? What does your instinct tell you?'

'My instinct?'

'Yes,' replied Fletcher. 'How genuine is this woman? The memory loss. Is she putting it on?'

Pope wondered why Fletcher hadn't asked her the question. Had the two been in communication about Brody's suspicions without her knowing? She made a mental note to find out as soon as she got the chance.

'I don't know, to be honest, sir. It's really difficult. She comes across as very genuine.' At this he looked at Pope, who stared at him with, she hoped, a neutral expression. 'But it's very convenient. She could well be playing us, although if she is, she's doing an extremely good job of it.'

'Pope?' Fletcher turned to her.

She turned from Brody to him, after a beat. 'I think Brody's right that either is a possibility. But if you want my opinion, I'd say she's genuine. She doesn't remember anything. Who she is, where she is, where she's been. She can't remember family, friends. It's as you said, total memory loss. And that's very difficult to fake. To maintain that level of subterfuge, of total amnesia, seems beyond what she's capable of at the present time. And she's been through something horrific one way or another. She's covered in blood and presents with all the signs of PTSD and abuse. That could certainly explain her symptoms.'

'Alternatively, she could be the perpetrator of a horrific act and this is simply an elaborate way of covering her tracks,' said Fletcher.

'As we said, either is a possibility.' Pope was irritated now. She looked at Brody to make sure he knew it.

'Right, so how do we find out?' asked Fletcher.

Pope spoke. 'We'll continue to look at the missing persons database and try to track the CCTV to see if that gives us anything. Hopefully the forensics will be back shortly, at least the initial report. She didn't have a phone on her, so we won't get any help there. I'm going to call Dr Tobias Darke and see if he'll come and speak to her, see what he thinks. He might be able to help us with the memory stuff, or at least recommend someone who can.'

Fletcher was about to speak when the phone rang.

'Hang on a moment.' Pope picked up the phone. She listened. 'Are you sure? Hundred per cent? OK. Thanks, and let me know when you have anything else.'

She hung up. 'That was Forensics. The blood taken from our woman is definitely not a match to the blood on her clothes.' Her admonishment of the Forensics officer had obviously had some effect.

'So, she's a suspect.' Fletcher sounded as if he wanted to prove a point.

'Not necessarily,' said Pope. 'Let's keep an open mind.'

'Right. But this young woman has most likely committed a serious crime and we need to treat her as a person of interest.' Fletcher directed this to Pope and it didn't invite discussion.

'We don't know that,' replied Pope.

'Don't know what? We know that she has someone else's blood all over her. That's all you need at this point.'

'As I said, we'll keep an open mind and investigate accordingly.'

Pope was combative, and the others in the room looked uncomfortably from her to Fletcher and back again.

'What other explanation do you favour, DCI Pope? You clearly seem very reluctant to face the obvious facts of this case.'

Pope was furious at the challenge to her professionalism and objectivity, but she was determined not to react. She had had a great deal of practice in restraining her anger in her dealings with Fletcher over the years.

'I don't favour any explanation at this point. I'll let the evidence lead my conclusions, rather than guesswork.' Fletcher opened his mouth to speak, but Pope continued. 'There are a number of possible scenarios, not least that she may have been attacked and had to defend herself. She has all the hallmarks of an abuse victim, and as such, we need to tread very carefully. The trauma she may have suffered, which could have triggered her current state, needs to be at the forefront of our minds. I don't want to make that worse.'

Pope could see him gauging his response. 'OK, DCI Pope. For the moment, we'll go with your approach.'

Pope was surprised. Maybe he was considering the potential negative publicity if the Metropolitan Police were seen to have treated an abuse victim as a suspect. It wouldn't be the first time.

Fletcher's face hardened. 'But I want her closely guarded at all times while she's in the hospital, then we'll decide where she goes after she's discharged. I don't want our feelings clouding our judgement.'

Pope wasn't sure exactly what that meant.

'There are two guards outside her room at the moment. The doctors will let us know if there's any change, or if they find out anything else that's of use to us.'

'I want to know when you know, DCI Pope.' He turned and left, his order hanging in the air.

After the others had moved back to their desks, Pope looked at Brody. 'Did you talk to him about this when we were at the hospital?'

'Of course not,' replied Brody, the shock showing in his expression.

'Well, he seemed to be on message with your scepticism before he even heard anything.'

'What? You think I'm the only one who doesn't believe her? You think I'm whispering to Fletcher to get him onside? To undermine you and forward my own agenda?'

Hearing it put like that, Pope realized how ridiculous she sounded.

She sat down in the chair behind her desk. 'I'm sorry. I know you wouldn't do that.' She ran her hand through her hair and around the back of her neck. 'It's just Fletcher. He always manages to say the wrong thing. I'm sorry,' she repeated.

'It's OK. It's a very odd situation. But Fletcher's right. It doesn't look good for her. The most obvious likely scenario is that she killed someone.'

She knew Brody was right. But she desperately didn't want him to be.

* * *

It was late and Pope needed to go home. Needed to sleep. Everyone else had left, agreeing to meet early the next morning. She had stayed on to finish the last bits of paperwork. Now she just needed to make one final call before she left. She picked up the phone and dialled a number from memory. The call was answered quickly.

'Tobias. How are you? Hope it's not too late to be calling?'

'Of course not. How nice to hear from you. How are things?' His booming voice was at once familiar and reassuring.

She could hear Tobias Darke's dogs barking in the background. He quietened them down, which took a while. She guessed he was about to take them out for a late-night walk in Richmond Park.

'Fine.' They weren't, of course. But she didn't feel like detailing the catastrophe of her personal life and her struggle to view her current case objectively. 'But I need your help with something.' Tobias Darke was a long-time friend of Pope and an excellent criminal psychologist who had assisted the Metropolitan Police on a number of occasions over the years.

'Of course, Bec. What can I do for you?'

Pope outlined the case and the apparent amnesia of the young woman currently in St Thomas' Hospital. She needed Darke to assess the extent to which her memory loss was genuine. He told her that he was happy to help and would meet her at St Thomas' at nine sharp tomorrow morning. She thanked him and replaced the receiver.

Pope leaned back in her chair and looked out of the window. The view wasn't much — her office wasn't high enough to see over the buildings opposite — but it gave some sense of space in this crowded and at times claustrophobic city. She considered what Fletcher had said, and what he had implied. She usually prided herself on her objectivity. Was he right that she wasn't seeing things clearly? But Pope was pretty convinced that the young woman's trauma was genuine. What could she see that Fletcher and Brody could not? Was it to do with gender politics, or was it simply investigative and personality differences entirely unconnected with the fact that she was a woman? She wasn't sure.

It was also the case that the last woman Pope had been responsible for in a hospital, Karen Tarling, had died. Were the events of the previous autumn clouding her judgement? She thought back to the Tina Waterson case, and was suddenly struck by how long had passed since Tina had been found dead, and how many years since Pope had failed to find her killer.

There were too many unanswered questions, the most personal of which was why this case was so problematic for her. She needed to get her head out of it and leave. Pope closed down her computer, made a half-hearted attempt to tidy her desk and turned off the office lights.

As she walked down the main stairs she signed out, said goodnight to the officer at the reception desk and headed down to the underground garage. She opened the door to the concrete enclosure and was hit by a wall of heat as she walked towards her car. The garage was dimly lit, the lights casting a yellowish glow, and it struck her how alienating a place it was to start and end every working day. She located her car, spent some time searching her bag for the keys and, once she had eventually found them, got in and started the engine.

As she pulled out of the automatic gates and on to Agar Street, a drunk walked out in front of her and she had to brake hard. He stuck his middle finger up to her and shouted a string of obscenities she couldn't really hear. She didn't react. Her mind was elsewhere, now narrowing in on one thing. Where the hell had she seen this woman before?

CHAPTER SIX

The drive home was quick and quiet. Unusually so. Once she was off the Old Kent Road there was little traffic. She'd spent too much of the day, and evening, at work. She threaded through the smaller streets that led home, her driving memory taking over. It almost surprised her when she realized she was pulling into her street.

Pope parked and got out of the car. As she walked up the drive, she noted the total darkness of the house. Most other houses either side of hers had lights on, cars in the drive or on the streets. Pope's showed no signs of life. It was a building, not a home. She knew it was her fault. That she had caused this.

She found her keys and let herself in, closing the front door behind her. As she walked in, again the heat hit her. Turning lights on at least gave the place a slightly more welcoming feel and she could almost pretend that things were normal. Almost.

The stale, dry air of the hospital had given her a headache, one that the lingering heat did little to improve. She knew that the sensible thing to do would be to drink several glasses of water, take a shower and go straight to bed. Instead she opened a bottle of red wine, poured herself a large glass and put her vinyl copy of *Kind of Blue* on the turntable. She fell into a deep armchair, took a sip of wine and let the first track wash over her. It didn't help her headache, but she felt herself start to relax.

She looked around the room. She was living in someone else's house, sitting in someone else's chair, drinking out of someone else's glass. At least the vinyl belonged to her.

Alex and his daughters had left around the time of her father's funeral last year. Though Pope could pinpoint exactly the date they'd moved out, it felt much longer ago. She and Alex had been in regular contact, they were still trying to sort things out. But she'd put them all in terrible danger and he could no longer accept that as part of their relationship. Hannah and Chloe had gone with him, of course. Hannah had emailed her a number of times, but she'd heard nothing from Chloe. Pope understood. When things had gone so very wrong, you needed someone to blame. That someone was Pope.

It wasn't over with Alex. At least she didn't think so. But exactly how they were supposed to recover, how he could trust her again and move back in, that was the issue. She didn't have any answers other than the ones she had already given him. She was sorry and it wouldn't happen again. She thought he believed the first part.

Alex, Hannah and Chloe were currently living with his parents just outside London. Not far, but as she felt the emptiness in the house, and the echo of the music around the otherwise silent rooms, it could have been another country. When this case was over, she vowed that she would go to see Alex and really work to establish a new sense of trust. She would make him believe that she would prioritize him and the girls, rather than her job. How many of Pope's resolutions began *When this case is over* . . . ? She took another drink of wine, bigger this time.

She closed her eyes and let the music and the wine work together to take the edge off. As ever, her mind drifted to her current case. She thought about the young woman in the hospital and how terrified she must be. The complete absence of memory, the loss of self, the lack of familiar people or situations. Alone in the hospital bed, guarded by police officers. It was unthinkable. Pope tried to think of what she could do to alleviate the woman's fear but knew that what she needed to do was find out what had happened. The rest was outside her control. Only when this woman knew who she was and why she had ended up in Pope's arms on the floor of Charing Cross Police Station would she be able to begin to recover from this ordeal.

Pope knew a little about memory — how unreliable it was and how reliable most people thought it was. This often created problems, not least with police witnesses who could be absolutely positive about something they had remembered, a whole scene or a tiny detail, and be completely wrong in their recollection. But she knew little about amnesia and would need to get up to speed on that quickly. What she was sure about, however, was that she believed this woman, though she couldn't put her finger on why her belief was so complete.

Something was niggling away at Pope, something disjointed. She couldn't quite explain it. It wasn't so much that she knew the woman, that she had met her before. But there was a familiarity. That was the only word she could find. Familiarity. She thought again but couldn't get anywhere. As she got older, this seemed to happen with increasing regularity. A piece of the puzzle that she couldn't quite fit into place. Was it age, stress, overwork? Probably all three.

Pope sent a text to Adam Miller to cross-reference her past cases with the details of the woman, just to feel like she was doing something about it. Then she parked the thought, knowing that she would return to it and hoping the answer would reveal itself with a bit of distance.

She looked at her watch. Midnight. She knew she should sleep but was too wired. Instead she went to her laptop and opened the web browser. Where to start? She could only access the missing persons database at work and had never really needed to use it from home. Most of the time she left that type of work to others, Adam Miller or Stephen Thompson. But she needed to be doing something.

Pope typed "Missing woman, 20 years old, London" into the search engine and pressed enter. Her browser refreshed and informed her that she had 190 million hits. She took a deep breath and began to click on the links on the first page. She had planned to look at the first few, but as she moved down the list, she became more and more engrossed in the stories she was reading. Most had pictures of the missing women, and she would check the picture, skim-read the first paragraph and move on. But some were so tragic, so powerfully described, that she ended up reading whole reports. Pope knew the statistics, knew how many women went missing in and around London each year. But reading the individual stories, seeing the photographs, was a different thing. She hadn't been responsible for finding missing persons for many years and this was hard.

One story in particular caught her eye. The picture at the head of the story showed a young woman, about the same age as their case. She had shoulder-length brown hair and was wearing jeans and a T-shirt. She was holding a glass of wine and dancing in a garden with several friends, seemingly without a care in the world. Pope read the text. According to the parents, the young woman had left the house to go grocery shopping and never returned. The parents were frantic, distraught, and had heard nothing since. The photograph was taken three days before she had disappeared. Pope checked the date and saw that the woman had been missing for over two years. She knew it was unlikely the police were actively investigating the case, although it would still technically be open. She knew why it had stood out from the others. It reminded her of the young woman in the hospital. Same age, physically similar. She, too, had to have parents searching for her somewhere. There had to be someone who was waiting for this woman to return. Someone who had contacted the authorities, desperate for news.

She tried to think of ways to narrow the search, to focus in on their case. She tried adding "blonde hair" to the search.

This didn't help much. She started scrolling down, but by the time she'd skim-read the hits on the first three pages, she realized it was a pointless exercise. She would need to leave this to her team and the database in the morning.

Pope checked the clock on her laptop and saw that it was 2.30 a.m. She'd lost track of time. She groaned and closed the browser window. It was still uncomfortably hot, even at this late hour. She looked at her phone and saw no messages waiting or missed calls, and decided it was time to go to sleep.

Lying in bed, Pope closed her eyes, but, as so often happened, sleep eluded her. She guessed she wasn't the only Homicide detective with insomnia. All she could think about was the woman. What was it about her that she felt she knew, but couldn't articulate? Why was Pope so convinced that she was genuine in her amnesia, while both Brody and Fletcher were so sceptical?

She got nowhere, and eventually found sleep, with too many unanswered questions in her head.

CHAPTER SEVEN

After too little sleep, Pope was up early. Eager to get to the hospital, she showered quickly and grabbed a slice of toast and a coffee. She usually skipped breakfast, but she hadn't eaten last night and she needed something. All her work suits had been worn already, so she chose the one that showed the fewest creases and made a mental note to visit the dry cleaners as soon as she got the chance.

The drive to St Thomas' Hospital gave her time to wake up properly and put together her plan for the day. The first thing was to meet Tobias Darke and try to get his observations. He knew much more than she did about memory and there was no one she trusted more to assess this young woman. Then she would need to get back to the station and see how the investigation was progressing.

As she approached the hospital, she noticed a young family walking along the pavement. The two adults were dressed in business wear, the two young children carrying school backpacks. She assumed the parents were dropping their children at a breakfast club before school, on the way to work. As she drew closer, the mother laughed at something the younger child had said and ruffled the girl's hair.

Pope felt a pang of jealousy. This should be her and Alex, Chloe and Hannah. Was this what she wanted? The traditional family unit? It seemed an impossible dream under the current circumstances. She passed the family and pushed the idea out of her head. Something she was very good, and very practised, at doing.

She pulled up, found a parking space and entered reception. It was already warm and Pope knew it was going to be another oppressively hot day. She went to the main desk and explained who she was and that she was expecting a visitor. She briefly described Tobias Darke and asked that he be directed to the appropriate room when he arrived. Pope took the lift to the fifth floor, and as the door opened, she was greeted by the sight of the two officers outside the room.

'Morning,' said Pope. 'All OK?'

'Yes, ma'am. She's been asleep most of the night,' replied one of the officers. 'She woke up around three, but a nurse came in and talked to her. She went back to sleep pretty quickly. I think the sedative must be doing its job.'

Pope nodded and walked past the officers. She looked through the window and saw that the woman was, indeed, still asleep.

Just then she heard the lift doors open and turned to see Tobias Darke stride into the corridor. Darke hadn't changed in the months since Pope had seen him. Still a little overweight, still the full beard, and still an expensive three-piece suit, this time in a smart navy. He was a constant in her ever-changing, unpredictable world. He walked towards Pope and gave her a robust hug as the two officers looked on. Darke then nodded to them, said hello and followed Pope's eyeline into the hospital room.

'Is this our patient?' he asked.

'Yes. Slept most of the night apparently. She's been lightly sedated. We can find the doctor and get her woken up. Shall we have a quick chat before you speak to her?'

'Absolutely,' replied Darke.

Pope led him along the corridor to the chairs she had been sitting in yesterday. They both perched and Darke took a notebook and a pencil out of his briefcase.

'So, what do I need to know?' he asked.

'Well, I gave you the gist on the phone. She turned up at the station yesterday afternoon. Her dress was covered in blood and she collapsed into my arms asking for help.'

Darke was listening, making notes in a cloth-bound oxblood A5 notebook.

'We brought her straight here to get checked over. She seems physically OK. Unhurt. But she claims total amnesia.'

'Did she tell you her name?' asked Darke.

'No. When I say "total", I mean it. She hasn't been able to answer any of the questions I've asked her.'

Darke raised his eyebrows. 'What does your gut tell you?'

'About whether she's genuine?'

'Yes. What sense do you get?'

Pope paused, hoping to indicate a considered response. 'I believe her. I think. She's very convincing. I mean, I'm not an expert on memory. But I'm used to being lied to, and I'm pretty good at spotting that. With her . . . I don't know. If it's not genuine, it's an extremely good act.'

Darke nodded slowly, then smiled. 'Right, well, I'll go in and have a talk with her. Bear in mind, though, that memory is a funny old thing. Very erratic and unpredictable, and unfeasibly complex. I can't guarantee that I'll be able to tell you anything beyond what you already know.'

'I just need an informed opinion, really. We don't know anything other than what I've told you, so anything you can get would be great. And it's sort of your area of expertise, isn't it?'

'Well, assessing prisoners to ascertain if they are competent to stand trial is rather different, but I suppose the principles have something in common. What you really need is a neuropsychological assessment, but you need a specialist for that. That will take a bit of time to organize. In the meantime, I'll do my best.'

'Oh, one more thing,' said Pope.

Darke waited.

'She seems to react badly to men. She's been quite clingy with me when there have been male doctors, police officers, paramedics. So bear that in mind.'

'Are you thinking abuse?' asked Darke.

'Yes, possibly. Of some form. We'll see how she reacts to you.'

He nodded his understanding. They stood up and walked back towards the room where the woman was sleeping. Pope went to find someone to wake her up and check it was OK to talk to her. She returned with the same nurse who had brought the food yesterday.

Pope and Darke let the nurse go in first. She had no trouble waking the young woman, who seemed immediately alert, eyes searching the room then landing on the people standing outside. When the nurse had performed some checks, she came back outside.

'You can go in now.'

'How does she seem?' asked Pope.

'Surprisingly together, considering she's been given a sedative,' replied the nurse.

'Ready?' Pope asked Darke.

'I am.'

Pope went in first, followed by Darke. The girl looked first at Pope, then looked warily at this newcomer.

'Hi,' Pope whispered. 'This is a good friend of mine, Dr Tobias Darke. He's come to have a chat with you this morning, to see how you're getting on. It won't take long.'

'Good morning. Pleased to meet you.' Darke wore a disarming smile.

She still looked wary. 'Will you stay?' she asked Pope.

Pope looked at Darke, who nodded his agreement.

'Of course. If you'd like me to.'

They pulled up chairs and sat down. The woman leaned back against the pillow and shielded herself with the bed covers. She couldn't have pushed herself further away if she had tried.

'How are you feeling this morning?' asked Pope.

The woman didn't say anything.

'Any better than yesterday?' continued Pope.

She returned her gaze. 'A little.'

'That's good.' Pope looked at Darke, indicating he should take over.

He looked down at his notebook, then back up to her. 'DCI Pope said you were having a little difficulty remembering things yesterday.'

The woman looked at him but did not reply.

Darke continued. 'How is that today? It sounds like you had a good night's sleep. Has that helped at all?'

She shook her head slowly.

'Can you tell me your name?'

Again, she shook her head but said nothing.

Darke smiled. 'OK. That's fine. What about your date of birth?'

She seemed to be thinking, searching, but again shook her head.

Darke reached down and withdrew a sheet of A4 paper from his briefcase. Pope hadn't seen this before.

'I'm going to ask you a few questions to try to see if we can work out what's going on with your memory. No problem if you can't answer them, it's just to try to help you. Is that OK with you?'

She nodded.

'Right.' Darke arranged the sheet on his notebook. 'First, can you tell me the date today?'

After a pause, she shook her head.

'Can you tell me who is the prime minister of the United Kingdom?'

Nothing again.

'What about the president of the United States?'

She looked blankly at him.

Darke made a note on the sheet. 'I'm going to name three objects and then I want you to repeat the objects back to me. Let's start with apple, chair, dress.'

The woman was wary, but repeated the words with little hesitation.

'OK, that's good. Very good,' said Darke. 'Now, can you take away seven from one hundred?'

'Ninety-three.'

'Can you take seven away from that figure?'

'Eighty-six.'

'Take seven away again.'

'Seventy-nine.'

'And once more.'

'Seventy-two.'

'Good. Well done.' He shot Pope a look.

'Right. Can you name the three objects I asked you to remember just now?' asked Darke.

She seemed to be thinking hard. It showed on her face. Eventually she shook her head.

'Can you remember any of the objects?' asked Darke.

She shook her head again.

Darke made some notes on the sheet, then continued. He held up his fountain pen. 'What's this?'

She looked at him as if this was a ridiculous question. 'A pen.'

'Good. And this?' He pointed to his wristwatch.

'A watch.'

'And what about this?' he asked, taking his wallet from his jacket pocket.

'A wallet.'

'OK. That's really good. Well done. That's all I need to ask you at the moment.' He stood up.

Pope also got up. 'I'm going to have a chat with Dr Darke and find your doctor. See how long you might have to stay here. I'll be back in a little while. Is there anything you need?'

She looked at Pope warily and shook her head.

'OK, see you in a little while.'

Pope felt the woman's eyes on them as they left the room. She closed the door gently behind them.

'So, what do you think?' she asked Darke.

39

'Shall we go downstairs and have a coffee?'

They took the lift to the ground floor and once they had collected their drinks sat down at an empty table in the hospital cafeteria.

'So?' said Pope.

'Interesting case,' replied Darke. 'As I said, we really need to get her seen by a specialist. Memory is not easy.'

'I know, but what did you think?' Pope was eager to get his opinion.

'First of all, bear in mind that it is very difficult to clinically detect if amnesia is genuine or not. The questions I asked come from a basic test to check short- and long-term memory loss symptoms, not to establish the veracity of the memory loss. It's just an initial idea of the type of amnesia the subject is suffering. From what I saw in there, I would agree that your patient appears to be suffering global memory loss.'

'"Appears" to be?'

'Yes. Appears. You will need a much more detailed assessment if you want to see if it is genuine. There are a number of quite complex and detailed tests that can be carried out, but these are time-consuming and require a specialist. However, no test is one hundred per cent accurate, and a good actor or skilled manipulator can fool the tests and even the most competent neuropsychologist.'

Pope thought for a moment. 'Is there any way to make these tests more reliable?'

'Well, ideally you would need a psychiatric history and a range of detailed reports to be carried out.'

'If you had to put your money on it?' Pope asked.

Darke hesitated. She could see he didn't want to commit himself. 'Genuine amnesia is often blurred. What some call "islands of memory". Feigned amnesia is often described as sudden onset and, in criminal cases, often limited to the recent past and the circumstances of the crime itself. But you have the added complication here of possible PTSD.'

'You mean if we're right about her being an abuse victim?'

'Exactly. PTSD makes examination and diagnosis difficult because it carries its own set of symptoms, which can vary in different patients.'

'Vary in what way?' asked Pope.

'Research shows us that psychological trauma, such as PTSD, can have huge effects on the brain. The hippocampus is thought to be very sensitive to stress and can in some cases suffer neural degeneration as a result of sustained stress. There is some dissent about this in the medical and scientific community, but it is generally accepted that physical or emotional trauma can greatly affect one's memory. Some think it is a temporary way for the brain to cope with the memory of the trauma and protect us from psychological damage.'

'So you mean that amnesia allows us to temporarily forget details of an event to give us the time and distance to start the recovery process?'

'Yes. It's called repressed memory syndrome.'

'But this isn't just short-term memory loss. She can't remember anything about herself.'

'Indeed. She appears to be suffering from global amnesia. This can include the loss of personal identity. It's very rare, though. Genuine dissociative global amnesia is highly unusual and we're still learning about it and the links to PTSD.'

'How long can it last?' asked Pope.

'Can be a few hours, can be a few months. Or longer. Impossible to tell. And even then, not everything is likely to come back all at once. Some parts of the memory may return long before others, some may never return at all.'

'Is crime-related amnesia common in criminal cases? You know, to claim no knowledge of the crime?'

'It's not. Certainly not genuine cases.'

'You didn't tell me what you thought,' said Pope.

Again, Darke considered before answering. 'I genuinely don't know, Bec. She didn't hesitate with the mathematical questions or the naming of basic objects. I might expect a brief indication that she was working out whether she should answer those questions if she was faking it. But she could be a very skilled manipulator, in which case . . .' He left the sentence unfinished. 'As I said, this was a preliminary test to establish the type of amnesia the patient is suffering. I didn't go into detail with the questions as she just didn't seem to remember anything, which told us what we needed to know. Her cognitive function is fine, but the memory — nothing.'

Pope waited, hoping to tease out something firmer from Darke.

'OK. I think, on balance, she seems genuine. I would say that she has been traumatized and is almost certainly suffering with some form of PTSD. There is a strong possibility that she has repressed everything, to protect herself from the cause.'

Pope nodded, encouraging him to continue.

'But I would keep an open mind until we know more. Do you want me to arrange for someone more specialized to see her?'

'Yes, that would be great.'

'I know a woman who is one of the best in this field. I'll give her a ring and try to get her over here as soon as possible. As I said, though, it might take some time to arrange.'

'That's great. Thanks, Tobias. I need to get back to the station now.'

'I'll come out with you. I have a lecture at King's in an hour.'

They walked to the hospital entrance and exited into the stifling heat. Darke, despite his three-piece suit and tie, looked fresh and ready to face the rest of the day. Pope felt like she had started sweating the moment she left the building.

'I'll be in touch, Bec.' He paused. 'Interesting case.'

'Thanks again. I'll talk to you soon.'

They went in opposite directions. Pope found her car and as she opened the door was hit by a wave of heat from inside. She left the door open to let in the fresh air, such as it was, and stood looking towards the skyline for a moment. She thought about the woman in the hospital bed, how she must be feeling. She agreed with Darke's assessment of the genuine nature of the amnesia, but she could tell that he wasn't entirely certain. She got in the car, closed the door and started the engine, trying to ignore the kernel of doubt that sat somewhere in her brain.

CHAPTER EIGHT

Pope arrived back at her office to find that, if anything, it was hotter than yesterday. She nodded hello to Brody and Miller, who were sitting at their computers, then made a beeline for the water dispenser and drank three glasses in quick succession.

She collapsed into her desk chair and switched on the floor-standing fan just as her phone started ringing. She picked it up, had a brief conversation and replaced the receiver.

'That was Fletcher,' she said to Brody. 'He wants to meet me in half an hour for an update.'

'Did Tobias Darke talk to her?' asked Brody.

'Yes. He says that he thinks she has global memory loss, everything, and it's his opinion that she's genuine.'

Brody raised his eyebrows. 'How sure did he seem?'

'Well, he said that the test he gave her was only preliminary.' Pope filled Brody in on Darke's assessment of the patient.

'How did she seem this morning?' he asked.

'OK. Much the same. She slept well, I think, with the sedative. Woke up once but went back to sleep pretty quickly.'

'How did she react to Darke?'

'Pretty warily. I stayed in the room. She certainly isn't comfortable around men,' said Pope.

'That was pretty clear yesterday.'

'So, where are we?' She looked at both Brody and Miller.

'I've been checking missing persons. Nothing so far. I'll keep extending the net, but each time it simply takes longer and longer to cross-reference. We haven't got anything useful to narrow the search,' said Miller.

'What would you need?'

'Name would obviously be helpful. But seriously — age, location from where she went missing, identifying marks, tattoos, etc. Any of this would help, but without even one of those it's like a needle in a haystack.'

'And that's if she was even reported missing,' said Brody.

'Why wouldn't she be?' asked Miller.

'Well, it's happened before. If she was the subject of abuse in the household, then maybe she ran away, and her abuser may not want to report her missing and get the police involved. Or there may have been other problems — drugs, prostitution — and her family are glad to see the back of her. We've all seen these kinds of cases before.'

'That's true,' said Pope. 'And if the blood on her is that of her abuser, they may not be around to call in a report at all.'

The three of them considered that for a moment.

'You're just going to have to keep looking, Adam. We'll have to hope she shows up on some report somewhere.'

'Yes, boss.'

'Do you know how Thompson's getting on with the CCTV?'

Miller nodded. 'I spoke to him just before you got here. He has her walking along the Strand, then on to Agar Street and into the station. But it's a bit of a mystery before that. He's still looking at the possible cameras, but as yet, nothing.'

Pope looked puzzled. 'That's strange. She must have come from somewhere pretty visible.'

'Thompson is also working with some pretty sophisticated reverse-ageing software at the moment and hopes he can get us something we can use.'

'Reverse-ageing software? I've heard about that,' said Pope.

'Yeah, it's pretty cool. There's a possibility she went missing some time ago, maybe years. If that is the case, it'll be difficult to identify her from any photographs or descriptions that are in the system. So it would really help to have a more accurate image of her to cross-reference with missing persons reports.'

'Is that where the software comes in?' asked Pope.

'Yup.'

'Is it any good? I haven't seen it used before.'

'I've only seen it used in practical demonstrations and training, but apparently so. Ageing software is obviously much more common. But recent developments have used the same idea to reverse-age photographs. It's essentially the same process, just done backwards. The computer algorithm identifies key features of the face, such as the shape of the cheeks, mouth and forehead to produce photographic images of the subject as a younger person. It's been shown to be fairly accurate and has been used successfully in some cases.'

'How long does it take?' Pope asked.

'Miller says he should have something this morning, or early this afternoon at the latest.'

'Good. That will at least cover one possibility if it turns out she's been gone longer than we think,' said Pope. 'Have we got anywhere with the blood on her clothes?'

'No,' replied Brody. 'We know it's not hers, but until we've got anything to compare it to, there's not much we can do. Once we've identified her, it gets a bit easier. We can look at family members, boyfriends, co-workers. But until then . . .'

'OK. Brody, can you get on to 999 and check the domestic abuse calls in the past, say, forty-eight to seventy-two hours. We need any that sound like they're from a woman of similar age and in shock. As in, more terrified than you might expect. Someone who might have been involved in an attack.'

'Will do,' said Brody. 'Are you still thinking abuse? What did Darke think?'

'He thought she was presenting with symptoms consistent with a diagnosis of PTSD, and that could be as a result of abuse. He was telling me that trauma can sometimes result in the brain shutting down to block out any memory of the traumatic event.'

'You mean repressed memory syndrome?' asked Brody.

She shouldn't have been surprised that he knew all about it. 'Yes, that's right.'

'It's pretty unusual though, isn't it?'

'Yeah, that's what Darke said. But it's possible. The jury's still out, I guess,' admitted Pope reluctantly. 'Right, I've got a date with Fletcher.' She got up from her desk, catching a few breaths of cool air from the fan.

'Have fun,' said Brody.

She had even less enthusiasm for this than she had for the prospect of a discussion on the vagaries of global amnesia.

* * *

Pope knocked on Fletcher's door. Initially there was no response. She was just about to knock again when a voice from inside invited her in. She rolled her eyes. Fletcher was sitting bolt upright behind his expansive but strangely empty desk. His hair looked like it had just been combed in preparation for the meeting. He indicated the two chairs on the other side of the desk and Pope sat down in the nearest.

'Bring me up to speed,' said Fletcher.

'We still don't have an identification for our mystery woman.'

'I hope that's the bad news before the good news.'

'We're looking at all possible scenarios.'

'What scenarios?' asked Fletcher. Pope knew that he was almost certainly prepping for a press conference later today.

'We're working on the possibility that she went missing a long time ago — years, maybe. Thompson is running some reverse-ageing software to get a photofit of what she might have looked like when she was younger. That way we can look at old missing persons reports and maybe have some luck there.'

'So is she victim or perpetrator? Can we be any clearer on that at present?'

Pope knew that this was the key question. It determined how the woman should be handled. How the case was to be presented to the media.

'Not at the moment. Until we have blood to match up against, or she remembers what happened, we can't be definitive.'

'And she still hasn't remembered anything?'

'Not yet, no. Tobias Darke saw her.'

'What was his opinion?' asked Fletcher. Pope knew that he respected Darke's work. 'Is she genuine?'

'He thinks so.'

'With what degree of certainty?' asked Fletcher.

'Darke said that memory is complex and so it's very difficult to be certain. But as far as he can tell, in his professional opinion, he thinks she is telling the truth. She really has lost her memory.'

'And you agree?'

'I do. It's the hypothesis we're working on.'

Fletcher looked at her. She couldn't read him this time, although usually she thought she could.

'OK. I need to talk to the press. I'll try to keep it circumspect. The last thing I want to do is present her as a victim and then find out she killed someone. It will make us look like fools.'

Pope was about to say something but decided against it.

'I need you to be very careful here, DCI Pope. Clearly you are aware of this, but if anything changes about the veracity of this woman's claims, I need to know immediately. And I want you to keep an open mind until we know for sure.'

'I will.'

'I want to hear the moment we have anything. This will quickly become high profile once I've spoken to the media.'

'Got you.' Pope stood up, nodded at Fletcher and closed the door behind her. She shook her head. Why did she always leave these meetings so irritated?

* * *

Pope returned to her office and sat down at her desk. She drank from a bottle of water sitting next to her computer, but it was from yesterday and was the temperature of bath water. She grimaced and replaced the cap. She looked at her watch: 11.30 a.m. Realizing she hadn't eaten much in the past twenty-four hours, she took herself to the small fridge at one end of the shared office. She saw several packed lunches that more organized members of her team had brought to work and several open cartons of milk. A half-empty packet of cheese slices and a tub of margarine sat alone on the middle shelf. It wasn't haute cuisine. She decided on a black coffee and, once she had made it, returned to her desk.

She looked around the office. Brody and Miller sat at their computers. Brody looked up. 'How'd it go with the boss?'

'Fine. I took him through what we were thinking and he worked out how he could spin it at the press conference.'

Brody smiled. 'At least you can be useful to him sometimes.'

'Indeed I can. Furnisher of information.'

'Did he ask if Darke thinks she's telling the truth?'

'Yes, of course. That's his main concern, really.'

'I bet it is,' said Brody.

'He doesn't want to stand up in front of the media and paint her as a killer and then have to explain how she was a defenceless victim. That wouldn't play well at all.'

'No. And nor would it sound too good the other way around. I can see his dilemma.'

'Fletcher's always got one eye on his stripes. He wants it too badly and it colours everything he does. It's irritating.' Pope had never had a career plan and each promotion she'd received had been almost incidental. She'd infuriated Alex last year when she'd refused the offer of a promotion to a managerial role, essentially a desk job. Working with Fletcher for the past four years had put her off management for life. Detective chief inspector seemed to her the perfect combination of leading a team but also being at the forefront of investigative work.

'Stripes aren't always a bad thing,' said Brody.

'Maybe you should join Fletcher's golf club. How's your Masonic handshake these days?'

'I'm a quick learner,' said Brody, contorting his hand into a painful-looking shape.

'You're halfway there already.'

Miller's phone rang and Pope watched him answer and have a brief conversation. He replaced the receiver.

'That was Thompson. He's on his way up with the results of the reverse ageing.'

'How's it looking?' asked Pope.

'He says it's come up with a couple of possibilities at different ages. We'll see how it looks in a minute.'

Pope was impatient. She hated waiting around for information, preferring to go after anything she needed immediately. She stood by her desk, watching the door. She was unsure exactly what she would be able to do with the images once they arrived, but in the absence of facts, of any real information, this was at least something.

After a couple of minutes Stephen Thompson came into the office, two pieces of A4 photo paper in his hand.

'How did it go?' asked Pope before he had even closed the door.

He looked hot and bothered, sweat patches under his arms and fine beads of sweat on his forehead. He wiped his shirt sleeve across his face and positioned himself in front of one of the tall fans, a look of relief on his face. 'They seem OK, quite clear. The software's produced one image at approximately ten years old, and one at about fifteen. That's working on the assumption that she's twenty years old now. We're not sure about that, of course. It doesn't look that much like the current photo of her, but then there are a lot of physiological changes that take place between those ages, so that's to be expected.'

'What's the quality like?'

'Have a look yourself,' said Thompson, handing them to Pope.

She took the two pages and looked at the first picture. This was the one of the woman at approximately ten years old. She paused, her look darkened. They all noticed.

'Everything all right?' asked Brody.

Pope didn't answer but slowly brought out the other photograph, the fifteen-year-old version of the woman in the hospital bed.

'Jesus Christ.' Pope continued to study the picture.

Thompson looked confused. Brody and Miller rushed over and looked at the photograph in her hands. She was holding both edges tightly.

Brody looked up at her. 'What is it? What have you seen?'

Pope took a step back from them, still holding the photographs.

'It's Alice Lowrie,' said Pope in a quiet voice. 'Jesus Christ.'

Everyone waited but no explanation was forthcoming.

'Who's Alice Lowrie?' asked Brody.

Pope returned his gaze. She shook her head. 'We found Tina, but never Alice. My God. It's Alice Lowrie.'

CHAPTER NINE

Eight years ago

It was the phone call that no Homicide detective wanted to take.

Bruce Phillips drove, Pope in the passenger seat, less than a week in Homicide, not knowing what to say.

As they pulled into the street that led to the reported crime scene, Pope saw that there were two marked cars already there. Four police officers were cordoning off an area around what Pope could already see was a body. She started. Phillips pulled up behind the other vehicles and turned off the engine. He faced his passenger.

'You going to be all right?'

'Yes. Of course.'

He raised his eyebrows. 'Stick close to me. Don't be afraid to walk away if you need to,' he said. 'I don't want you throwing up on our crime scene.'

Pope didn't know him well enough to tell if he was joking. She scanned his face but got no clue.

She got out of the car and gently closed the door. She followed him towards the officers placing the tape.

The scene was a large patch of wasteland by the river, just north of Bermondsey. It was seven in the morning and she felt the chill of pre-sunrise, amplified by the wind whipping off the Thames and right into their faces. Pope turned up her collar, as much against the scene they were walking towards as the bitter wind. She walked several steps behind Phillips, watching, trying to gauge the appropriate way to handle herself. How do you approach a possible murder scene? Do you show confidence or humility? These are the things you don't learn on a normal beat. Phillips stopped when he reached the tape, then lifted it and ducked under.

'Morning, sir,' said the officer nearest him. He then nodded at Pope. She nodded a return greeting.

'What have we got?' said Phillips.

'Teenage girl. Maybe thirteen or fourteen. Looks like the cause of death was suffocation.'

'You a medical expert now? Shall we cancel the coroner?' said Phillips.

Embarrassed, the officer looked down at his shoes. 'Sorry, sir. Just trying to—'

'Do your job. Don't try to do other people's.' The officer looked away and apologized again. Phillips walked past him towards the body.

Pope thought Phillips had been unnecessarily cruel. The officer was clearly trying to impress the DCI and didn't deserve that kind of treatment. But she said nothing and followed her boss.

The girl was lying on her side in the mud and scrub. Her clothes were filthy. She wore corduroy trousers and a light blue sweatshirt. Her fair hair was matted and caked with mud. Pope agreed with the assessment that she was around thirteen or fourteen. Obviously dead. She and Phillips both stared at the body. Suddenly Pope felt bile rising in the back of her throat. She wanted to turn away, walk away. But she couldn't. Phillips had offered her the get-out, but she knew it was a test to see if she could handle the job. Phillips hadn't been too keen on a woman on the team but had been over-ruled in the interests of gender balance and optics. She was determined to show it had been the right decision. Pope steeled herself, swallowed and fixed her gaze on the body.

Phillips kept his eyes on the girl. 'What do you see?'

Pope looked at him, then back at the body on the ground. Phillips said nothing, waited. Pope took a couple of deep breaths. Desperate to show no sign of weakness.

'He's right, I think. Early teens.' She looked around. 'No obvious signs that it was done here. No drag marks, no blood. So maybe she was killed somewhere else and dumped here.'

Phillips continued looking at the body. Wanted more.

'The contusions on her face suggest a violent attack. Her clothes look intact, so no obvious sexual assault.'

'The medical examiner will determine that,' said Phillips. It sounded like a reprimand.

'Yes, of course,' said Pope.

'She's not wearing any jewellery,' said Phillips. 'So robbery could be a factor. Although I doubt it.'

'Why?'

'Most thirteen-year-olds don't wear the kind of jewellery you'd want to nick. And she doesn't look like a rich kid.'

Pope thought about that.

'So, what's next?' he asked.

'Fingerprints, photographs and get the medical examiner to look at the body,' said Pope, again aware that she was being tested.

'Right. Sort it out.' Phillips turned and started walking back towards the car. As he walked, she heard him mutter something under his breath.

'What did you say, sir?'

He stopped and turned, looked right at her. 'I said I fucking hate kid cases.'

Pope's first Homicide case had begun.

* * *

Pope had joined the police force twelve years ago. Her promotion to the Homicide squad had come as something of a surprise to her. Several years after becoming a sergeant, she had taken her detective exam. But being promoted to Homicide had taken some time. She had friends in the force who told her this was because she was a woman, and others who told her it was the "type" of woman she was. She wasn't sure what that had meant. Either way, she spent a few years with a qualification and not a lot to do with it.

But now she was here. Where she'd wanted to be from the day she joined the academy. Seven days ago she had felt elation and excitement. Then, on her first day, one of the men on the new team — forties, all brown corduroy and twenty a day — told her that she had only been recruited to Homicide because she was a woman, as a token to placate the political correctness lobby. They'd told her she wouldn't last, it was a man's world and women were not cut out for this type of work. Pope had felt instantly deflated. She was used to the casual, institutional sexism of the Metropolitan Police. But this level of attack, so direct and brutal, was a shock. She hesitated to take it on initially. She knew she had to prove herself first, establish herself in Homicide. Then she would deal with this.

In the car on the way back to the station, elation and excitement were most certainly not what she felt. She thought she would feel a thrill, the frisson of a new case, a real homicide. But she was overwhelmed with a sadness so profound that she wasn't sure how to deal with it. Phillips talked about the way the investigation would start, and she listened and took it in. But she didn't say anything. Didn't contribute. When they arrived back at the station, she went straight to the bathroom, locked herself in a cubicle and sobbed. She was furious with herself but could do nothing to stop it. Eventually she regained control, unlocked the cubicle door and washed her face in front of the mirror. There was absolutely no chance that she was going to let anyone in Homicide see her like this on her first case. That kind of introduction never went away. Pope checked in the mirror to see if she looked OK and left to return to the squad room. Nobody commented or indeed showed any interest whatsoever when she returned. She walked to her desk, the smallest in the room, tucked away in the corner, acres away from the nearest window. Phillips was about to lead a briefing and she found her pen and flipped to the next clean page in her notebook.

Bruce Phillips was a legend in the Met Police. Thirty-five years on the job, twenty in Homicide. He was what you thought of when you thought of a 1970s detective working in London. He was sexist, homophobic, incredibly insensitive. But he was also tough, loyal and looked after his team, protecting them from any outside interference or obstruction. It was assumed that he had dirt on one or more of the bosses, which allowed him to act with impunity, so long as the successes kept coming. And they did. Phillips had the best clearance rate of any Homicide detective in the Met. His team loved him, worshipped him and accommodated his methods and idiosyncrasies as if they were the price of being on the best team in London. Pope knew his reputation when she joined up. Also knew that he was close to retirement. She thought she would learn a lot before then.

Phillips's popularity and success were also his key problems. He believed his own press, and when he had a suspect in his crosshairs, he could find it difficult to listen to anyone who disagreed. In most cases he was right. He had a knack for quickly eliminating the wrong leads, homing in on the suspect and forensically pinning down their guilt. But not always.

The body they had found was quickly identified as Tina Waterson. Thirteen years old, lived in Bermondsey. Her parents, Mick and Trish Waterson, had reported her missing the day before. Very quickly, Phillips homed in on Mick Waterson as his chief suspect. Too quickly, in Pope's view. Waterson was remarkably hostile to the police. That got Phillips's back up and he wouldn't entertain the idea that he was on the wrong track. He put all of his resources into Waterson.

Waterson had no real alibi to speak of. Time of death had been established as late evening, between 8 p.m. and 11 p.m. He had told the officers who interviewed him, in what was reportedly a very difficult conversation, that he had worked late, then gone to the pub, alone. Waterson worked as a mechanic in a small automotive repair business based in one of the arches in Peckham. He owned the business and had sent his colleague home earlier but had stayed at work to finish a job that had taken longer than he had expected. When he had finished, at around seven thirty, he had gone to a nearby pub, where he spent a couple of hours drinking and reading the paper, before arriving home at 10 p.m. The problem was, nobody who had been at the pub could remember Waterson being there. The landlord thought he might have seen him but couldn't be sure. It had been a busy evening and he was rushed off his feet, he said. None of the regulars remembered seeing him either.

Three days after Tina Waterson's body had been found, Phillips and Pope took a car and headed to the Watersons' house. Pope had reservations, but Phillips wouldn't even begin to listen. He drove quickly, explaining his thinking to Pope on the way.

'Mick Waterson has no alibi. He says he was in a boozer near his garage. But it wasn't his regular and nobody remembers seeing him. First, why didn't he go to his regular? Second, I don't believe you can spend two hours drinking in a pub and be seen by nobody. Third, the officers who interviewed him described him as hostile, aggressive, uncooperative. Who the hell is uncooperative with the police trying to find their kid's murderer? Unless they have something to hide?'

'He said he had had an argument with a regular in his local a couple of days before, so he fancied a change. That could explain why he went to a different pub,' said Pope.

'A local's a local. You go there after a hard day's work. Waterson isn't the type to hide away from an argument.'

'Maybe. But it's not inconceivable that nobody remembers him, if he was sitting quietly in a corner having a couple of pints and buried in a newspaper.'

'Or he wasn't there at all.'

Pope could see that Phillips had made up his mind and she wouldn't be able to dissuade him from this course of action.

'His hostility screams guilt,' said Phillips, as if it were fact.

'He might have a complex relationship with the police. He's been in trouble before,' ventured Pope, aware that she needed to navigate this with care.

Phillips smiled and shook his head, keeping his eyes on the road. 'This is no time for bleeding hearts. "Complex relationship" or not, he's definitely in the frame.'

* * *

They had arrived at the house, but there was no one home, much to Pope's relief. She hadn't relished being the referee between a driven Phillips, convinced of his suspect's guilt, and an aggressive Waterson, wary of the police and distraught with grief for his daughter.

Pope wanted to confront Phillips about his bias in the case, but she knew he wouldn't listen. She simply didn't see Waterson murdering his own daughter and dumping her body on waste ground near the Thames. The evidence was circumstantial at best and he had no motive. Phillips had found a suspect and constructed a flimsy case around his initial gut feeling. Her initial instinct was to go to his superior officer and voice her concerns. But Phillips was very unlikely to be taken to task and she would probably suffer as a result. Seven days on the job was not the ideal time to be taking on your boss. Pope vowed that if she ever got to his position, she would listen to her officers and avoid the level of tunnel vision she saw in him.

So she decided to avoid the confrontation, keep her head down and focus on learning as much as possible from Phillips and the rest of his team. She would follow the evidence and trust the Homicide squad to do the same. If Waterson was guilty, they would find evidence. If he wasn't, they'd prove it and shift the focus of the investigation. There would be other suspects and they would solve the case.

Pope's optimism was fleeting. Phillips announced that he wanted four of the squad at Tina Waterson's funeral the following day. Pope would be one of the four. Phillips wanted to rattle Mick Waterson, see how he acted under pressure. Pope was appalled but everyone else seemed enthusiastic about the plan. She was beginning to realize that Phillips could suggest anything and his team would get behind it without question.

The funeral was held at the Watersons' local church in Peckham. All Saints was a hub for the local community and Trish Waterson, in particular, seemed to know everybody there.

When they had questioned Trish she had taken an instant dislike to Pope, recognizing and then dismissing her as inexperienced. Pope was hoping to avoid her today. She felt very uncomfortable being there.

They hung back until the other mourners had entered the church, then they quietly walked in and took the final pew on the left-hand side. It was about three quarters full, and Pope hoped this might provide some anonymity. Phillips watched Mick Waterson like a hawk throughout. But when the service finished and the parents turned, they noticed the police officers at the back of the church. Pope was expecting Mick to do something stupid, but when he left, he simply walked past all of them, staring at Phillips. The two locked eyes but said nothing. Pope was relieved. But this was short-lived.

She was standing outside the entrance as Trish walked past. She stopped, looked at Pope.

'Enjoying yourself, are you?'

'Our condolences, Trish,' said Pope.

'It's Mrs Waterson to you. You don't know me.'

Pope said nothing.

'Why aren't you out doing your fucking job, instead of wasting your time here?'

'We wanted to pay our respects.'

'Yeah, right. Fuck you.' With that she suddenly balled her hand and swung it at Pope's face. Pope stumbled back as Trish's fist connected just below her left eye. She steadied herself on the handrail by the side of the steps, but she was disorientated. Trish Waterson could hit hard. Before she could gather herself, she was stunned by another blow, quick and firm, to the same place. Again, she was knocked back, vaguely aware of several people stepping in and standing between the two women, holding Trish back. The woman was hustled away, followed by the remainder of the mourners, all staring at Pope. She put her hand up to her face and winced with the pain. Phillips and the other officers were there then, supporting her and talking of arresting Trish Waterson. But Pope shook her head vehemently, insisting with more force than her junior standing allowed. Pope knew they had invaded the Watersons' privacy and grief, and she deserved what she had got. She was furious with Phillips, not Trish Waterson.

* * *

Within the next week three more teenage girls disappeared. About the same age as Tina Waterson, and from the same area. The media went into a feeding frenzy. The cases were quickly linked although there was no concrete evidence, and the press, in particular, zeroed in on Pope and Phillips. By now they knew what had happened at the funeral. Trish Waterson had talked to the papers, and as far as she was concerned, Pope's inexperience had certainly let the killer escape justice. She also told them how Bruce Phillips had become fixated on her husband. Mick Waterson had a solid alibi for two of the other missing girls, and the Homicide squad had wasted their time, allowing three other abductions. It was an irresistible narrative and it filled the front pages of the London papers, then the nationals and television news, for weeks. Pope had reporters camped outside her front door, following her car, trying to get up to see her at Charing Cross Police Station. Her picture, along with that of Bruce Phillips, was on the front page of the *Evening Standard*. People started looking at her in the street.

This was the toughest time Pope had ever had on the job. She knew it would pass, but it didn't help. She should have talked to Phillips's boss and voiced her concerns more forcefully. Inexperience wasn't an excuse. Trish Waterson had been right: her inexperience had contributed to the abduction of three more girls. She would have to live with this.

Bruce Phillips was characteristically unrepentant. At least in public. Pope very much doubted if anyone with any integrity could fail to be affected by what had happened. But he had no other leads and nowhere to go. They continued to investigate, but eventually the case was put on the back burner as the murder rate in London continued to rise and the cuts to policing kept coming.

For both Pope and Phillips this was the one that got away. For Phillips it turned out to be his final big investigation. Pope thought it was simply too much for him, the not knowing. Just over a year later, he retired. A hero to most and his reputation largely intact, though Pope suspected he privately felt it tarnished by the inability to solve the case. They had had no contact since.

Pope couldn't forget Tina Waterson and the other girls. She lobbied for the case to be kept active, but there were no resources allocated. She revisited it on occasions, although they became less and less frequent. She developed insomnia, spent her nights thinking through the evidence, the possibilities, trying to open it up in a million different ways. But apart from sleepless nights, she had nothing to show for it.

Her first case in Homicide.

Four missing girls. Three never found. Not a trace. No witnesses, no suspect.

Until eight years later when one of them walked into Charing Cross Police Station.

CHAPTER TEN

Pope was vaguely aware that Brody was waiting for her to say more. She simply stared out of the window. Alice Lowrie had changed so much in eight years. Almost unrecognizable. But now Pope had seen the younger image, she knew.

'Tina? Tina Waterson?' Brody said. 'Didn't we question her father last year?'

'Mick Waterson. Yes, we did.'

'So, what's this got to do with the girl we found?' asked Miller.

Pope took a deep breath. Her mind was elsewhere, but she brought herself back into the room. 'We talked to Mick Waterson last year about another matter. It was nothing to do with him. But I knew him from a long time ago. His daughter, Tina, was abducted eight years ago. We found her body dumped just outside Bermondsey. We never found who killed her.' She paused, steeling herself. 'There were three other girls linked to the case. Taken at the same time, from the same area.'

Pope took a beat. She knew all the names by heart but hadn't said them out loud in a very long time. She felt that she needed to now. 'Sarah Banks, Belinda Forsyth. And Alice Lowrie. She was the fourth girl.'

Everyone in the room was now looking at her.

'Did you have any suspects at the time?' asked Miller.

'Not really. My boss thought Mick Waterson looked likely. We stayed on him, but it turned out it wasn't. There was no other evidence, no solid leads, no suspects.' Pope decided to give them the short version. She didn't feel like laying out the team's failings in detail.

'From what I remember Mick Waterson saying last year, the other girls were never found, right?' asked Brody.

'No. No sign. And it seemed to end there. No more missing girls fitting their descriptions taken locally afterwards.'

'So, the case is technically still open,' said Brody.

'It is,' replied Pope.

'Wow. Serious cold case!' said Miller, with a little too much enthusiasm.

Pope looked at him disapprovingly, then away.

'Sorry,' said Miller.

'This is a lot to think about,' said Pope. 'Miller, I want you to trace Alice Lowrie's parents. Up to eight years ago they'd lived in Bermondsey all their lives, so I'd start there. I need to know where they are now, what they're doing, and find out if there's anything on them in the last eight years.'

'OK.'

'Brody. Can you get the details on the next of kin for Sarah Banks and Belinda Forsyth? Check what they've been up to as well.'

Brody nodded, and both he and Miller sat down at their desks and brought their computers to life.

Pope left the office and went to the bathroom. She went straight to the taps, splashed water on her face and around the back of her neck, and held her wrists under the stream of cool water until she felt like she wasn't in an oven. She turned off the taps and then leaned with her back against the wall. All she wanted to do was slide down and sit on the floor. That was all she had the strength for.

But she knew she had to get moving and get a blood sample from Alice Lowrie and hope there was a DNA reference somewhere from the original investigation. Then, if she could confirm that, she had to visit Lowrie's parents and break the news. How that conversation would go would depend largely on where Alice Lowrie had been for the last eight years.

* * *

Pope returned to the office. Four floor-standing fans and two desktop models couldn't alleviate the heat to any great extent. She billowed her shirt to generate something approaching a breeze.

'Not good news, I'm afraid,' said Miller.

She turned to him.

'Both of Alice Lowrie's parents are dead.'

Pope felt an immediate sharp stab inside. Maybe guilt, or sorrow, or pain.

'What happened?' she asked.

'Michael Lowrie had a massive heart attack and was dead by the time he arrived at the hospital. His wife, Emma . . .' He paused and looked up from his computer. 'She took her own life.'

Pope was silent for a moment.

'When was this?' she asked.

Miller checked the screen and scrolled down to find the information. 'Michael Lowrie died a year after Alice Lowrie went missing and his wife took her own life the year after that.'

Pope thought back. 'We told them we had moved resources away from the case about a year or so after her disappearance. They took it really badly. Shit.' She now knew what had happened. The news had killed her father, and his wife had lasted barely a year longer. It was simply too much grief to bear.

'You can't blame yourself for that,' said Brody. 'That's the way it goes sometimes. Cases can't stay on the gas for ever.'

'I know,' said Pope. 'But that doesn't actually make this any easier. It still happened.'

'I can see that,' said Brody.

Why hadn't she known that Alice Lowrie's parents were both dead? How could she have missed that? The family of a missing child in a supposedly open case. They had failed to find the girls, or the person who abducted them, in time to give Alice's parents some peace of mind. And the grief had killed them.

'Miller, can you check on the case files and find out if we have a sample of Alice Lowrie's DNA? I'm pretty sure her parents gave us one at the time. Hopefully it will still be OK. We need to match that with a sample from our girl, to make sure. Can you get the lab on to it ASAP?'

'Yes, no problem.'

'Brody, we need to go and have a chat with our favourite Peckham mechanic.'

'Oh. Great,' said Brody. Pope knew he'd remember their last encounter with Mick Waterson in an interview room downstairs. It was fair to say that they hadn't hit it off.

'And this time you might get to meet his wife.'

'What's she like?' asked Brody.

'Like her husband. Only without the self-restraint.'

Brody raised his eyebrows.

'You think I'm joking?'

* * *

The drive to Peckham was slow, with too much traffic as they inched across the Thames and then hit the Old Kent Road.

'It's your great white whale, isn't it?' said Brody as he drove, his eyes on the road.

Pope was silent.

'Your first case, right?'

'In Homicide, yes. I'd only been in a few days when I caught it. I say "I" caught it. It was Bruce Phillips's case all the way. I was very much the newbie.'

'I've heard of Phillips. Never met him, but he has something of a reputation,' said Brody.

'Yeah, he does. All well deserved. He was quite the boss.'

'In what way?'

'He was old-school. His attitudes and methods were 1970s all the way. Dress sense too, actually. No concessions to the modern world.'

Brody smiled. 'Apart from the clothes, how did that go down?'

'Well, he got results, so they left him to it. There were all kinds of rumours about how he managed to get away with some of the things he did, but I think his clear-up rate just got him a pass on everything else. His team loved him.'

'Did that include you?'

Pope thought for a moment. 'I only worked with him for a little over a year. He retired.'

'That doesn't answer the question.'

'He was good at his job, but he was a man out of his time. As a woman in the team, that made it hard. It's always difficult to balance professional success with how you achieve it. How far can you separate the man, his methods and his results?'

'To what extent does the end justify the means?'

'Yes, exactly.'

'So, where did you get to?'

She thought again, trying to decide. 'He relied heavily on his instincts. Which, to be fair to him, were usually excellent. He was pretty good at reading people. But if that's what you primarily rely on, they have to be pretty much foolproof. Which, of course, they aren't. He lost the thread in the Tina Waterson case. He leaned too heavily on Mick Waterson, and by the time he realized we were on the wrong track, it was too late. Everything had gone cold and three more girls had gone missing in the meantime.'

'Did that contribute to his leaving, do you think?'

'I'm sure it did. He realized his mistake and it cost him. If not personally, then definitely professionally.'

'Do you keep in contact?' asked Brody.

'No, I haven't spoken to him in years.'

They were both quiet for a while.

'Can I ask you something?' said Brody.

There was something ominous in his tone. Pope looked over. 'Go on.'

He hesitated, clearly unsure whether to ask the question. Pope nodded her encouragement.

'Do you think it's possible to have relationships, doing this job? I mean, I know how difficult it's been with Alex. Do you think it can work?' He kept his eyes on the road.

'That's coming out of left field.' Pope thought for a minute. She knew the answer, but hoped to find a different one. It didn't come.

'I don't know. From my experience, it's . . .' She tried to find the right words. 'Let's just say I haven't mastered the art yet. Why do you ask?'

For the first time in a long time, Brody seemed awkward.

'It's just, I've been out on a couple of dates with someone. I really like them, but I'm not sure if it's fair to take them into a relationship I can't commit to.'

Pope looked at Brody again. When was the last time he had discussed his private life? They worked so closely, but he never shared things about any partners. This must be serious.

'I wouldn't take my situation as any kind of example. You're probably asking the wrong person.'

This seemed to close down the conversation. It's not what Pope had intended, but she felt that the only things she could say would put Brody off, so she decided to say nothing.

Brody stared ahead and put his attention into driving. They drove the rest of the trip in silence.

* * *

The car pulled into Mick and Tina Waterson's road, and Pope's heart suddenly started to beat faster. She remembered being here all those years ago. Turning into this road, Phillips at the wheel. She'd been here a number of times, and it had always ended badly. She found herself hoping there was nobody home, then quickly put that out of her mind. She needed to talk to them.

Pope indicated the house to Brody and he pulled up outside. The last time she had seen Mick Waterson had been almost a year ago. That, too, had not been a positive encounter. But it was Trish she was really not looking forward to seeing. Trish hated Pope, which was not wholly unusual for a police officer. But deep down, Pope still believed that Tina's mother had a point. She knew they had got it wrong. She knew that her inexperience had prevented her from calling out Phillips and she knew that might have allowed Tina Waterson's killer to go free. Her nightmares over the last eight years reminded her of that on a regular basis. She took a deep breath and opened the car door.

Pope walked to the front gate and undid the latch. The house was a typical 1930s London workers' house. Small, two up, two down. What front garden there was was messy, the rest mostly concrete. Pope couldn't remember what it had been like before the couple lost their only daughter, but she doubted that she would prioritize gardening in similar circumstances. She walked up to the front door. Before she knocked, she turned to Brody behind her.

'Ready?'

'Yup. Let's go.'

Pope nodded and knocked on the door, then took a step back on the pathway. There was a short pause, then she could see a figure inside coming towards the front door. She steeled herself. The door opened.

Mick Waterson, all six foot of him, was wide enough to fill the small doorframe. Like the last time she had seen him, he was still sporting the neo-Nazi look: faded jeans, Fred Perry polo shirt, crew cut. He hadn't changed. Waterson took a moment to register. He stood still, a look of distaste forming. He said nothing.

'Hello, Mick. How's it going?' asked Pope, attempting to adopt the appropriate tone for the greeting.

He paused, looked over her shoulder at Brody, then back to Pope. 'What do you want?'

'I need to talk to you and Trish about something, Mick.'

'What is it? Have you found Tina's murderer?'

'No, we haven't. But I do need to talk to you.'

'If it's not about that, I've got nothing to say to you.' He went to close the door.

A voice from inside. 'Who is it, Mick?'

Pope felt suddenly nervous. Mick turned. 'It's nothing.'

'Mick. It is about Tina. Sort of. Can we talk inside?'

'What do you mean "sort of"? What the hell does that mean?'

Just then, Pope heard footsteps inside and Trish Waterson arrived at the front door. Her shock was evident. She hadn't seen Pope for six years. Once the shock had registered, hatred quickly took over.

'Hello, Trish.'

'Bitch,' said Trish Waterson, and spat at Pope's feet. 'What the fuck do you want?'

Brody made to walk forward, but Pope shook her head. 'Trish, I need to talk to you. It's important.'

'We've got nothing to say to you. Fuck off.'

'Trish. I need to talk to you about Tina. Something's happened.'

That made her pause. Her body changed, a different kind of tension.

'Have you found him?' she whispered.

'No, Trish. But I think we have something. I need to talk to you both. Can I come in?'

Pope knew that the last person Mick and Trish Waterson wanted in their home was her, the woman they hated more than anyone. But she also knew that Tina was their Achilles heel. Trish looked at her husband. It was clear that it was her call. She threw a glance at Pope, full of hate and malice, but moved slowly away from the door. Pope knew it was as good an invitation as they were likely to get. Mick stepped back about a foot, which meant that Pope had to squeeze past him to get into the house. When Brody walked in behind her, the two men didn't take their eyes off each other until he was past.

The front door led straight into the living room. Although she had little recollection of the outside, she remembered this very clearly. This was where she and Phillips had delivered several doses of bad news, and it was burned into her memory. It hadn't changed a bit. Pope and Brody sat on two of the chairs at the small table in the corner. Trish sat opposite, while Mick Waterson stood a few feet away, watching them carefully. Pope looked around the room and her eyes landed on a photograph of the three of them, Mick, Trish and Tina. Smiling and carefree. It hurt Pope to see that.

'What is it? I've got things to do,' said Trish. The hostility was obvious, but her interest was now piqued.

'I'll get straight to the point,' said Pope. 'You'll remember that after we found Tina's body, there were another three missing girls linked to the case? All from around here?'

Trish looked at her. Nodded slightly. 'So?'

'We think we may have found one of them. She's alive.'

The expressions on the two of them suddenly changed. Trish leaned forward, while Mick took a step towards the table.

'What do you mean? Where?' asked Trish.

'I can't go into the details yet . . .'

'For fuck's sake! You're talking about my daughter. Tell me!'

Mick walked to her and put a hand on her shoulder.

'I will, Trish. I will. But at the moment, we're still checking the details, and I can't tell you too much until we know more.'

'Where did you find her? Was she with someone?'

'No, she was on her own. She came to us, but we haven't got anything else yet. We're on it.'

'"On it". Like you were "on it" last time?'

'I know it's frustrating, Trish. But you have to trust me and let us do our job.'

'Trust you? Trust you!' she shouted, standing up from the table. 'You must be fucking kidding me! You come here and then tell me nothing, and I'm supposed to trust you? Idiot!' she spat.

'Trish.' Pope also stood up, took a step towards her. 'Listen. I'm here, aren't I? I will let you know everything when I can. I promise you. But you have to give me a bit of time.'

Trish shook her head dismissively. 'Time,' she muttered, shaking her head.

'Trish.' The woman refused to look at her. 'Trish,' she repeated, this time with more authority. She turned her head to Pope.

'Do you remember the name Alice Lowrie? From back then,' asked Pope.

Trish and Mick looked at each other, a faint spark of hope between them.

'She was one of the other girls. The ones you never found,' said Mick.

'Yes. She disappeared a couple of days after Tina. We're matching the blood samples, but I can see it's her.'

Trish was clearly frustrated. 'I want to talk to her.'

'No,' said Pope, a little more firmly than she had planned. 'I need to talk to her. Why not?'

'She's still being questioned and checked out. But I'll let you know if we find anything out about Tina, I promise.'

Trish looked at her. 'It's been eight years.'

'I know it has, Trish.'

There was silence between the two women. The tension still real.

'I need you to do something for me. Contact Tina's friends from back then, their parents, anyone you're still in contact with. Ask them if they knew Alice Lowrie. She was around the same age as Tina.'

Trish nodded slightly. Pope took out a card and handed it to her. 'Anything you get, call me on one of these numbers. Any time.' Trish looked at the card, then back at Pope.

Pope was pleased she didn't screw it up and throw it on the floor, which was the least she'd expected. The four of them stood in the living room, nobody speaking. For Pope, a very strange moment.

'We'll let ourselves out. I'm sorry I couldn't bring you anything concrete, but I wanted you to know that we're doing everything we can. As soon as I have anything I can tell you, I'll be in touch.'

Trish opened her mouth to say something but seemed to change her mind. She simply nodded at Pope. Mick just glared at her.

Pope walked to the front door and she and Brody left, closing the door behind them. They were silent as they got in the car. Brody started the engine and pulled away.

'No doubt Bruce Phillips would have a hip flask in the glove box for moments like these,' said Brody.

'Bloody right he would.'

* * *

Pope and Brody went straight to Fletcher's office when they arrived back at the station. He'd asked to see them both as soon as they got back. The desk sergeant had emphasized "as soon as". The door was open, which was unusual for Fletcher. He liked a closed door. Pope knocked and they went in.

Fletcher was sitting behind his desk and in the middle of a phone call. He motioned for them to sit down. They sat and watched him as he finished up. Eventually he replaced the receiver.

'Bec, James. Tell me where we are with the investigation. You've got a connection to an old case?'

'Yes. We think the woman is actually Alice Lowrie. She went missing eight years ago. We investigated out of here at the time,' said Pope.

'Bruce Phillips, right? And it was your first case in Homicide? Tina Waterson.'

Fletcher had clearly done his homework.

'Yes, that's right. Phillips was the lead. We found Tina's body, but three other girls, presumed linked, were never found.'

'How do you know it's Alice Lowrie?'

'I recognized her from the reverse-ageing software that Miller used.'

'Have we confirmed this?' asked Fletcher.

'Miller's sorting the DNA now. Hopefully by later this afternoon. But I'm certain it's her. I didn't see it at first, but it's clearly her in the picture.'

'And what are we thinking? Have you talked to her parents?'

Fletcher clearly didn't know everything.

'Her parents both died some years ago. We've just got back from talking to Tina Waterson's parents. They're going to ask around Tina's friends from the time, their parents. I'll get Miller chasing other contacts, teachers, and clubs she belonged to.'

'Good. So, what are we thinking?' Fletcher asked.

'At the moment we're still not sure. This clearly changes everything, not least because we're now looking at where the other two girls might be. But we're still not getting anything from Alice Lowrie. At least we know who she is.'

'Do we know whose blood it is yet?'

'Still on that. Now we've potentially identified her, we can start compiling a list of people close to her to check against. But otherwise, if we have any pre-existing matches on file, we'll know sometime today, I'd hope.'

Fletcher thought for a moment. He leaned back and steepled his hands in front of him. Pope knew this was his tell for broaching something difficult.

'Is she telling the truth?'

'You keep asking me that and I still don't know,' said Pope. She stared at Fletcher. He stared back.

'James, has your opinion changed?' Fletcher's eyes remained on Pope.

He was about to answer, when Pope interrupted. 'What do you want him to say? That I'm wrong, that she's lying and is actually a murderer? That would certainly be a simple solution to a complex case.'

'Bec, that wasn't what—' Brody started.

'Yes, it was.' She stared at Brody then turned back to Fletcher. 'You think she's lying. You haven't even seen her, and you've already made up your mind because it's the easiest thing to say to the media. How about we wait and see what the evidence tells us?'

Fletcher opened his mouth to say something.

'I'm going to go and do some work. To find out the truth of this.'

With that, Pope got up and left the office.

Fletcher and Brody watched her leave. Then, after an awkward silence, Brody got up.

'James. What's your take on DCI Pope on this case?'

'She's working too hard and this is bringing back too many bad memories. The Tina Waterson case is still a bad one for her. With that and the family difficulties . . . I don't know. She'll be fine.'

'I want you to keep an eye on her. She could be right about the girl, but you know as well as I do that, all things being equal, there is a more plausible explanation. The fact that she can't seem to accept this suggests that she might have lost perspective on this case, and I can't have that. Not from a DCI. Do you understand?'

'Yes, sir,' said Brody. 'I'll keep an eye on her. But she'll be fine. She just wants to get this one right this time. It means a lot to her.'

'Make sure I know anything I need to know immediately. There's a lot of eyes on this one and that's going to increase exponentially once the connection to the old case is out. It won't take long.'

'I will, sir,' said Brody.

'OK. That's all,' said Fletcher, dismissing him.

Brody closed the office door behind him and took a moment to consider what he was going to say to Pope, who was sure to ask him what Fletcher had said as soon as he walked back in the office. That was a line to tread very carefully.

CHAPTER ELEVEN

Eight years ago

It was cold as she left the house, the early-morning cold of late autumn just before it changes to winter, and she pulled up the zip of her coat, holding the collar up to her chin. This afforded some protection, but it was more a means of occupying her hands and keeping her mind from racing. Trying to keep calm despite the pounding of her heart in her chest. She looked back and saw the door close. Then she looked around and checked that there was nobody nearby. Both sides of the street were empty. She abruptly turned around, crossed the street and walked back in the direction from which she had come.

Was she doing the right thing? Should she turn around and run? This was her last chance. She didn't take it.

As she approached the car, the driver's side door opened and a man got out. She smiled shyly, and her smile was returned with a confidence and assuredness which immediately quelled her anxiety. She was nervous, yet excited. He continued smiling and indicated the passenger side of the car. She stepped into the road and opened the door, placed her school bag on the floor and got in. He followed suit and they both closed their doors.

'Don't forget your seat belt,' he said.

She nodded, and as she reached behind her the car engine started and the man immediately pulled the car out into the road. He seemed to be in a hurry. As she fixed the seat belt, she looked at him and he gave her that same smile, the one that always seemed to put her at ease. She leaned back in her chair. This was a good idea. The right thing. And even if it wasn't, she could simply come home. Her parents would be angry at first, but also relieved, and it would all be fine. This was a win-win situation.

As they reached the end of her street and pulled out into the stream of traffic on the main road she watched the familiar landmarks drift by. The newsagent's where she often met her friends, the grocery shop where her parents sent her to pick up items they needed from time to time. She felt a pang of fear as they moved past these but reminded herself again that she was in control, she was in charge. This was just change and her teacher had told them that change was good.

'Are you thirsty?' he asked, reaching between the seats and bringing out a bottle of water. She nodded and he handed it to her. Again, this prop would occupy her and calm her nerves. She unscrewed the cap and took a long gulp. The cold weather had kept the liquid cool and it felt good. She drank some more.

Slowly, the area became less familiar until she could see they were leaving the city and she didn't recognize any landmarks.

'Will it take long?' she asked.

He kept his eyes on the road and shook his head. 'No, we'll be there soon.'

Looking out of the window, she suddenly began to feel tired. She seemed to be having difficulty keeping her eyes open. Not surprising, given the lack of sleep she had had last night. She had been so excited. After her parents had said goodnight and closed her bedroom door, she had quietly got up and packed her bag. She removed all the school books and equipment and hid them under her bed. Then she packed the clothes and toiletries she would need. She had planned this down to the last detail, so it didn't take long. But now the lack of sleep was catching up with her. She had thought the adrenaline would keep her awake. They had learned about that in biology. But for some reason, this didn't seem to be working. Suddenly she felt an extreme wave of exhaustion wash over her and she had trouble holding the almost empty water bottle upright.

He reached over and caught the bottle, took it from her hands just before it fell to the floor. He replaced it between their seats. Then he looked over and watched as Alice Lowrie's eyes finally closed and she slumped like a rag doll in her seat.

* * *

The first thing she was aware of was a sharp headache, followed by the harsh light of early afternoon as she tried to open her eyes. She closed them again, processing the pain. Then she realized the urgency and opened her eyes fully. It hurt, but she rubbed them as if by reflex and struggled to push herself up on one shoulder. She looked down and saw that she was lying on a bed. A thin mattress, with a slightly raised metal frame. She leaned one hand on the frame and brought herself upright. She winced as her eyes let in more light and looked at her surroundings.

She was in what looked like a small dormitory. Maybe an old school or hospital? She had seen something similar in a television drama she had watched with her parents. It had been set in a rural boarding school and the story told of the brutality of the housemasters towards their young charges. The room was rectangular and she counted the beds. Eight, including the one on which she was sitting. It looked like five of them were currently in use, made neatly with covers tucked in and pillows carefully positioned. The other three were stripped and held only a bare mattress. Next to each bed was a bedside table and a chest of drawers. A few personal possessions sat on the bedside tables. With her slowly recovering vision she could make out a watch, several items of jewellery, a couple of soft toys. There were also a number of books.

She took in the room again, this time more carefully. The walls were painted white and looked like they had recently been decorated. The lighting was two bare bulbs, but no lampshades. Her mother would not approve; she was very clear about good-quality lampshades. The floor was covered in vinyl, beige and rather old, with a V-shaped pattern. It was an odd contrast with the newly painted walls. Then she noticed the windows. There were two, both at the far end of the room. They were barred outside. She frowned and her heart beat a little faster. Why bar the windows?

She lifted herself off the bed and stood up. It took a few moments to balance, and she leaned on the metal bedpost for support. It felt cool and smooth in her hand, but unfamiliar. Where was she? Was this the place he had described? She realized that he hadn't said much about it in their discussions. It was only then that she began to wonder why she felt like this. If this were a movie, she would assume that she had been drugged. That couldn't be right.

She stumbled towards the nearest window and put her face close to look out. It seemed odd having the bars in the way of the view. She could see what appeared to be the countryside. A very large, lawned area, fairly well looked-after. Beyond that were woods. All she could see there were trees. There didn't seem to be anyone about, certainly not in the area she was looking at. It looked very peaceful. Just as he had described it. She wasn't sure how she felt.

Then she remembered her phone. She reached into her pocket, but it wasn't there. What had she done with her phone?

She looked towards the door and made the decision to go outside this room, to find out where she was and where he was. She walked, still a little unsteadily, towards the far end of the room. She reached the door and turned the handle. It moved, but the door didn't open. She pulled again. Nothing. She saw that there was a lock just below the handle. Why would it be locked?

'Hello? Hello? Can anyone hear me? Is there anybody there?'

She had raised her voice a little, although she didn't want to shout. But nothing came back. Nobody answered. She attempted to open the door again.

'Hello? Can anyone hear me? Hello!' Slightly louder this time.

Silence.

Her pulse quickened. Every sinew was now telling her that something had gone badly wrong. That she had made a terrible mistake. All she wanted was to be back home with her parents. She turned and walked back towards the bed she had woken on and sat down. What else could she do?

* * *

It was sometime later, maybe half an hour, that she heard footsteps. She instinctively stood up next to the bed. They came closer and she heard a key turn in the door. She was suddenly very nervous. The handle turned and she watched the doorway carefully as it opened. A man entered, looked at her and smiled, closing the door behind him. But he didn't lock it.

He strode towards her, exuding confidence in every way. She watched, said nothing. He was dressed in a suit, but with no tie. He approached her, stopping to pick up a chair that was beside the next bed. He placed it down at the end of her bed and sat down carefully. He smiled at her.

'Hello, Alice. Why don't you sit down so we can have a chat?'

She stared at him for a moment, then did as he suggested.

'Where's Nicholas?' she asked.

'Nicholas will be along a little later. He's got some work to do.'

She looked at him, then nodded. 'Where am I? Nicholas didn't say we'd be coming to a place like this. I thought we were going to a house.'

'This is a home, Alice. There's an important distinction.'

She nodded. He spoke with a slight hint of an accent, but she couldn't quite place it. His voice was calm and deep. He smiled again. She relaxed a little.

'This is your home now. As you discussed with Nicholas. I think you'll really like it here. It will take you a while to get used to the way we do things, which will probably be a little different to the way you're used to. But we have a purpose here. Everyone is valued and everyone is respected. And we know that there is a chaotic, unjust and violent world out there. In here, things are different. Things are much, much better.' He smiled, leaned forward a little.

He was saying many of the things Nicholas had said and it made her feel better. She just needed to see him and everything would be all right.

'Is it OK to call my parents?'

He clasped his hands in his lap. 'No, that's not a good idea. You'll feel homesick for a while. That's only natural. Perfectly normal. But it will be easier if you don't contact them now. We'll let them know you're safe and well, and when the time is right you can talk to them. Once you're settled. It will be easier that way.'

Alice wasn't sure what to say, but she got the distinct impression that this wasn't up for negotiation so she simply nodded. She would talk to Nicholas about it. He'd sort it out.

'How are you feeling?' he asked.

She thought about her sleep and her headache. Considered her vague idea that she might have been drugged, but didn't want to ask outright in case she appeared stupid.

'I feel OK. A bit tired,' she ventured, wondering if he would pick up on it.

'That's to be expected. You've had a journey and are in new surroundings. It's very common to feel disorientated when you first get here. Many of our group felt the same way at first.'

'How many of you are here?' she asked.

'How many of "us", Alice. Not "you".'

She nodded. 'How many of us are here?'

'You'll meet the others soon. They're working or studying at the moment, but they won't be long.'

'Is this where they sleep?' She looked around the dormitory.

'Some of us sleep here, yes.' He had corrected the pronoun again. 'Are you hungry?'

She thought. 'A little, yes.' She had had breakfast, but she had no idea what the time was now.

'It will be time to eat soon. Someone will come and get you.'

'OK. What shall I do in the meantime?'

'Relax, Alice. Take some time to think about what you really want from your life. Our purpose here is to be happy, and one of our fundamental beliefs is that if you want to be happy, you have to truly understand what you want. One can't exist without the other.'

This was almost exactly what Nicholas had said to her. It had been one of the things that attracted her to this group of people. She wasn't sure what to say to this.

'OK. I'll do that,' she said.

He stood up and smiled at her again. 'I have to go now, but I'll see you a little later and we can talk some more. We'll sit down with Nicholas and then we can answer any questions that you might have. I'm sure you'll have many. This is a place for answers, Alice.'

She nodded. The thought of seeing Nicholas cheered her up.

He turned and walked towards the door. Without saying anything, or even turning around, he left the room and closed the door behind him. She heard the key turn in the lock and his footsteps trailed softly away.

She wondered why he had locked the door. Maybe that was just how it worked here. Wherever "here" was. She stood up and walked back to the window at the end of the dormitory. There was still no one in sight, no cars, just nature. It certainly looked beautiful outside. Peaceful. Maybe she could be happy here for a while. She felt a tense pain in her stomach and concluded that it was almost certainly the nervousness she felt. She rationalized that if it didn't work out she could always leave, return home and pick up where she'd left off. Plenty of young people left home, ran away for a while, then returned. Their parents always understood, were always happy to have them home. This wasn't permanent. It was an adventure. Something to tell her friends at a later date.

Nicholas had prepared her for the initial feelings she was likely to have. He'd said it was not going to be easy at first. But he'd assured her that the benefits would vastly outweigh the difficulties. Nothing good came easy.

Alice Lowrie resolved to embrace this adventure. What else could she do?

CHAPTER TWELVE

Present day

Pope watched Brody as he returned to the office and pro-
ceeded to make himself a coffee. He avoided eye contact.
She considered starting an argument, pressing him to say
what he was thinking and what he had said to Fletcher after
she had left, but decided to avoid it for the time being. They
had work to do and she needed everyone focused on the case.
Best to let it go.

'Could you make me one of those?' she said. His shoulders seemed to relax a little and he turned and nodded his
agreement. He made the drinks and brought one to her desk.
She took it and sipped. It was what Pope needed and she was
glad to have moved on, if only a little, with Brody. At that
moment Miller came in and headed straight to his desk.

'Adam, where are we on the blood test?' she asked.

He took a seat. 'Hang on.' He clicked his computer
mouse and carefully scanned the screen. 'Nothing from the
lab yet. I'll give them a call.'

Pope watched him as he talked on the phone. This was
the most promising lead at the moment. If they could identify the blood on Alice Lowrie, they could begin to find out

what had happened to her. As he spoke, Miller seemed to nod at Pope and he wrote something in his notebook.

'OK, great. Can you send me the details straightaway? Thanks.' Miller replaced the receiver and finished what he was writing. 'Good news. The lab have identified the blood. The sample that wasn't hers. It belongs to a Nicholas Cooper,' he read from his pad. 'I'll look him up.' He returned to his keyboard.

Pope's heartbeat immediately quickened and she felt the thrill she only got with progress in a case. She and Brody walked quickly over to Miller's desk.

Miller found the details and brought them up on screen. 'Here we go. Nicholas Cooper. Date of birth, third of December 1980. Six foot one. Born in the States. San Francisco. Apparently lived in Paris for two years before moving to the UK in 2010. No record while he's been here, but immigration have the visa and entry information. US police have his blood records.'

'Do we know why?' asked Pope.

'No. Can't see an explanation here. There's a picture from his passport, I think.' He turned the screen towards Pope and Brody.

Pope saw a handsome man, shoulder-length dark hair and brown eyes. She did a mental calculation; he looked younger than his years. At least at the time the photograph was taken, a decade or more ago.

'Do we have an address?' asked Pope.

Miller scrolled down the record on his screen. 'Last known address is in Lenham, Kent. Those are the details he gave when he entered the UK. Nothing since then.'

'Where's Lenham?' asked Pope.

Miller checked something on his computer. 'Looks like around an hour and a half, a bit less. Straight down the A2.'

Pope considered this for a moment. She could call the local police and send them on a recce. But there was no guarantee they'd be quicker, and she was too fired up to sit around and wait.

'Miller, print off his photo and bring it with you.' She nodded at Brody. 'Let's go and see what we can find out about the mysterious Mr Cooper.'

* * *

The drive down the A2, then M2, was not the most visually stimulating. Kent may be known as the Garden of England, but this did not lend itself to attractive scenery. Rather, they found the endless fields flat and uninspiring. Luckily, Pope, Brody and Miller had the prospect of finding out more about Nicholas Cooper to keep them occupied en route. Brody drove, while Miller looked up the place where they were going.

'What have you got?' Pope was impatient. She'd been waiting a while for Miller to find something of interest.

'Lenham is a pretty small place. Around three and a half thousand people live in the village. A couple of pubs, a restaurant and a church. That's about it. Commuterville, by the look of it.'

'What about Cooper's address?'

'Well, it seems to be a few miles outside the village. It's called "The Old Schoolhouse", although it's not clear if it's actually an old school or not.'

Pope thought for a minute. 'What's the nearest station to Lenham?'

'Maidstone,' said Brody.

Pope didn't ask how he knew that so quickly. He seemed to know a lot of odd stuff. 'Do either of you know anyone at Maidstone?'

'Yeah, there's a guy I trained with at Hendon. Pete Fraser. I think he's still there,' said Miller.

'Give him a ring. See what you can find out.'

Miller nodded and found the number, then dialled and waited to be put through. After briefly catching up he explained the situation to Fraser, who evidently didn't know anything about Lenham but said he would talk to a couple of colleagues and call back. Miller made sure Fraser knew that it needed to be quick, as they were already well on the way.

Pope was surprised at the speed with which the call was returned, and she watched Miller carefully as he nodded and wrote in his notebook. When Fraser had finished, Miller thanked him and made promises to catch up soon.

'What?' Pope knew she'd said this unnecessarily, but the anticipation had clearly got the better of her.

'A bit odd, to be honest. He said he hadn't heard of the place but it's apparently quite well known.'

'In what way?'

'It did use to be a school. Old Victorian place, but no one remembers it actually working as a school in recent years. It's used by a religious missionary group known as "The Collective". Ever heard of them?'

Both Pope and Brody shook their heads.

'Sounds like some kind of cult,' said Brody.

Miller nodded. 'This group use it as a UK base for their travel abroad. They work as missionaries in far-flung parts of the world, although Pete didn't know where exactly. Keep themselves to themselves. No trouble to anyone. He said they don't really interact with the community. Very self-contained, rarely seen. Local police know about them, but rarely have any contact.'

'And this is the address we have for Cooper?' asked Pope.

'Last known address, yes. But bear in mind it's ten years old.'

'So, Cooper travels from the States to Paris, then heads to England and lands in an old schoolhouse inhabited by a group of secretive missionaries?'

'Seems that way,' said Miller.

'And his blood ends up all over Alice Lowrie's dress.'

'A strange one.'

Pope nodded. 'The more we learn about this case the more we don't know. More questions than answers.'

'You never know. He might be there when we arrive and he can clear everything up for us,' suggested Miller.

'You never know,' replied Pope.

* * *

Brody guided the car off the motorway and followed his sat-nav towards Lenham. The house seemed to be on the other side of the village, and as they drove through they saw that Miller's description had been pretty accurate. A small place, with a modest road through the centre. There was one pub on either side of the road, only separated by a few hundred yards, and a quaint tea shop that looked more like a kitsch tourist attraction than a useful hangout for locals.

They were soon out the other side and back into the countryside. Here it was more appealing, with green meadows either side of the road. Pope couldn't live here, but she was beginning to see why some people might. Maybe.

Brody was the first to see the sign and pulled up at the closed gates. An old plaque that simply said *The Old School* was attached to the wall. Next to it was a postbox, so that the person delivering the mail wouldn't have to walk up the drive. Miller got out and released the catch, pushing the large gate back and walking with it. He got back in the car and they drove slowly up the long, gravelled drive. For a few moments they couldn't see the property and Pope noted how private the location was. If you wanted to live apart from others and maintain your privacy, this would be a good place to do it.

Then the building came into view. It was a large, one-storey, brick-built property, Victorian in style and construction. It was L-shaped, with a large main section and a smaller part forming the perpendicular of the "L".

As they pulled up Pope saw that there was a car parked at the far end of the driveway, an old blue Volvo estate. Brody stopped the car just in front of it and the three of them got out. The first thing Pope noticed was that all the windows had bars over them. They were old and were starting to rust at the bottom, where the water would have pooled in the rain. It seemed odd and suddenly she was wary, her senses pricked.

She stopped. 'Brody, Miller. Look at the bars on the windows. They're pretty heavy duty for home security. And the locks on the door look pretty serious too.' There were three separate locks: one at waist height, one at shoulder height and one at knee level. This is what security companies often recommended where above-normal protection was required. It was very difficult to kick in a lock at shoulder or knee height. Pope looked back at the Volvo. She suddenly regretted that she had not thought to bring any armed backup. She had absolutely no idea what was waiting behind the barred windows and tightly secured front door.

She indicated to the others to look towards the left of the building, while she moved to the right. She walked slowly, taking in every detail. The windows were large, as you'd expect in a building like this. But there was a wide hedge bordering the entire length of the wall, making it impossible to look inside. Pope tried, but she simply couldn't get close enough. She walked as far as she could, then came up against a large, solid, locked gate joined to a wall — the border to a walled garden, she guessed. She couldn't see over and, again, she was struck by how much this seemed to be set up for maximum privacy. Pope turned and went back to the centre of the house.

'The bars on the windows, the locks on the door. Do you think Alice Lowrie could have been held against her will? Is that what this is?' asked Brody.

'Maybe. It might just be heightened security, particularly if they're abroad for long periods of time,' said Pope.

'Is that the feeling you're getting?' said Brody.

'No. Not really.'

'So, how do we get in? *Do* we get in?' said Miller.

Pope walked up to the front door. As she peered at the locks, she suddenly stiffened and turned to the others. 'The door's open.'

Brody and Miller walked forward and inspected it for themselves. The door was indeed very slightly ajar.

'If you're this security-conscious, why leave the door open?' asked Brody.

'Good question.' Pope raised her eyebrows, shrugged her shoulders and slowly pushed the door. It was silent as it opened. She took a step inside and looked around. The entrance hall was vast, with high ceilings and deep red tiles on the floor. The walls were painted white. Along the sides of the room were simple wooden benches, which reminded Pope of church pews. That would fit with the missionary idea.

She called out. 'Metropolitan Police. Anybody here?' No reply. The words echoed around the space. She repeated them. Then, 'Metropolitan Police. We are entering the premises. Please identify yourself.' Still silence, after the echo. Pope looked at Brody and Miller, who both nodded. Technically they didn't have authorization to enter the building, but the nods agreed: something was wrong and that gave them reasonable grounds.

Walking into the large central area, Pope saw that there were several doors leading off. All were closed. She indicated to the left and the three of them approached the first door. It was old, stripped wood, either original or a very effective reproduction. Pope's knowledge of Victorian architecture and fixtures and fittings wasn't good enough to tell the difference. She gripped the handle, opened it and moved inside, followed by Brody then Miller. Pope looked around and saw that this was a larger room. A dormitory. The room was a rectangle and stretched to a wall at the far end with two large, barred windows. On either side were simple, metal-framed beds with what looked like thin, functional mattresses. She counted eight beds, but only three looked like they were currently in use. They were neatly made with a floral cover tucked under the mattress. The other beds were bare. Beside each was a bedside table. Most were empty. Pope walked further into the room, taking in the surroundings. She had a thought and glanced back to the door. She hadn't noticed, but it had a formidable lock. Again, more than you might expect in a community of missionaries or a school dormitory.

'It doesn't look like there are many people staying here at the moment,' said Brody. 'Could be away, I guess. On a trip somewhere?'

'Maybe,' said Pope. 'But look at the lock on the door and the bars on the windows. This doesn't feel—' she searched for the word — 'voluntary. I get the austere living conditions, the few belongings. But why such a serious lock? Why the bars? It doesn't feel right.'

Brody was looking out of the window. He turned back. 'We need to find out a bit more about this missionary society, the Collective. This feels like something else.'

'Like what?' asked Pope.

'I don't know. But I've read about cults and their living conditions. This doesn't seem too dissimilar to some of that stuff.'

'It could explain Alice Lowrie. This definitely feels like somewhere you'd want to escape from.'

'Yes. But what did she have to do to make that escape?'

Pope nodded. 'Let's check out the rest of the place.' She led them out and back into the main atrium. Pope walked towards the next door and knocked. No answer. She opened it slowly and saw that it led into a large, open kitchen, dominated by a huge, dark blue farmhouse-style range cooker. It looked like it could provide for a significant number of people. In the middle of the room was a substantial island, holding a knife block and several wooden chopping boards. Suddenly she froze. 'Blood.' She indicated the corner where the island met the floor farthest from where she was standing.

Pope gathered herself and walked carefully around to the other side of the island. On the floor was a body. A tall man, short, dark hair, lying on his back as if he had fallen awkwardly. His white shirt was now largely a very dark red, as whatever wound had been inflicted had released enough blood to stain the entire shirt and form a sizable pool on the floor. It was obviously several days old, as it had now dried, but it was clear enough what it was. And he was very evidently dead.

Brody kneeled down, checked his pulse to confirm. Miller took the photograph from his jacket pocket and looked carefully at it, then again at the corpse.

'It's Cooper.'

Pope nodded. She watched as Brody used his pen to open Cooper's shirt a little, while preserving any trace evidence that might be present. He looked carefully under the shirt.

'It looks like he was stabbed multiple times.' Pope could see he was counting. 'I can see at least seven stab wounds, although there could be more. I don't want to disturb it too much.'

She knew what this meant and what was coming next.

'I think this tells us all we need to know for the moment about how to proceed with Alice Lowrie,' said Brody, still examining the body. He didn't look up at Pope. 'Seven stab wounds takes us a world away from self-defence. This is a frenzied attack.'

Pope watched him. And she didn't argue.

Brody stood up and put his pen away. 'We need to check the rest of the place. I'm guessing there won't be anybody else here now. Not after this.' He looked down at the body.

Pope nodded. 'You and Miller do that. I'm going to call it in. I want our guys down here looking at this, not the locals.'

'They won't be too impressed by that.'

'It's our case, they can be as unimpressed as they like. That's not my main concern.'

Pope took out her phone and dialled Fletcher back at the station while Brody and Miller left to check the rest of the building. She explained what they had found and what she needed. Fletcher, like Brody, initially suggested that the local station might be able to handle the scene. But when Pope described the scene in detail, how many times Cooper had been stabbed and the dormitory they had discovered, Fletcher began to see that this might be something they wanted to handle themselves. Eventually he agreed to send a Scene of Crime unit and a medical examiner as a matter of urgency. Pope said that they would wait there until they arrived, brief them and return to the station. She also asked Fletcher to check who was currently on duty outside Alice Lowrie's room at St Thomas' Hospital. After a few moments and a discussion with his PA, Fletcher found what she needed and passed on the information. Pope ended the call and immediately dialled another number. The call was answered after three rings.

'Is that McEwan?'

'Yes. DCI Pope?'

'Where is Alice Lowrie? Is she still in her room? In bed?'

'Yes, ma'am. She's asleep.'

Pope breathed a sigh of relief. 'OK, good. Look, I need you to keep a very close eye on her.'

'We are, ma'am. She's fine. The doctors and nurses here seem to be doing a pretty good job, they're regularly in and out.'

'That's good. But things have moved on. There's a good chance that she might have attacked someone before she arrived with us. It's serious. So we now have to treat her as a possible perp.'

'Oh. OK.'

The officer sounded a little unsure now.

'Basically, keep an eye on her when the medical staff are in there. Don't say anything to them about this. But be vigilant when anyone comes or goes. And under no circumstances let her out of your sight.'

'Right. Understood.'

'Thanks, McEwan. How long are you on for?'

'Another four hours.'

'Good. I'll be there before you finish. Call me if there's any change.'

'Will do, ma'am.'

Pope hung up. She looked down at Nicholas Cooper, or what was left of him. This was a vicious attack. Like Brody,

93

the coroner would call it "frenzied", she had no doubt. Could Alice Lowrie really have done this?

Just then, Brody returned.

'Anything?' asked Pope.

'Miller's having a look around outside. There're another two main rooms off the entrance hall, and a bathroom. One is an office, looks set up for quite a few people. Four or five desks in there. There are several computers, printers and a load of box files. Off that room is another bedroom slash study, but looks like it's just for one person. Male, judging by the contents of the wardrobe. Double bed, though.'

'Cooper's, maybe?'

'Yeah, that's what we thought. Couldn't find a wallet or anything with ID. Fingerprints will probably confirm when the techs get here.'

'They're on the way. We'll wait here until they arrive but not much point in us all staying after that. Miller can wait here to liaise. We need to get to the hospital and have a chat with Alice Lowrie. We may be able to jog her memory with what we've found. Can you make sure you take some pictures of the place before we leave?'

'Will do,' said Brody. 'So, what do you think?'

'It seems likely, although not certain, that she stabbed Cooper. There's a possibility that she just found him like that and that would account for the blood on her. But I think we have to accept that she might be dangerous. I've talked to McEwan, who's outside her room at the moment, and filled her in.'

'Good. It does change how we approach talking to her going forward.'

'To a point, yes. But this place looks like some kind of a prison. Self-defence is definitely still a possibility if she was held against her will.'

'Stabbing someone seven times? That's a stretch for self-defence. She wanted to kill this guy. Really wanted to kill him,' said Brody.

'Alice Lowrie disappeared eight years ago. If she's been here ever since, under God knows what circumstances, she would have been prepared to do whatever it takes to get out. Any good defence barrister could make a strong case.'

Brody thought for a moment. 'There's another possibility, of course.'

'What's that?' Pope's tone was combative.

'This certainly looks like she might have been held against her will. The bars, the locks on the doors all suggest that. But if that were the case, then we could easily be looking at a cult situation.'

'A cult?'

'More common than you might think. There have been quite a few cases in the UK in recent years.'

'I didn't know that,' admitted Pope.

'And if we are talking about a cult, brainwashing is their stock-in-trade.'

'What's your point?' Pope was impatient, although she realized where Brody was going with this.

'If Alice Lowrie has been held here for eight years, then she must have had the opportunity to escape before. And if she didn't then, why now? What's her agenda? And why did she turn up at our police station and fall right into your arms?'

Those were questions that Pope, as yet, was unable to answer.

CHAPTER THIRTEEN

Pope waited for the forensic and Scene of Crime technicians to arrive. She explained that Miller would stay there until they had finished and would accompany the body of Nicholas Cooper back to London. She wanted everything kept in-house. Once she had briefed Miller, she and Brody got in the car. Brody drove.

As the car pulled out of the driveway, Pope turned around for a final look. She was beginning to get a clear sense of what had gone on here. That Alice Lowrie had been taken against her will eight years ago and kept in this place. Probably by Nicholas Cooper. And eventually, she had found the strength to fight back. If Pope was right, it might hold the key to what had happened to the other two missing girls. Though the thought of what she might discover worried her greatly, she was desperate to give answers to the parents of Sarah Banks and Belinda Forsyth. And to find out what had happened to Tina Waterson.

As he steered the car towards London, Brody broke her train of thought. 'Back to the station?'

'No, I want to go straight to the hospital. I need to talk to Alice Lowrie as soon as possible.'

'What's your plan?'

'I'm hoping that now we know where she came from, it will jog her memory. I want to show her a picture of Cooper, and of the schoolhouse, to see what that shakes free.'

'When are you going to tell her we think we have her identity?'

'I want her to see the pictures first. I'm hoping she'll remember herself when confronted with that. It might be better that way.'

'You still think the amnesia is genuine?'

'I don't know. But I'm hoping her reaction might tell us. If she sees these images, I think we should get a pretty good idea of whether she killed him.'

'Are you beginning to think she did? Have you changed your mind?' Brody sounded tentative.

'If she killed him, or even saw someone else do it, then that would fit with what Darke said about PTSD. I mean, that's enough to send anyone over the edge.'

'It fits,' agreed Brody. 'Possibly a little too conveniently.'

Pope ignored his cynicism. 'Hopefully she'll be able to answer some questions and we can find out what the hell went on here.'

They drove the rest of the journey in silence, each lost in their own thoughts.

* * *

When they walked out of the lift, the first person Pope saw was PC Ana McEwan, sitting with another constable outside the room. She got out of her chair as soon as she saw the detectives approach.

'How's she doing?' asked Pope.

'She's awake now. Just had something to eat. The doctor was in with her about an hour ago. He didn't tell us anything.'

'And she's been in the room the whole time?'

'Yes. She hasn't left the bed while we've been here.'

'Have you been in?' asked Pope.

'No. Only hospital staff — the doctor, a couple of nurses and the person who brought in her lunch.'

'OK.' She turned to Brody. 'Ready?'

He nodded. 'Yeah. Let's go.'

'We're going to have a chat with her. No one comes in, OK?' said Pope.

'Yes, ma'am,' replied McEwan.

Pope walked past the constable and gently opened the door to Alice Lowrie's room. The woman was sitting up in bed, staring blankly out of the window. What she could see of the London skyline from there was holding her attention. She turned to take in Pope and Brody.

'Hi. How are you feeling?' asked Pope, pulling up a chair. Brody closed the door behind them and remained standing.

'I don't know. OK, I guess. The doctors haven't really told me anything. I feel a bit—' she searched for the word — 'a bit spaced out, really.' Her voice sounded small, light, detached. *Fragile*, thought Pope. Could she really be responsible for such a ferocious act of violence? Could she have stabbed Nicholas Cooper to death?

'We visited a place today that we think you might know.' Lowrie's gaze suddenly sharpened. Pope wanted to turn to Brody to see if he had noticed it too, but she kept her eyes focused on the woman. 'We also have a picture of someone to show you. We want to see if you recognize him.'

Lowrie's eyes glowed with an intensity that Pope hadn't seen before. Was it that she thought this might activate her memory? Or was it something else?

'Are you happy to look at some pictures now?' asked Pope.

Lowrie sat frozen with that laser focus in her eyes. Brody handed Pope his phone, cued up on the first picture of the schoolhouse. The look he gave her told Pope that he had picked up on the change in the woman. Pope checked the image and turned the phone around. It was an outside shot of the building in Lenham, taken from the driveway. She offered the phone to Lowrie and let her look at it for a moment.

98

'Do you recognize this place?' She almost used the name Alice, but stopped herself just in time. Lowrie stared intently at the picture but said nothing. 'Do you know this place? Have you ever been here?' Still no response. Pope brought the phone back and scrolled to a picture of Nicholas Cooper. Miller had sent them all a copy of the shot they had on file. It was old, but very clearly him.

'This is a picture of a man we think you might know. His name is Nicholas Cooper.' Pope watched her carefully, but didn't see a reaction. 'Have you seen this man before?' She showed Lowrie the phone.

It was as if a switch had been flicked. The woman let out a scream and pushed violently backwards. She hit her head against the raised back of the hospital bed, but instead of stopping, she continued pushing backwards, hitting herself each time. She continued screaming.

Both Pope and Brody rushed towards her and attempted to restrain her. She began to fight with them rather than herself and tried to tear free of their grasp. The door flew open as McEwan saw what was happening from outside.

'Get a doctor!' shouted Pope. Both officers were used to restraining recalcitrant suspects, but Lowrie seemed to have the strength of several. It took all of their combined might to keep her in the bed.

Then a doctor and two nurses came rushing in. He saw what was happening and ordered one of the two nurses to obtain a drug with a name Pope didn't catch. They held Lowrie down, with difficulty, then the nurse returned and handed a syringe to the doctor.

He swiftly administered an injection, with some difficulty, to Lowrie. She shouted 'No!' several times, but the drug was fast-acting and she soon slumped back in her bed. Pope and Brody stood clear while the two nurses arranged her more appropriately.

'Thanks,' said Pope, looking at the doctor. 'What did you give her?'

'Diazepam. It's the only thing that works this quickly.'

'How long will she be under?'

'Probably around twelve hours. But I can administer flumazenil if you need her earlier. It reverses the sedative effect.'

'I'll need to take you up on that, and soon. I can't wait another twelve hours to talk to her again.'

The doctor nodded his agreement. 'Let me know when.' After checking their patient, both he and the two nurses left the room. McEwan went back outside, leaving Pope and Brody with the sedated Alice Lowrie.

'I think it's safe to say she knows Nicholas Cooper,' said Brody.

'Yeah. I think you're right.'

'Did you buy it? Do you think she's acting?'

'Looked pretty real to me,' said Pope. She leaned against the wall, palms flat against the surface as if she were holding on to steady herself after the drama they'd just witnessed. 'She was in a panic.'

'Yes. But because of what he did to her in the past, or because of what she's done to him? Does she know we're on to her?'

Pope considered that. 'We need to talk to her again. Hopefully she'll be a bit calmer next time.'

'A politician's answer,' said Brody.

'Maybe. I'm going to go and speak to the doctor.'

'Already? She's only just been put under.'

Pope ignored him. 'Stay here and keep an eye on her. I'll be back in a bit.'

She left the room and walked past the officers outside. She briefly explained the situation, reinforced their instructions and headed towards the nurses' station.

She found the doctor, who told her that he could administer the medication to wake her up at any point, and agreed to meet her back at Lowrie's room in a few minutes.

When Pope arrived back Brody was in the corridor talking to the officers on guard outside. He took a step towards Pope. 'Did you find him?'

She nodded. 'He's just sorting out the meds and then he'll wake her up.'

'How are you going to play it?'

'I'm going to talk her through what we've found, tell her we think we know what her name is and then show her the photographs again.'

'What if she reacts the same way?'

'We're just going to have to deal with it. I can't wait any longer on this. We'll have to manually restrain her until she calms down this time. She recognized Cooper. She'll have to tell us what she knows.'

Just then the lift doors opened and the doctor walked out accompanied by a nurse. 'Ready?' he asked Pope.

She nodded and they went to follow him into Alice Lowrie's room. He stopped at the door and turned. 'I think it might be better if you wait out here. We'll wake her up and check her out. It works quickly. I'll let you know when it's OK to talk to her. It shouldn't be long.'

Pope was irritated by his tone and considered taking issue, but thought better of it. She, Brody and the other two officers stood outside and watched as the doctor and nurse set about waking up their patient. He attached a small vial to her intravenous drip, then carried out a number of tests before he administered the drug. It only took a minute for the young woman to begin to stir and soon she was sitting up, drinking water and listening to the doctor. Pope assumed he was explaining what had happened. Then he asked her some questions while the nurse made some notes in the chart. After a few minutes, they opened the door and came outside.

'She's OK,' the doctor explained. 'She should be fine now, but be careful what you say to her. We really don't want to have to go through this again. It wouldn't be any good for her.'

Pope nodded her agreement.

'Kathy will stay outside just in case you need anything.' He indicated the nurse standing next to him. She smiled at Pope.

'OK, that's great. Thanks.'

With that he left and Pope and Brody entered the room again. The woman looked a lot calmer this time and Pope wondered how much of the previous conversation she recalled. Did she remember seeing the photo of Nicholas Cooper?

Again, Pope sat down while Brody remained standing by the door. Pope was impressed that he had the emotional intelligence to stand back and make this less intimidating for the woman. She checked herself; of course Brody had the emotional intelligence for that.

She still had Brody's phone in her pocket. She held one hand on it while she spoke. 'How are you feeling?'

'I've got a headache and I feel really hot,' she said. 'The doctor said those are side effects of the drug they gave me.'

'Yes. They had to sedate you just now. Do you remember?'

'Sort of. You were talking to me, then I can't remember much after that.'

'We were trying to work out where you've been and see if we could get your memory working again. I'd like to carry on with that, if it's OK with you?' said Pope.

The young woman nodded, less wary this time, which Pope took as a good sign.

'We think we know your name now,' said Pope.

'What is it?' She was direct and clear.

Brody watched her carefully.

Pope decided to be equally direct. 'We think we have identified you as Alice Lowrie. From Bermondsey, in South London.'

The woman seemed to be thinking carefully. It wasn't the epiphany that either Pope or Brody were expecting. But then she nodded slowly.

'Yes. That's my name.'

Pope started. 'You remember? You remember your name?'

'Yes. I'm Alice Lowrie.' She looked straight at Pope. 'That's my name,' she repeated.

'OK. Well, that's good, Alice. That's really good. Is anything else coming back to you?'

'You showed me some pictures before. Can I see them?'

She hadn't answered the question. Pope pulled out Brody's phone and got him to unlock it and find the first picture again. She showed her the picture from before, of the outside of the schoolhouse in Lenham. She leaned forward and looked at the picture.

'That's the Collective,' she said. Her voice was quiet.

'What's the Collective?' asked Pope.

'It's where I lived.'

Pope noticed the past tense.

'Can I see the other picture you showed me? Of the man,' asked Lowrie.

Pope threw a glance at Brody. Would Lowrie react the same way? She found the picture of Cooper. She turned the phone around and braced herself, but this time Alice Lowrie was calm, quite subdued. She stared at the image, a deep frown appearing on her face.

'Do you know this man?' asked Pope.

Lowrie slowly nodded.

'Who is he?'

'That's Nicholas,' she said.

'And who is Nicholas?'

'He looked after us at the Collective.'

'Do you know what happened to Nicholas?'

There was a pause, during which Alice Lowrie didn't take her eyes off the photograph on Brody's phone. Then she said, 'I killed him.'

This time there was no dramatic reaction. Pope thought maybe there should have been.

'Why did you kill him?' Pope tried to make the question sound casual, despite the confession of murder.

Now Alice Lowrie looked at Brody, then straight at Pope. She held her gaze while she spoke. 'I . . . I had to.'

'Why did you have to, Alice?'

'He was keeping me prisoner. He locked me in there. And he . . .' Her voice trailed off, but she still looked at Pope. It was disconcerting.

'And he what?' asked Pope.

Lowrie shook her head. 'He did things to me.'

She didn't elaborate, but Pope had a pretty good idea of what she was talking about. They would come back to that later.

'How did you kill him, Alice?'

'I stabbed him.'

'What did you stab him with?' Pope wanted to make sure.

'I took one of the knives in the kitchen,' she said quietly. 'And I stabbed him.'

'How long have you been at the Collective? How long have you lived there?'

'I can't remember.' She looked into the middle distance, seemed to be trying to reactivate the memories.

Tobias Darke had told Pope that sometimes parts of the memory returned before others, sometimes long before. He had said that some memories never came back. Pope thought that maybe that was a good thing.

'Do you remember how you got there?'

'No. I only remember being there. Sorry.'

'That's OK. I think it will take time for your memory to return to normal. You're doing really well.'

Lowrie smiled a little. Or as close to a smile as Pope had seen from her.

'Who else was there? At the Collective?' she asked.

Again, Lowrie seemed to be trying to search her memory, her concentration showing in her furrowed brow.

'I can't remember. I can't remember much before I . . .' She didn't finish the sentence. She didn't have to. They all knew what she had done.

Pope debated telling her about her parents. But as she didn't ask, and didn't currently seem to remember anything concrete beyond a couple of days ago, it seemed best to wait.

'How did you get to the police station in London yesterday?' asked Pope.

'I don't know. The first thing I remember after stabbing Nicholas is waking up here. In the hospital. I don't remember anything else.'

'OK,' said Pope. 'We're working on that, so hopefully we'll know soon. And hopefully your memory will get stronger and you'll remember all those details before too long.'

Alice Lowrie looked down, then at Pope. She had tears in her eyes.

'Hey, it's all right. Don't worry.' She put her hand on Lowrie's arm to comfort her. She passed her a tissue from the table next to her bed. Lowrie dabbed her eyes.

'I killed him. I killed Nicholas,' she said.

'Now's not the time to think about that,' said Pope. 'You need to focus on resting and getting your memory back. We can talk about that later.'

'But I'll go to prison.'

'Don't worry about that now.' Pope leaned towards her. She rubbed Lowrie's upper arm, as the woman looked her in the eyes.

'I didn't mean to do it. I just . . . he just . . .'

'I know,' said Pope. 'There are reasons why you did what you did. A judge will see that and I'm sure you won't go to prison.' Pope caught the flash of warning in Brody's eyes but ignored it.

'Do you really think so?' she asked Pope.

'Yeah, I'm sure of it. You were defending yourself from him. Anyone will be able to see that.'

Brody looked at the floor and shook his head. Pope didn't see it, but she didn't need to.

'You need to get some rest now. I'm going to talk to a few people, then we'll be back later. In the meantime, there'll be officers outside if you need anything.' Pope pulled out a card and put it on the table by the bed. 'If you need anything, just give me a call. Anything. You can get the officers to contact me. OK?'

Lowrie nodded. She wasn't crying now. Pope's reassurances had calmed her down.

'We'll be back soon.' Pope smiled and got up. She avoided eye contact with Brody as she walked past him and opened the door. Brody watched her walk down the corridor and press the elevator button, having just promised a self-confessed murderer that she wouldn't go to prison. She didn't look back.

CHAPTER FOURTEEN

Eight years ago

Alice was hungry. It had been several hours since she had woken up, and she had eaten at least a couple of hours before that. She didn't know the exact time. She didn't wear a watch, and looking around she saw no clock in the room. She wished she could use her phone. She picked up her bag and searched for it there, turning the contents upside down on the bed. No, not there. The phone and the charger were missing. She considered this and, again, felt a knot of tension in her stomach. Who had taken her things?

* * *

When she had first met Nicholas in the online chat room, she immediately knew she had found a kindred spirit. She argued with her father so much, about seemingly everything, that she was very happy to meet an older man who was so different. He seemed to understand her problems and, crucially, didn't seem to judge her. He had experienced something very similar with his own father — lack of understanding, lack of connection. One thing she certainly had with Nicholas was a connection.

It turned out that they had a great deal in common beyond father issues. Both had similar tastes in music and in film. They were also both interested in politics and the environment. He absolutely understood that climate change and inequality were the two most pressing global problems. They talked for hours, always online, about the problems and about possible solutions. Alice would often lie awake for hours after they had finished talking, inspired by the optimism and creativity he brought to bear on each problem they discussed. Nicholas was a visionary. And he knew so much.

Alice wanted to experience something better. She had outgrown her parents and wanted to live a different life. She wasn't interested in the lives her friends and classmates led. They were shallow, vacuous. She wanted something "real". And he was the first person to understand how she really felt about life. So, when Nicholas told her about the group of people he lived with just outside London, she was instantly hooked.

Nicholas was American and had left the States looking for something better — another desire they had in common. He'd travelled to Paris and then to England. Here he had found a group of people so different, so special, so wonderful, that he instantly knew he had found his spiritual home. Here he had found inclusion, trust, respect and equality. True equality. Everyone was focused on a better life for all. This group rejected party politics and cynicism, and instead embraced an agenda that foregrounded collaboration on issues such as the environment and social justice.

The more Alice heard about this group of people, the more she knew these were "her" people. They thought the same as her and rejected all the things she hated. They prioritized mutual support and free will. They focused on solutions to the problems everyone else just talked about.

So when Nicholas suggested they meet, despite some initial misgivings — Alice had heard a million times about the dangers of meeting strangers on the internet — she agreed. If it was somewhere public, she would be fine. She could get up and leave if she wanted to. But she knew it would be fine. She felt like she had known Nicholas all her life.

She agonized for days about what to wear. How much make-up to put on. Eventually the day came. Alice told her parents she was meeting friends at the park and took a bus to the café where they had arranged to meet. She was incredibly nervous. But as soon as he walked in and started talking to her, Alice knew she had done the right thing. Nicholas was tall and handsome. He was a little older than she had thought, though not by much. But he was also very easy to talk to and instantly put her at ease. They talked for two hours, and by the end she was utterly in thrall to him.

They met several more times, and each time they told each other more about their lives, confided secrets. Nicholas told her all about where he lived, the other people there, and eventually she asked the question. Was there a place for her there? Nicholas said he was very much in favour, that he knew she would love it there, but he needed to ask the others. They didn't let many people in. They had to be very special individuals indeed.

Two days later, two agonizing days where Alice was sure they had said no and Nicholas was working out how to break the news to her, she received a message that confirmed that she could come and stay with them. With him. She was unbelievably excited. She was also scared. But she knew she'd say yes. Nicholas arranged how and when it would happen. And then Alice was leaving her house with a school bag packed with clothes, saying goodbye to her mother, and heading not towards school but rather a new life full of promise and excitement.

* * *

A key turned in the lock and the door opened. Two men entered the room and closed the door behind them. One was the man Alice had spoken to earlier, and the other was Nicholas. She was so pleased to see him she almost jumped up and gave him a hug, but something about the presence of the other man told her it might not be a good idea. She smiled at him and he returned it, walking up and handing her a glass of water. The two men sat down on the bed next to the one she had been allocated, and she took her cue to sit too.

'Alice. How are you feeling?' asked the man she had seen earlier.

She looked at him, then at Nicholas. 'Fine, thank you.' She didn't know what else to say.

'Are you hungry?'

He had asked her that earlier. 'Yes. A little.'

'Good, we'll be eating soon. You can meet the others.'

Alice wondered why Nicholas wasn't saying anything.

'I'm so glad you've decided to come and join our group. I think you'll be very happy. Did you have a think about what we talked about earlier?' he asked.

Alice looked confused.

'I asked you to think about what you really want from your life. What you think will make you happy.'

She remembered. She hadn't really thought about it. Thoughts raced in her mind. 'I suppose I want everyone to be happy.' He looked at her without any real expression and she realized what a silly thing that was to say. She needed something more concrete. What *did* she really want? 'I want everyone to see that solving the problems we have with the environment, with poverty and with inequality are more important than watching reality TV and buying a new outfit every weekend. I want us to work out the real problems, not distract ourselves from them.' Yes, this was what she wanted.

He looked at Nicholas and smiled, then turned back to her. 'That's excellent, Alice. Really excellent.' He looked happy with her.

She smiled. Nicholas nodded at her.

'That's exactly what we want here too. We want to challenge the current social narratives of right-wing ideological shifts and environmental decline and bring about real change in the world. In short, we all want to make a difference here. Does that sound like something you can support?'

Alice nodded. She didn't understand exactly what he meant, but she got enough to know that she was on his wavelength. 'Yes, I really can. That's what I want too.'

He nodded thoughtfully. 'Our philosophy here is that we must learn as much as possible. "To know is to exist." There is a truth, but you need to find it for yourself. You can't rely on a god or a government to find it for you. And we will help you with that. But you must move forward. Always. Here there is no looking back. We must cut off everything in our past in order to truly develop. Unlearn everything you thought you knew, and the path forward is much easier.'

Nicholas was nodding. It made sense to Alice. She could totally see what he meant. She nodded too.

The man looked closely at her. He had a very intense gaze. 'I must say, Alice, I think we have found someone very special in you.'

She smiled shyly. He was very handsome. His deep, blue eyes seemed to be locked on to hers.

'You seem to have all the attributes we look for. Intelligent, thoughtful and keen to learn from everyone. I think you're going to really love it here. And something tells me you're going to be very popular with the others.' He smiled.

Alice smiled again. She had never really been popular, never had that many friends. And she had never had a best friend. All her friends seemed to have other, better friends. She'd always felt secondary to their lives.

'Tell me, Alice. Do you like reading?'

'Yes. I love reading,' she enthused.

'I had a feeling you might say that. I'm going to give you a couple of books to get started with. To get you thinking about a few of our key ideas. But first, let's meet the other girls and get you something to eat. You must be starving.'

Alice was indeed. She got up and followed the two men to the door. Nicholas had not spoken a word.

The dining area was in a large atrium in the middle of the building. A long, rectangular oak table sat in the middle of the room, with twelve chairs around it. The table was laid out with simple crockery and cutlery for nine of the spaces. Sitting around the table were two girls who looked to be slightly older than Alice. They turned when they saw her and smiled. One of them motioned to sit next to her. She looked at Nicholas, and he nodded his agreement. As Alice sat down, she saw two other girls, maybe her age, come in carrying a pot each. They laid them down on the table and removed the lids. Alice leaned up to see in and saw one filled with rice and the other filled with what looked like a vegetable stew. There was also bread on the table and two jugs of water. Nicholas and the other man — Alice realized she didn't know his name — sat at opposite ends of the table. They served themselves first, then the girls took their turn. Alice did the same. By now she was ravenous, and the food tasted good. The man suggested that everyone introduce themselves to the newcomer, which they dutifully did. But they mainly ate in silence, with only a little conversation about the state of the gardens and the work the girls had been doing today. Alice wanted to ask a great many things, but she sensed that now was not the time.

When they had finished, the two girls who had brought in the food removed the dishes and went next door to clear up. To Alice's surprise, the others moved to the dormitory and chose a book. They sat on their beds and began to read.

'Why don't you go and join the others, Alice?' said the man.

She nodded and left the table.

Alice felt incredibly self-conscious as she walked into the dormitory where two girls were sitting, watching her every move above their books. She walked past them and perched on the side of her bed. But all of a sudden, the others got up and crowded around her. Then the other two girls arrived and before long there were five of them spread across Alice's bed and the one next to it.

The chatter was incessant. They wanted to know all about her, where she had come from, what it was like at her school, if she had a boyfriend. They were lovely, and she soon felt more at ease than she had for a long time. Her friends at home never talked to her like this. It was like a Victorian portrayal of a girls' boarding school.

When talk eventually got to the group, their home and the two men, the girls suddenly became more serious. Almost reverential. They explained to Alice that this was the best thing that had ever happened to them. They all had their stories and each one had a happy ending. They told her that they referred to themselves here as "The Collective". This, one of the older girls said, was because generally decisions were made collectively and democratically. There wasn't a hierarchy in the traditional sense. But when it was needed, it was clear that the other man was in charge. Nobody referred to him by name. It almost seemed a joke that he didn't have a name, but everyone referred to him as "Sir". This sounded pretty hierarchical to Alice, but she didn't say anything. When he wasn't around, which was quite often, Nicholas was in charge of the day-to-day running of the group. But decisions, in the main, were democratic.

The girls told Alice that in the mornings they looked after the outside and the gardens. There were lots of fruit and vegetables that needed tending, picking and storing. There were also animals that needed to be looked after — sheep, goats, chickens. Alice loved animals. They were more or less self-sufficient, with Nicholas taking care of getting anything else they needed. Afternoons were spent on study. Nicholas and the other man took care of some sessions, with the rest self-study and directed work. There was a plenary held at the end of each afternoon to discuss what had been learned and any issues or questions that had arisen during the learning. Alice was thrilled. She didn't enjoy school and the idea of not having to attend, even if it was only for a while during her stay here, was fantastic.

Alice asked if it was always only girls here. One of the girls explained that Sir felt society was inherently patriarchal and gender-imbalanced. He saw the role of the Collective was to challenge that with a female-only environment that wasn't repressed by men. He wanted them to develop their own ideas, within the Collective's own framework, and take them out into the world free of the systemic bias that encumbered other women. Alice loved being treated like an adult and felt thrilled that people were talking about sophisticated ideas with her as if she were an equal. That didn't happen at school or with her parents.

Alice asked the other girls if there were any rules. She was used to environments with rules. At this they became noticeably more serious. The tone changed. There were some rules. Sir and Nicholas explained that it was counterintuitive, but only with rules could we become genuinely free. If we don't have to worry about the little things, we can concentrate on the big ideas. Alice could sort of see the logic in that, she thought. So, what were the rules? The most important one was to respect Sir and Nicholas. They worked on their behalf, so they respected them. The next was not to talk to outsiders from the village. Sir told them that, because they lived differently, some people would always view them with suspicion. The easiest way was to avoid others and let Sir and Nicholas handle them. The final key rule was not to contact parents, relatives or friends. This was the most important. They would worry and try to close the Collective down. This would ruin what they were trying to achieve. Alice asked what happened if you broke a rule. The girls insisted that you shouldn't, but if you were to break a rule, you were "aloned". That, as far as Alice could work out, meant essentially solitary confinement. One of the girls appeared to hint that there were more serious consequences for infractions of the rules, but the others looked at her in a way that made her stop talking and Alice didn't push it. She didn't want to think about that now. Everywhere had rules.

That first night, Alice went to bed with feelings of excitement and hope. Everything she had heard, almost everything, was so far from what she was used to. How long she stayed, well, that remained to be seen. But in that moment, she was thrilled to have been chosen. Her mind filled with all the possibilities that now opened up before her, it took her a long time to get to sleep.

CHAPTER FIFTEEN

Conditions at the Collective were in many ways idyllic. The way the girls had described it to Alice was essentially accurate. They got up early and worked outside when the weather allowed. Alice loved working with the animals and quickly began to see their personalities and develop favourites. After lunch, which the girls cooked on a rota, they would study. But this was not like any study she was used to. Nicholas described it as "Socratic". They would read suggested passages of text and then discuss them, asking questions and trying to decide what they felt about a particular idea and issue and how it might relate to the organization of contemporary society. There was an emphasis on the seemingly paradoxical notions of sharing ideas and ideals as a group, while also developing and maintaining an individual philosophy of life. Alice noted that sometimes she felt guided towards a particular view that concurred with the majority. But most of the time she felt that she made up her own mind and was happy with the group consensus.

Sometimes the texts they read were written by Sir, but none of them by Nicholas. Still with no name on the books, these were clear and lucid accounts of particular issues in life and society. It was rare that anyone disagreed with the ideas in these books, especially when Sir was teaching. At the end of each session was a plenary, where the leader of the group summed up and drew conclusions.

After that was creative time. There was no television, radio or other means of consuming popular culture. But music, singing and art were actively encouraged. Sir told them that one of the ways to true understanding was through creative expression. Alice loved art and spent many happy hours painting and drawing, eliciting praise and encouragement from the others.

During these sessions, some of the older girls would be summoned for a private tutorial with either Sir or Nicholas. Sir said that this was a great privilege for the girls, as they had demonstrated that they were worthy of individual time with him. It was to be seen as a reward for good thinking and learning. They had a private study where Nicholas slept and worked and this is where these tutorials would take place. Afterwards, the girls never talked about what went on in these sessions. Sir always left at the end of the day. He never stayed the night there. Once Alice had asked one of the girls what happened. She had burst into tears but refused to discuss it. She had curled up on her bed and Alice hadn't known what to say. The girl was older and had been there longer. What could Alice do to help her? Alice assumed that the girl had said the wrong thing or been scolded for an idea that did not make sense. But she also had a deep sense that something was more wrong.

Then one day Alice was told that she would have a tutorial with Sir. She had expressed some really interesting thoughts in the afternoon session and Sir wanted to follow up individually so they could really focus on some of the finer points of the thinking. Alice was initially thrilled to be chosen. But then she noticed that the other girls were looking at the ground rather than congratulating her and she remembered the older girl sobbing on her bed after her tutorial. She began to feel nervous. But she could trust Sir, she thought, so it would be all right.

She followed him to his study and the first thing she saw when she walked in was a double bed in the corner of the room. Her heart thumped in her chest and she immediately knew what was coming. How had she been so stupid? She didn't want to admit it to herself at the time, but seeing the older girl, curled up and crying on her bed, she should have known why. Maybe she was wrong.

Sir indicated for Alice to sit on the bed. He took the only chair, a few feet away from her. Maybe he did just want to talk. Or maybe she could talk her way out of this.

'So, Alice. How are you settling in? You've been here a while. How are you finding it?'

She considered how to reply, but decided that being honest was probably the way to start. 'I really like it.'

'What do you like?'

Alice thought. 'I like the people, the other girls, you and Nicholas. I've learned so much. Much more than I did at school.'

'I must say, Alice, I'm very impressed.'

'With what?'

'Well, with you, of course. The way you've settled in and contributed so much. You've become such a natural part of the group that it almost feels as if you've been here for ever. Your ideas and intellectual capabilities are really very impressive. Very impressive indeed.'

Alice looked at him and blushed. She felt like she'd been wrong about his intentions. The praise was so unexpected and so important.

'I want you to read, Alice. You have the brain to really understand the ideas we discuss and maybe take them further. We must learn about as much as possible. When we learn with great breadth and depth, we have the context to move our intellect forward in ways that don't get boxed in. An open mind comes from breadth of knowledge.'

Alice nodded. She absolutely agreed with everything he said. He spoke in a way that dealt with complex issues but was easy to understand. Sir was a born teacher and so much better than those she had encountered before who called themselves by that name. He looked at her with an intensity that made her feel that he saw right into her soul. He really knew who she was and could see her potential like no one else.

He leaned forward in the chair, his voice barely a whisper. 'We must make our own rules and decide our own leaders, Alice. Nietzsche talked of the U*bermensch*, someone who doesn't adhere to the mediocrity of common people and ideas, but rises above falsely constructed notions of right and wrong to establish a higher set of values. The Collective must be a form of this. We devise our own, situationally specific rules and ways of being, our right and wrong.'

Alice had heard of Nietzsche. He was one of the thinkers Sir referred to regularly. She was keen to hear more, but suddenly he leaned forward, put his hand on Alice's leg and looked into her eyes. Then he kissed her.

When she left the room an hour later, Alice went straight to bed. It was quite late and nobody said anything. Alice couldn't articulate exactly how she was feeling as she lay in bed that night. She was so excited. Sir had been able to see her maturity and had treated her like an adult. They had made their own rules and that seemed absolutely right.

One thing Alice Lowrie was certain of: she was completely in love with Sir and couldn't wait to spend the rest of her life living with him in the Collective.

CHAPTER SIXTEEN

Present day

Pope and Brody didn't talk on the way back to the station. She knew what he was thinking, and she didn't want an argument. So she sat back and enjoyed the air conditioning in the car, a brief respite from the ongoing heatwave outside.

She wondered what Alex was doing. Wondered if he was thinking about her. They'd had good times. Really good times. She thought he would feel the same. And they'd managed to ride out the arguments, the petty squabbles of everyday life that everyone had to navigate. But she had messed up too many times and the big mistakes, her big mistakes, had all been around her work, which had always been their main bone of contention. She needed them to be able to come back from this.

She stopped herself from brooding, tried to clear her mind and stared at the clouds as they drove.

The first person they saw once they arrived back in the office was Miller.

'How did it go?' asked Pope.

'Fine. I waited until Forensics and Scene of Crime arrived and briefed them on the situation. They're working now, but they'll call if they find anything useful. We left with the body and I got a lift back with one of the techs who was bringing the computer equipment back. How was the hospital?'

Pope spoke. 'We showed her the picture of the house and she didn't seem to recognize it, but when we showed her a picture of Cooper she freaked. Absolutely uncontrollable. They had to sedate her. When she woke up she seemed much better. She recognized her name and confirmed that she is Alice Lowrie. It obviously jogged her memory sufficiently. She also recognized the schoolhouse. Said it was called "The Collective".'

'How about Cooper? Does she remember him?'

'Yes. She reacted totally differently the second time I showed her the picture. She confirmed his name was Nicholas and that she had killed him.'

Miller looked shocked. 'Did she say why?'

'She said he had been keeping her prisoner. And she implied that he had sexually abused her.'

Miller nodded.

'That's all she seemed to remember. She couldn't tell us anything else, who was there besides her and Cooper, how she escaped, how she got here.'

'Do you believe her?'

Pope glanced at Brody. 'Not sure yet.' Brody didn't offer an opinion.

'I've been looking into Nicholas Cooper and Thompson's been checking his online footprint. He's just updated me.'

'Anything we can use?' asked Brody.

'Well, he's an interesting character, although information is pretty sketchy. Born in San Francisco in 1980. Both his parents died and left him a lot of money. When he moved to Paris in 2008 he seems to have lived a fairly bohemian lifestyle from what his social media profile tells us. Plenty of pictures of him with lots of different women in Parisian bars. He presents himself as a sort of Hemingway character, American-in-Paris type of thing.'

'Did he work?' asked Pope.

'Doesn't seem to be any information on that. Looks like he might have just lived off his inheritance and enjoyed the good life for a while, until he moved to the UK in 2010.'

'Why the move?'

'Good question. What's interesting is he had a fairly prolific online presence while he was in Paris, but that comes to an abrupt stop when he arrives in the UK. Thompson can't find any social media at all since then.'

'Nothing at all?' asked Brody. 'Why the sudden change?'

'No idea,' said Miller.

'Unless he was doing something that he didn't want anyone to know about,' suggested Brody.

Pope nodded. 'If the Collective is what we think it might be, there would be good reasons for not wanting any scrutiny of the place. Or of him.'

'That's also interesting,' said Miller.

'What is?' asked Pope.

'The Collective. It represents itself as a charitable religious missionary organization. Basically, they work to raise money and charitable donations, and once they have enough they head out to distant places to work with those in need.'

'But?' said Brody.

'There's plenty of information about charitable giving *to* them. Companies are only too happy to tell anyone who cares to listen how much they donate to charity, and the Collective is registered with the Charity Commission. They get a fair amount of money each year. But there doesn't seem to be any record of the trips they undertake, any travel, any actual missionary work. I can't work out where the money goes.'

'That makes sense,' said Pope. 'I don't think they're a charity in anything other than name. From what we saw and from the little we got from Alice Lowrie, I think it's an organization to recruit young women. I think we're unlikely to find anything charitable about the Collective.'

'A cult,' said Brody.

'Maybe. That's certainly a hypothesis we need to explore now.'

'Another interesting aspect of all this is Nicholas Cooper's connections,' said Miller.

'Go on,' said Pope.

'Well, it appears that when he was in Paris he became involved with a number of individuals with links to terrorist organizations.'

'Seriously? How do we know that?' asked Brody.

'Thompson is following up the contacts he's found so far. But several of them are linked to some very nasty groups. We're not sure of the extent of his involvement, but there's clearly potential there. And one of the men he appears to have known was killed in the Bataclan attack in Paris in November 2015.'

'Christ.' Brody was visibly shocked.

'I know. It was a few years before, but still.'

'That changes our approach,' said Brody.

Pope nodded, deep in thought, trying to process this new information.

'If we're thinking that Cooper had links to terrorists, then that changes how we view the Collective. Maybe we're not talking about a cult, but a terrorist cell. Cooper could have been grooming and recruiting young girls.'

'We don't know there were other girls,' said Pope.

'Not yet, but it seems likely. There was a dormitory with quite a few beds. I don't think we've found everybody by any stretch.'

'Probably true,' said Pope. 'But just because he knew someone who was a terrorist, it doesn't mean he was a terrorist himself, much less anybody he recruited.'

'It doesn't. But it means that we have to consider the possibility that Alice Lowrie is not telling us the truth and that the real reason why she's turned up now might be much more sinister. And it also means that there might be more like Lowrie out there who we don't yet know about. And if so, where are they and what are they planning to do?'

The three of them were silent for a moment. 'I'll get on to Counter-Terrorism,' said Pope. 'Let's see what we might be dealing with here.'

* * *

DCI Mike West walked into Fletcher's office approximately seven minutes after Pope had put down the phone. A veteran of a number of different areas of the force, West was generally respected as a fair and committed police officer. He was a couple of years older than Pope but, unlike some of his colleagues, had embraced all aspects of modern policing and his career had developed well as a result. He wore a smart grey suit and his hair was sharply cut, very short around the sides and longer on top. It was a modern style that worked well on him and made him look younger, unlike Fletcher's side parting that aged him considerably. West shook hands with them both and took a seat next to Pope, across from their boss's chair.

Pope filled them both in on the details of the case so far, and the possible links with members of the group that attacked the Bataclan in Paris. West made notes on an iPad as he listened.

'What do you need from me?' asked West when she'd finished. He had a strong South London accent.

It was refreshing to have a senior male colleague ask Pope what she needed, rather than tell her.

'We need to work out Nicholas Cooper's contacts and establish the nature of his connections to any terrorist organizations,' said Pope. 'It would be useful if you could run the names we have and see if it raises any flags with you guys.'

'No problem, I'll get on to that. I can talk to the security services and see where they are currently on the Bataclan attack and if they're following anything from that.'

'That would be great. It might be unconnected, but there are some coincidences here that I don't like.'

'What do you mean?' asked Fletcher.

'Well, Cooper is in Paris hanging out with guys who later go on to commit a terrorist attack there. Meanwhile he's in the UK grooming young girls, recruiting them into some kind of shady organization masquerading as a missionary charity, but that doesn't seem to do any actual charitable work.'

'How many girls were there?' asked West.

'We only know of one so far, Alice Lowrie, but by the look of the place I'm sure there were more. We're working on finding where they went.'

'So you think Cooper was building a terrorist cell in the UK and was planning something?' asked West.

'Possibly. That's what we need to find out,' said Pope.

'I don't think it's on our radar, which would be unusual given that you say Cooper arrived here ten years ago. But I'll get my team on to it. What's your take on the girl?'

'Alice Lowrie is presenting with almost total amnesia. She claimed not to remember anything, but when we showed her a picture of Cooper, she recognized him and told us that he'd held her prisoner. She suggested sexual abuse.'

'Do you buy it?' asked West.

'The story? Yes, I do. Our psychiatric consultant talked to her and he confirms that her behaviour is consistent with memory loss caused by a traumatic event.'

'She admits she killed him?'

'Yes. I think that's the traumatic event. She says that it was her means of escape.'

'And she seems genuine?'

'As far as we can tell. If not, she's an excellent actor.'

West considered that. 'I've seen a lot of excellent actors since I've been working in counter-terrorism. Part of what these guys do in their grooming is train people in subterfuge and manipulation. I would absolutely expect that if this is indeed a terrorist cell. She could well have been trained to present with fake memory loss. They're sometimes very good at what they do. It's what makes it so damn difficult to track and assess the threat.'

'I'm aware that she might be playing us. My gut says she isn't, but we are keeping an open mind. And this new information adds another layer of complexity to the whole thing.'

'Do you want me to talk to her?' asked West.

'No, not yet. She has a big problem talking to men, which would fit with what she says happened to her at the Collective. I seem to have built a relationship of sorts with her, and I don't want to jeopardize that. What I would value are your thoughts about where we go next with the terrorist links.'

'Absolutely. There are two possibilities here. One: she was held against her will for a long time and ended up stabbing Nicholas Cooper to escape. If that's the case, it's murder. Two: she, and whoever else, were groomed by a terrorist organization and this is all part of a plan. What we need to find out quickly is which of those is true and, if the latter, what they're planning. Because if so, it's already started.'

'I want you both to keep in mind that this is now extremely time-sensitive,' said Fletcher. 'If there's God knows how many people out there planning a terrorist attack, we need to find them before it happens.'

Both Pope and West nodded.

'I'll look at the Collective and work on Cooper's terrorism links. If your guy can let me know the names you have so far and send over the material he's got, we'll get on to that. You could focus on the girl and try to get some more out of her,' said West.

Pope nodded. 'Great. Thanks for your help, Mike, I really appreciate it. We'll keep in touch.'

West left, leaving Pope and Fletcher. She got up.

'DCI Pope, this could be a big problem for us. I don't want to be the team that knew about a potential terrorist attack but didn't stop it.'

'I know.'

'I want to know anything you know immediately. And anything you need, just ask. We have to throw everything at this.'

'OK.'

Pope left and closed the door. At the end of the corridor, she turned the corner and leaned against the wall. She looked up, sighed deeply and closed her eyes, feeling every single one of her forty-two years on this planet, with another twenty on top. She felt an intense pressure on her chest and put her hand on her heart. There were times when she questioned why she had chosen this career. This was most definitely one of those times.

CHAPTER SEVENTEEN

'Right. I've had enough of this.'

'Had enough of what?' asked Brody. He could see the meeting with Fletcher and West had strained Pope.

'Of yo-yoing from here to the hospital to get tiny pieces of information each time. I think it's time we had a tougher chat with Alice Lowrie. I'm getting the sense she knows more than she's telling us. Come on.'

Pope grabbed a bottle of water and headed out of the door. Brody scrambled to catch up. She had got her head together and her frustration had turned into focus and drive. She was going to push Lowrie harder and find out what was really going on.

* * *

St Thomas' Hospital was quiet this evening. Even the accident and emergency unit was more hushed than usual. It would get busier. It always did. The early-evening lull would soon disappear as twilight gave way to night and, exacerbated today by the stifling heat, the stream of casualties would begin to arrive. A few of the staff took a break, knowing they would get no chance to do so later on.

PC Ana McEwan was getting ready to be relieved after a long shift. Superintendent Fletcher had ordered the other officer on duty to an incident near Leicester Square, with her holding the fort until her replacement arrived. It wouldn't be long. She looked through the window of the hospital room for the thousandth time today. Alice Lowrie was still asleep. She wondered what this woman had gone through to make her sleep for so long. There were a few rumours she'd heard from her colleagues, police gossip, but only Pope and her team knew what had happened and they were keeping a lid on it at the moment. That was fine. McEwan wanted to be a detective. In fact, she wanted to be on DCI Pope's team one day. She knew, hoped, that soon she'd be the one keeping things from the junior officers. It was just the way it was.

As she looked at the woman sleeping, a man came rushing out of the lift, sprinted down the corridor towards her. He wore scrubs, a surgical mask and hair covering, his hospital identity badge flying from side to side as he approached. McEwan was instantly on her guard, surprised by the sudden arrival on this calm corridor of a doctor who looked like he had just walked out of the operating theatre.

The man was breathless, barely able to speak. 'Officer.' He breathed hard. 'Officer. There's a man with a knife downstairs in A & E. He's threatening to kill someone if he isn't seen immediately. They need you.'

McEwan wasn't sure what to do. She obviously had to go, but she had also been told not to leave her post. 'I need to be on duty here. What about hospital security?'

'They need your help. I can watch her. I'm a doctor. I'll make sure she's OK.'

McEwan was torn for a moment.

'There are children down there!' said the doctor.

McEwan's own son was four years old. 'Make sure no one enters and she doesn't leave.' She pointed to the room as the man nodded his understanding. McEwan ran to the lift, which was still waiting from the doctor's arrival, and punched the button for the ground floor several times until the doors began to close. As the lift began to move she tried her radio to call for backup, but the device didn't seem to work in the lift. As she replaced it in her belt, she had the vague beginnings of a thought about how the doctor knew where she was and why he came instead of, maybe, sending a nurse or a porter, but then the lift doors opened and she didn't have time to finish it as she sprinted towards the A & E department.

Outside Alice Lowrie's room, the man who had sent PC Ana McEwan to a different part of the hospital turned from the lift to look at the patient. She was asleep. There was no one else on the corridor. He checked that the syringe was still in his pocket. This was easier than he had thought. One not-very-bright police officer, a sleeping target, an unusually quiet hospital. He pulled a pair of gloves from his pocket and slipped them on, then gently opened the door and walked in.

* * *

Pope was impatient for the lift to arrive. She pushed the button repeatedly.

'You know that doesn't make any difference?' said Brody.

Pope continued pushing.

He nodded towards the button. 'Pushing it once calls the lift, it's a waste of time pushing it again. Same at pelican crossings.'

'Thanks, Albert Einstein. Very useful.'

Pope had purposely used the hospital entrance that didn't take them past A & E. She really didn't want to wade through the crises that always manifested themselves there. Not today.

'Come on.' Pope knew one of her faults was impatience. Or was it a virtue in her job? Either way, the wait for the lift was interminable.

* * *

He watched her sleeping for a moment. He could afford himself this pleasure. It had been a while since he had seen her. What she'd done, how she'd done it. That couldn't go unpunished. But it was a great shame. A waste in so many different ways.

* * *

Eventually the lift arrived and Pope and Brody walked in. Brody pressed the button this time. The doors closed and the lift began to heave itself upwards, seemingly in slow motion. It was so hot, Pope felt herself counting the floors until she could escape.

'I bet the lifts in the Shard aren't this old and slow. Or the Empire State Building,' said Pope, her irritation palpable.

'That's a bit of a random pairing.'

'Private enterprise. Money moves things quicker than human life.' Pope was clearly distracted.

Brody smiled and looked up at the floor numbers as they passed. Then the lift stopped, and the doors creaked open. Pope sighed one last time at this manifestation of the under-investment in British public services and walked out into the corridor. Just as she did so, she heard an incredibly loud scream. Both Pope and Brody tensed as they saw that there were no officers on guard outside Alice Lowrie's room. They ran down the corridor, seeing a doctor apparently fighting with Lowrie as they passed the large window. In that first split second, Pope assumed that Lowrie was having another panic attack and the doctor was attempting to restrain her. But when she saw the man slap Lowrie around the face, she knew different. Whatever was happening, it wasn't a bona fide medical intervention.

Pope got in first and grabbed the man by the shoulders, attempting to pull him off the woman. He let go of Lowrie, turned and punched Pope on the side of the head. It was a hard blow and she fell, tumbling over the chair and falling to the ground, instantly stunned. Brody threw himself at the man and they fought. He attempted to land a punch but his

129

opponent sidestepped. Brody stumbled on the foot of the bed and the man hit him hard on the back of the head. He dropped to the floor as the assailant ran out of the room and down the corridor towards the stairs.

Brody and Pope were now both on the ground. It had all happened in a few seconds. Brody was up on his knees then, checking Pope.

'Get after him,' said Pope. 'I'll sort her.'

Brody gathered himself, tried to shake off the pain in his head and haphazardly ran out of the door. He looked both ways and saw that at the opposite end of the hallway to the lifts, the exit door was swinging. He ran in that direction and barged through the door. He heard but could not see the man, who was fast and had managed to get down several flights already. Brody's head was pounding and his shoulder, which he'd fallen on, was burning. But he ran down the stairs. He had to catch this man.

* * *

Pope was up now and sitting with Alice Lowrie. She was shaking, sobbing, unable to articulate. Pope put her arms round her and Lowrie leaned into her. Pope could feel the woman's body shaking and she wondered what this was all bringing back to her, what she was reliving.

* * *

Brody was hitting the corners as he ran down the stairwell, his balance and judgement thrown off. At least once he thought he had lost control and was about to fall headfirst down the stairs, but somehow he managed to keep upright. Then he heard a door bang and he knew he was near the bottom and the other man had run out. He reached the door on the ground floor and exited to a short corridor, with only one door at the other end. He ran through it into stifling heat and a brilliant dusk sky. He was in the middle of the hospital complex, surrounded by buildings. He couldn't see the attacker anywhere. Brody knew that one way led to Lambeth Palace Road and the other to Westminster Bridge Road. But he had absolutely no idea which way to go and no way of finding out. He'd lost this one. He bent over and rested his hands on his knees, heaved his shoulders and felt every pain in his body returning with a vengeance.

* * *

When he arrived back at Alice Lowrie's room he saw that Pope was sitting with Lowrie and an embarrassed PC McEwan was hastily tidying the room, replacing the things that had been knocked to the ground or out of position. The officer shot him a look that told him that she had already been admonished by their boss. He'd give the officer a break and wait until later to find out what had happened. Pope looked at Brody expectantly.

Brody shook his head. 'He got out. I lost him.'

Pope cursed silently. Brody could lip read well enough.

'I didn't get a good look at him. Did you?' he asked.

This time it was Pope's turn to shake her head. 'Only from behind, and only for a second. And he was wearing a mask.'

'I'll check the CCTV.'

Pope remembered a similar hope on a big case last year. That didn't work out so well. CCTV was not always as comprehensive or useful as you thought it was going to be.

'He was pretty strong and well built, that I can tell you,' said Brody, twisting to massage his shoulder.

'Are you OK?' asked Pope.

'Yeah, I will be. He knew what he was doing.' Brody looked at Alice Lowrie, who was still propped up on Pope's shoulder. He indicated her with a lift of his chin and posed a silent question with his eyes. Did she recognize him?

Pope spoke to Lowrie gently. 'Alice.' She didn't move. 'Alice.' She raised her head a little. 'Did you see the man who was here?'

Lowrie looked at Pope, but offered no reaction.

'Did you get a look at him? Did you recognize him, Alice?'

Lowrie stayed motionless for a moment, then shook her head slowly as she looked down at the bed sheets. She didn't raise her eyes to meet Pope's.

'You saw him, but you didn't recognize him? Is that right?'

She nodded, still avoiding eye contact. Pope had made the decision earlier to push harder with Alice Lowrie, but how could she do that now, with what had just happened? She had to do something.

'Alice, look at me.' She waited for the woman to lift her eyes. When she did, Pope saw tears welling up again. She handed her a tissue. 'Alice. Think really hard. Are you absolutely sure you've never seen him before? Not at the Collective?'

She shook her head. 'Please don't leave me alone again. Please stay with me.'

'There will be someone outside the door while you're here.' Pope cast another look of fury at Ana McEwan, who was standing silently in the corner of the room like a naughty schoolgirl.

'No! I want you to stay. I'm scared. You told me you'd make sure I was safe and I wasn't. You said you'd keep me safe,' she repeated.

Pope looked at Brody, who shook his head in warning. 'Ms Lowrie,' he began, 'don't worry. You'll be perfectly safe with—'

'I'll be here,' interrupted Pope. 'I'll keep you safe. I'm not going anywhere.' Lowrie burst into tears of relief and once again sobbed into Pope's shoulder. She looked at her colleague, whose total exasperation was readily evident.

CHAPTER EIGHTEEN

Brody took McEwan outside and asked her what had happened. The officer explained and, to be honest, Brody had a lot of sympathy with her. Faced with the prospect of an armed attacker and a doctor who offered to keep an eye on the patient, Brody considered that he may have done the exact same thing. He was not sure Pope would see it the same way, however. It had been an impossible choice, but faced with imminent danger to the public, that always took precedence if you were a police officer. McEwan had absolutely no reason to suspect a man in medical uniform in a hospital, especially in the heat of the moment. Brody could see she felt terrible about it.

It had taken a while, but Pope had eventually managed to get Alice Lowrie to let her leave the room. Under Brody's disapproving eye, she had placated the woman and pretty much agreed to everything she had asked of her. She explained that she would be just outside the door and Lowrie could call if she needed her. Pope had promised not to leave the immediate vicinity. Under Lowrie's wary gaze, she and Brody left the room and walked a little way down the corridor, out of earshot. McEwan had left to talk to the security guards downstairs to try to get access to the CCTV footage. She had been replaced by another officer. Before she had left, McEwan had made it very clear to her replacement what was required. Not to leave his post under *any* circumstances.

'What now?' asked Brody.

'We need a doctor to check her over.'

'I'll go.' Brody hesitated. 'You pretty much promised to be her bodyguard. How will that work?'

Pope knew he would disapprove. Knew he thought she had got it wrong. She avoided the question. 'She's not safe here. That much is clear. Even with an officer outside and security downstairs someone still managed to get to her.'

'That's not what I thought the problem would be. I thought we were making sure she didn't escape. I think McEwan thought that as well,' said Brody.

'We need to find out who that was. And why the hell he's after her. It doesn't make any sense.'

'Unless someone from the Collective doesn't want her talking to us. Maybe she needed to be silenced.'

The same thought had crossed Pope's mind. 'Her reaction was a little off when we asked her if she recognized her attacker.'

'Yes, it was.'

'We need to keep her close. Something's clearly very wrong here. One way or another. She's either in serious danger, or . . .' Pope trailed off.

'Or she's seriously dangerous?' offered Brody.

'Can you go and find her doctor? Let's get her checked over. And you might want them to look at your shoulder while they're at it.'

'It's fine, really,' said Brody, subconsciously rubbing it with his opposite hand as he waited for the lift.

It took a while for the doctor to arrive. A different doctor — female, young. Pope considered the phrase about knowing you're getting older when the police officers start looking too young and decided it also applied to doctors. She nodded to Pope as she walked into the room but didn't say anything. She read Lowrie's charts and then got to work examining her.

Outside the room Pope called Fletcher and updated him. He already knew all about the attack and congratulated Pope on preventing it. He also asked her to send PC McEwan to him as soon as she had finished with the CCTV footage.

After some time the doctor emerged from Lowrie's room.

'How's she doing?' asked Pope.

'Are you the officer in charge?'

'Yes. DCI Pope.'

'She's fine. A little shaken, obviously, and scared. But medically there's nothing wrong with her. I'm discharging. There's no reason for her to be here.'

Pope was surprised by the abruptness of the woman's manner, but she'd been expecting this. Memory loss was not really a reason to occupy a hospital bed.

'When can she leave?' she asked.

'I need to do some paperwork. It won't take long. A nurse will be along soon to discharge her.'

Pope thanked her as the doctor walked away. She turned and acknowledged with a nod.

'Short but sweet,' said Brody.

'Nothing more to say, I suppose. They can't cure what's wrong with Alice Lowrie in here.'

'That's true. So, what do we do with her now?' asked Brody.

'We need to get her somewhere safe as a priority.'

Brody showed his surprise. 'We need to arrest her.'

'Arrest? For what?' asked Pope.

'For the murder of Nicholas Cooper, to start with.'

'We don't know the circumstances of what happened yet. And what do you mean "to start with"?'

'We know she killed Cooper. She's admitted to murder. But we don't know who else was there, what happened to them, or what the link is to Cooper and his terrorist connections. There's a lot we don't know at this stage.'

'Cooper could well be self-defence. We know that. And that's all we know at this stage. We can't arrest her on what we don't know.'

'Seriously? You don't think we should arrest her?'

'No, I don't. I'm not putting that frightened young woman in a cell. She's terrified, and that would tip her over the edge. We need to tread carefully if she's going to open up to us. No way. It's not going to happen.'

Brody looked incredulous. 'She has literally admitted to murder. What do you plan to do with her?'

'I don't know. But she isn't charged with anything. And we'll keep it that way until we get the facts.'

'We have the facts. The problem is you're too emotionally involved in this.'

'What did you say?'

Brody was committed now. 'You're thinking of Tina Waterson and you can't admit that this woman is a killer. You think by saving her, you're saving Tina.'

Pope was furious. 'How dare you!'

'You can't make up for the failings on that case by saving Alice Lowrie.'

Pope was so incensed that she couldn't speak. She stared at Brody, fury in her eyes.

Brody saw that he'd gone too far. 'I'm sorry, Bec. It's just—'

'Fuck you. You of all people should know . . .' She couldn't finish the sentence. But she could see Brody understood.

He tried again to apologize, but Pope turned and walked away. Back towards Lowrie's room.

'Bec.' He called after her, but she ignored it, opened the door and walked in, closing it behind her.

Pope was incandescent with rage. Not because Brody had challenged her authority. That she could deal with. But because he had brought up Tina Waterson. He knew that was her Achilles heel and it was unacceptable to use it as leverage in this argument. That he had apologized so swiftly was little comfort.

The question now was what to do with Lowrie. She looked at the woman now asleep in front of her and considered her options. There was no way she was going in a cell. With the trauma she had suffered, a cell, guarded most likely by male police officers, would be beyond what this woman could take. Regardless of the morality of the decision, Pope was concerned that what little progress they had made so far with her would be destroyed if she was incarcerated. Pope feared a relapse in her mental state, and worried that her memory might once again fail. That couldn't happen. The other possibility was that she was dangerous, was part of some plot. This was certainly what Brody thought. If that was the case, Pope wanted to keep her close. They had developed a bond of sorts, and Pope wanted to be able to use that to her advantage if it transpired that the woman was playing them. And she had to find out what had happened to Tina Waterson and the other girls.

She had made up her mind.

Pope walked out of Lowrie's room and found Brody outside in the corridor. He went to speak, but she got there first.

'I've decided what I'm going to do. I'm going to take her home with me and keep an eye on her there.'

Brody's shock was obvious. 'What? Bec, you can't do that.'

'I *can* do that. She's not charged with anything. My house is empty. And I trust her. I know you don't, but I do, and it's my call. I'll have a couple of officers outside in case there's any trouble. It'll be house arrest. This way she'll be safe and I can hopefully get her to open up. That would never happen if we kept her at the station.'

'It's too dangerous. We still don't know what's going on here. She murdered Nicholas Cooper, for Christ's sake. She could be anybody. We know virtually nothing.'

'As I said, I trust her.' Pope turned, went back into the room and closed the door, putting an end to the conversation. She wasn't sure how much of this was to spite Brody after his previous comment. She saw him take out his phone and dial a number. He was then having an animated conversation with someone. Pope watched the woman still asleep and wondered if she was doing the right thing. Either way, she had made the decision and as soon as the nurse arrived she would be taking Alice Lowrie out of here.

Just then Pope's phone rang. She saw the number, then looked up to find Brody watching her. Feeling livid, she answered the call.

'Sir.'

Fletcher was completely against Pope's plan. He explained his misgivings in a long rant that Pope simply had to listen to. Eventually, when he ran out of objections, Pope ran through her reasons and told him that the gains they had made so far would be lost if they didn't use the relationship with Lowrie that she had developed. The woman was terrified, vulnerable and had potentially been the subject of an attempted murder. How would it look when the press got hold of the fact that the Metropolitan Police's response to that was to incarcerate Alice Lowrie? If you wanted to persuade Fletcher, point out the optics. There was silence on the other end of the line, then Fletcher relented grudgingly. He told Pope that he would organize two officers to be outside her house overnight, and unnecessarily emphasized caution in dealing with Lowrie. Pope conceded and ended the call.

When the nurse arrived to discharge Lowrie, Pope went into the corridor.

'You called Fletcher?'

'Someone had to make you see that this is the wrong move.'

'Well, I made him see that it's the right move.'

'What?'

'I'll be taking her home when the nurse has finished in there.'

Brody was blindsided. 'I . . .' He didn't finish.

'Next time, maybe you should talk to me and leave it at that, Inspector.'

The final word seemed to inflict more pain than the punch he'd received earlier that evening.

* * *

138

Alice Lowrie shuffled along the corridor, her arm inter-linked with Pope's. She looked like a rabbit in headlights, like a celebrity walking out of rehab, the camera flashes blinding her. But there were no cameras, no headlights. Only Brody and another officer walking behind, the nurse watching from the doorway of her room.

As the lift doors closed, once the four of them had squashed in, they stood in awkward silence. The lift began to descend and Lowrie leaned in towards Pope, away from the two male officers.

The doors opened on the ground floor and the four of them walked out and towards the main entrance of the hos-pital. Out of earshot of Lowrie, Pope warned the other two to be extra vigilant as they left. She wasn't expecting the attacker to be stupid enough to hang around, but she prepared for the worst. A police car was waiting outside the front entrance. As they arrived an officer got out and opened the door.

'Do you want me to drop you off?' asked Brody, surprised that Pope had organized a different car. They had, after all, arrived here together.

'No, it's fine.' She said it without looking at him.

'OK. Shall I meet you at your place?'

Now Pope turned to Brody. 'No, you should call it a night. I'll see you at the station in the morning.'

She could see that the sting had affected him, but she didn't care. She got in the car next to Lowrie, closed the door and felt the smooth engine of the police BMW come to life as the car pulled away.

Pope sat back in the seat. She watched Lowrie gazing out of the window. She had explained that they were going back to Pope's house for the night and Lowrie had seemed relieved that Pope wasn't leaving her. Outside the car window she saw the sun setting over the Thames, the light glinting gold and silver on the water. It looked beautiful, and she almost forgot for a moment the events of the last two days. Almost.

As they passed Bermondsey, where Lowrie and her par-ents had lived many years ago, she wondered if the woman recognized the area. She hadn't asked anything about her parents yet and for that Pope was extremely grateful. That was a conversation she was happy to put off for as long as possible.

Bermondsey was also where Tina Waterson had lived. And later where her body had been found. She considered what Brody had said about overcompensating for what happened to Tina. In her heart, she had a suspicion that Brody might be right. She had carried a crushing guilt over that case for years and it had affected her in more ways than she cared to think about. It had come to define her last eight years as a police officer. She had become so focused on the job, so single-minded. Her career had benefited and she was known as tenacious and talented. But her personal life had suffered, as had those around her. Chloe had almost been killed as a result of her job, and it had been nearly a year since Alex moved the family out. Pope had no idea if or when they would return. She couldn't really blame them.

Brody had been right to call Fletcher, although she hadn't seen it at the time. She wouldn't have involved the boss herself, but that possibly said more about Pope's attitude to authority than any sense of duty. But Brody was a different person, and when he thought something was wrong he called it out whatever the cost. Pope respected him for that and made a mental note to apologize when she saw him in the morning.

Pope knew that she had to get her life back on track somehow, although at this particular point in time she had absolutely no idea what that even meant, let alone how to accomplish it. What she did know was that it involved Alex and the girls, and that involved her attitude to the job. If she could find out what had happened to Alice Lowrie, and find out if it was linked to Tina Waterson and the other girls, then maybe she could eventually be free of the weight that was holding her down.

Pope realized she had been thinking about this all the way home and now the car was pulling up outside her house. She saw that Lowrie seemed to be getting agitated as the car pulled to a stop. She put her hand on the woman's shoulder.

'It's OK, Alice. This is where I live. We're going to go in there.'

Lowrie nodded. Pope got out of the car and walked round to let her out. The two women walked up the path to Pope's front door. She turned and indicated the police officers who were still sitting in the car.

'They'll be outside all night,' said Pope. 'They'll keep an eye on the place to make sure everything's fine.'

Pope found her keys and unlocked the door, ushering Lowrie inside. She closed the door, placing her keys on the table.

'I'll show you where everything is, then maybe you'd like to take a shower while I sort us out with something to eat,' said Pope.

Lowrie just stood there, looking around, and Pope felt vaguely awkward with this stranger standing in her hallway. Had she done the right thing? A bit too late for reservations. She showed Alice the downstairs rooms and then took her upstairs.

'This is the bathroom. The shower's in there. This is my room. And this is where you'll be tonight.' Pope indicated the spare room.

'What happens after tonight?' asked Lowrie.

Pope smiled. 'Well, we'll think about that in the morning. I think you've had enough for one day.'

'But where will I go?'

'A lot depends on when your memory recovers.' Pope's tone was gentle. 'That will help us piece together exactly what happened to you and we can take it from there.'

In reality, Pope had not even thought about what would happen the next day. But she was hopeful that it wouldn't involve a prison cell.

'I'll get you some clothes to wear and a towel,' said Pope. Lowrie went into the spare bedroom and walked over to the window. When Pope returned with a pair of jeans, a long-sleeved shirt, some underwear, a pair of pyjamas and a towel, Lowrie was still staring out of the window. She hadn't moved.

'Best I can manage,' said Pope as she placed the clothes on the bed. 'My wardrobe's not exactly Paris catwalk, I'm afraid. I'll leave you to shower and change. Come down when you're done and we can have something to eat. Are you hungry?'

'Yes. Very.'

'Pasta OK?'

'Yes. Thank you.'

Pope left her alone and went downstairs. It was an odd situation. She poured herself a glass of red wine and took a big drink. She felt it going down and instantly it began to take the edge off. She could feel her shoulders start to relax a little. She checked the fridge and found half an onion and a red pepper. Luckily the cupboard yielded a prepared pasta sauce and a packet of spaghetti. It wouldn't be fine dining, but it would do the job.

As she prepared the food she could hear the shower running. She realized she could really do with a shower herself and began to think again about her guest. She had invited a stranger to share the one space where her work didn't encroach. At least not physically. She looked around and felt the echoes of Alex, Chloe and Hannah all over the room. The sofa where they sat to watch TV, the table where they ate on the rare occasions that they had all been here together, the photos on the mantelpiece of the four of them on holiday and Alex and the girls together before Pope had entered their life. Were they better off somewhere else without Pope? She hoped not, but hope, she knew, wasn't the same as truth. She had played this game almost nightly for months: list as many ways as you can that you have ruined everything. It was a game she was getting very good at playing. Coming home to this empty house every night was a constant reminder of her perceived failings with her family. Maybe it was time to move on. After all, it wasn't her house, but Alex's. She had no reason to be here beyond squatter's rights.

Her phone buzzed with a text message. It was Brody asking if everything was OK. Her reply was a brief *Yes*. She felt a little guilty, but she wasn't quite ready to offer the olive branch just yet. She put the phone away as she heard the shower being turned off. She put the spaghetti into the boiling water and put on the timer for ten minutes.

Just then, she heard a sound outside and was sure it sounded like someone trying to put a key in the lock. She immediately tensed and crept into the hallway. A thousand thoughts crowded in. Why had the officers outside not stopped the intruder? Who was trying to get into her house? Was it the same man who had tried to attack Lowrie at the hospital? Was he armed this time? She heard the bathroom door open upstairs and cursed the timing. Lowrie needed to be away from the upstairs hallway, but as she passed the top of the stairs, walking towards her room, she stopped, seeing Pope and knowing immediately that something was wrong. Pope indicated with a frantic gesture that Lowrie should move away from the line of sight of the front door, but the woman was rooted to the spot, glaring back in fear.

Just then Pope heard a key turn in the lock and saw the door begin to open. She was confused and in a heightened state of alert. She stared at the door and could not have been more surprised when it opened fully and she saw Alex standing in the doorway, Hannah, Chloe and one of the police officers behind him. She saw Alex's eyes dart to the top of the stairs to see a young woman wrapped in a towel standing upstairs in his house.

'Hello, Bec.'

CHAPTER NINETEEN

Pope could scarcely believe it. She hadn't seen Alex and the girls for almost six months. They'd visited sporadically in the months after her father's funeral, and had spoken on the phone with reasonable regularity, but that had tailed off in recent weeks and she had begun to fear the worst.

'Alex,' was all she could manage to say.

'Shall we come in?' Pope was standing in the doorway, effectively blocking their entrance.

'Yes. Of course. Sorry.' Pope moved aside and let them through. 'Hannah, Chloe.'

Hannah smiled at Pope, looking like she'd missed her. Chloe gave a curt nod of the head. At seventeen, it would be a little tougher.

The police officer stood at the doorway. 'He told us he was your partner. Hope that's OK?'

'Yes, of course,' said Pope. 'Thanks.'

The officer turned and walked back down the pathway. Pope closed the door as she realized that Lowrie was still standing at the top of the stairs clad only in a towel.

Pope gave a slightly embarrassed smile to Alex and the girls. 'Alice, why don't you get dressed and come down when you're ready? I'll introduce you.'

Lowrie turned and walked into the bedroom, without acknowledging either Pope or the new arrivals.

'Who's that?' asked Chloe.

Pope paused, considering how to explain the rather odd situation. 'She's from work. Why don't we get your stuff in and get you settled, then I'll explain everything.'

Alex shot Pope a look that was all too familiar: *What have you done this time?* She smiled and took Hannah's bag. Chloe held on to hers.

'There's some more stuff in the car. I'll get it later,' said Alex, putting his bag on the floor. He walked over to Pope and put his arms around her, gave her a kiss on the cheek. She couldn't believe how good that felt after so long and realized how much she had missed it. Throwing yourself into work could only mitigate the effects of solitude up to a certain point. Pope realized she had reached that point some time ago. They broke off.

'How are your parents?' asked Pope.

'They're fine. They send their best.'

Pope could only imagine what thoughts Alex's parents were sending her.

'Why don't you two take your stuff upstairs and unpack, then we'll see about getting you something to eat?' said Alex. If Hannah and Chloe realized they were being packed off so Alex and Pope could talk, they didn't show it. The whole situation was painfully awkward, and Pope thought they were probably glad of the excuse to disappear for a few minutes.

When they'd left, Alex spoke first.

'We've got lots to talk about, but let's start with who that is upstairs. You said something to do with work?'

Pope knew where this would end up, but she didn't have any other choice than to be honest. Reasonably honest. If she told Alex everything, he would probably grab the girls and their bags and leave immediately.

'She's a witness in a case. I brought her here to keep an eye on her. She's terrified and has grown quite attached to me, so I thought it was the best place for her to be.'

145

'A witness to what?'

'We're not quite sure.' That part, at least, was true. 'She seemed to be held by some kind of group in the countryside but she has amnesia and we need to find out what actually happened to her.'

Alex's expression told Pope that she needed to tread carefully.

'I think she may have suffered some form of abuse. She's very jumpy around any men, much more comfortable with women, and that can be quite a typical sign.' Pope felt bad pulling the emotional strings, but she wasn't saying anything that wasn't true.

Just then they heard footsteps coming down the stairs. Alice Lowrie walked to the threshold of the room and stopped. She looked warily at Alex. Pope walked to her, put her hand on her arm and guided her gently into the room.

'Alice, this is Alex, my partner. Alex, this is Alice, the young woman I was just telling you about.'

'Hi, Alice. Nice to meet you.'

'Hello,' she mumbled, looking at the ground.

Alex took a step towards the woman, but she took a step back. She turned to Pope. 'I'm going to lie down for a while.' She turned and walked out, and Pope could hear her walking quickly back upstairs.

'I see what you mean,' said Alex. 'She seems terrified.'

'That's why I brought her here. I wouldn't have if I'd known that you were coming back, of course I wouldn't . . .'

'It's OK, Bec. But we will need to talk. We need to set some ground rules, the first of which will be some firmer boundaries between work and home.'

It wasn't really okay. Pope could see that Alex was trying to rein in his reaction and was grateful.

'Yes, I get that. Do you want a glass of wine?'

'I think that'd be a very good idea,' said Alex.

They stood in the kitchen as Pope poured him a glass and handed it to him, then topped up her own.

'Why didn't you call? Let me know you were coming?'

'I was going to, but I didn't want to disturb you in the middle of work, and figured it wasn't the kind of news to leave on an answerphone. Plus I just thought . . . I suppose I thought it might be a nice surprise.'

'It was. It is. A lovely surprise.' She walked over to him and this time they kissed properly, hugged tenderly, and all seemed well with the world for a moment. Pope couldn't remember the last time she could say that about her life.

'How have the girls been? Has school been OK?' she asked.

'Yes, they've been fine. Chloe has been seeing more of Tyler lately. They seem to be getting on. Hannah's doing really well at school. Got her mother's brains.'

Pope realized that she should have kept in better contact with the girls while they were away.

'How did they feel about coming back?' she asked.

'Well, you know teenagers. Any change is a crisis. But Hannah was really pleased. They were keen to get back to their own house. Living with grandparents when you're their age is tricky. At my age too, actually.' They both smiled. Alex's parents were opinionated and slightly overbearing. Pope regretted putting him and the girls in that position.

'It's great to have you back,' said Pope.

Alex took a beat. 'How long is she staying?'

'Just a couple of days, if that.'

Alex looked surprised.

'I can't put her anywhere else. She remembers nothing so I can't trace any relatives or friends she can stay with. But we're investigating her background and as soon as I can work out what's happened, I can sort her out with something more permanent.'

'Bec Pope, social worker. That's a new one.'

'I know. But it's just this once. And it won't happen again. Especially now you're back.' Pope paused for a moment. 'Are you back? I mean, really back? For good?'

'I don't know, Bec. I want to be. We all want to be. The girls have really missed you. But we'll see how it goes. Let's take it slow.'

'OK. Slow sounds good.'

'The most important thing is that I can't have the girls put in danger again. I can't have a repeat of what happened last year. It took Chloe a long time to get over it. She's still not, really. But she's getting there and I can't jeopardize that.'

'Absolutely. I understand. I want that too. Their safety is the most important thing.'

'You need to leave work at work, and you need to make sure that you don't put yourself or any of us in that position again. How you do that, well, that's for you, for us, to work out.'

Pope nodded, although she wasn't entirely sure exactly how she could do her job without putting herself in danger. It was an occupational hazard. But she would try to keep Alex and the girls away from it. Although, having Alice Lowrie upstairs at this particular moment maybe wasn't the best way to start.

'Why do you have officers outside the house, Bec?'

She wondered how honest to be. She had to try.

'If I'd known you guys were going to come back, I never would have brought her here.'

Alex looked at her. Said nothing.

'She was attacked at the hospital. Someone came into her room and Brody and I interrupted them.'

'Did you catch them?'

'No. They got away. But we will.'

'That explains it!' Alex's voice was rising now. 'You think this person is going to come after her again, so you brought her here to protect her? Is that it?'

'Alex.' Pope put her hand on his arm, but he backed away from her.

'You haven't learned a thing,' he said. His tone was disappointed, resigned. It was hard for Pope to hear.

'Alex, I'll sort this out tomorrow. I can't do anything now. We're perfectly safe. As you said, there are officers outside. And, again, it never would have happened if I'd known you were coming back.'

'So it's my fault?'

'No, of course not. But you have to give me a chance to make this right. Let me show you I can sort this out. I promise I won't put anybody in this house in any danger.' In the forefront of Pope's mind was the fact that Alice Lowrie had almost certainly murdered Nicholas Cooper by stabbing him with a kitchen knife. She looked at the knife block just next to Alex and decided now was not the time to mention that fact.

'OK, Bec. I'll give you that chance. Obviously turning up unannounced has made things a bit awkward. But we need to establish some ground rules if this is going to work.'

'Yes. Of course.'

'Because if there's any repeat of the kind of thing that happened last year, that's it. I have to prioritize Hannah and Chloe.'

Pope was irritated by the repeated ultimatum, but she knew now wasn't the time. She adopted a conciliatory tone. 'I know I've messed up in the past, and I know I've got to put things right. I'm totally committed to that. And once this case is over, I'm going to make some big changes. You have to believe me.'

'"Once this case is over" is something I've heard many times, Bec.'

'I know. But I get it now. Last year was a wake-up call for me. Things will be different. You just have to give me a chance.'

'That's why I'm here.'

She smiled, just as the pasta pan began to boil over and water poured all over the cooker. 'Top up the wine, I'll make sure there's enough pasta for all of us.'

As Pope got to work on dinner, working with the little she had in the house and giving herself yet another reason to feel guilty, she heard footsteps down the stairs. Chloe came into the kitchen and stood against a worktop.

Pope felt the tension, the unfamiliarity of the situation. 'How have you been, Chloe?'

'OK.'

'How are your grandparents?'

'Fine. They go on a bit.'

'I think that's in the grandparents' job description.' Pope's attempt at humour fell flat with both Chloe and Alex. 'I'm glad you got to spend some time with them.'

Pope was surprised how difficult this felt. Nobody seemed to know what to say. She felt that she needed to do the work as she had caused the problems in the first place.

'How's Tyler?'

'Tyler's good. He's going to art school next year. He wants to design skateboards. He's really talented.' Chloe was sounding more animated now.

'That sounds interesting.' Pope avoided looking at Alex, who she felt sure would disapprove of pretty much anything his daughter's boyfriend chose to do. 'Where does he want to go?'

'He's not sure yet. But he's thinking of staying in London. It's the best place to study art.' Pope doubted that was the reason Tyler wanted to stay in London. But she was glad Chloe had some stability in her life.

'Who's that upstairs?' Chloe abruptly changed the subject.

Pope glanced at Alex. Knew this was another test of her ability to adequately fulfil the role of step-parent.

'Her name is Alice. She's had a really rough time so I'm keeping an eye on her for a couple of days, just until I can get something more permanent sorted out.'

'What do you mean by a rough time?'

'Well, she was taken from her family by a group of people some time ago and we think she was held against her will.'

'Who took her?'

'That's what we're trying to find out. We know where, we just don't know who's involved.'

'So, is it like a cult?' asked Chloe.

'Chloe . . . Bec can't really tell you too much about the case.' Alex was already enforcing the separation between family and work.

'It's OK,' Pope said to him. 'I don't know if it's a cult exactly.'

'I saw *Once Upon a Time in Hollywood* with Tyler. It was about a stuntman in Hollywood in the sixties, but they had a sort of cult in it.'

'It's probably nothing like that. We're not sure yet. But whatever's happened has affected her quite badly. She's very nervous, very scared.'

'What's she scared of?' asked Chloe.

'I think she's suffering from the trauma of being held against her will. But she has amnesia, so she remembers very little at the moment.'

'Is it PTSD?'

'It could be. How do you know about PTSD?'

'We studied it in science last year.'

'Sounds more interesting than the science I studied at school.'

'Why are there police outside our door?'

'Just a precaution,' said Pope, hoping to end the discussion there.

'A precaution against what?'

'Well, it's complicated.' Chloe stared at Pope. 'We don't know where the people who held her are now, so it's just to make sure.'

'Because you think they're going to turn up here looking for her?' Chloe was sounding agitated now.

'No, no. I'm sure they're not. As I said, it's simply a precaution.'

'You think someone's going to come after her.'

Alex moved towards Chloe. He tried to put his arm around her but she ducked away. 'No. This is going to be like last time.'

'Chloe, I promise you—'

'What? You're going to keep me safe? Like last time? It was your fault! And it's your fault again.'

Alex attempted to calm her down. 'Chloe, nothing's going to happen.' It didn't work.

'You don't know that. I'm not staying here while she's here. I'm going to see Tyler. Get her out of here.'

'Chloe, we've only just got back.' But Alex's words were too late. Chloe was off and out of the front door.

Pope was mortified. This was the worst possible start to the resumption of their life together.

Alex looked apologetic. 'She's still raw about what happened. I told you that. She'll be fine once she calms down. She's seventeen, it'll take a while.' He paused. 'But she does have a point.'

'I know she does. I'm sorry. I'll talk to her when she gets back and first thing in the morning I'll sort something out.'

'I'm going to see how Hannah's getting on with her unpacking.'

The look he gave her as he left said it all: *Don't screw this up*. Pope wondered if she would.

CHAPTER TWENTY

Brody was at the station early Thursday morning. He had sent Pope a text the previous night to try to begin a dialogue, but she had responded with a curt, single-word reply. He had wanted to see how she was getting on with Alice Lowrie, but also to make it right with her after his inappropriate comments at the hospital. He had slept badly knowing he would have to wait until he got into the office to sort it out.

He'd arrived at work at 7 a.m. to find Miller already at his desk, buried in his computer.

'I got an alert last night that some of the forensics had come through on the schoolhouse in Lenham, so I came in to see if there's anything interesting,' he explained.

'And is there?' asked Brody.

'I'm just going through it now. Seems there were a number of prints found in the other bedroom there. Not the main dormitory, they haven't processed that one yet. They took a million from there. But in the smaller room they found two main recurring sets. One matches Nicholas Cooper's prints that were taken from the body yesterday. But the other set doesn't have a match in the database. At least not one we've found so far.'

'So, it looks like there could be another player alongside Cooper?'

'Maybe. The number of prints suggests that this person was in that room a lot. I've asked Forensics to see where else in the house they occur, whether they're also in the dormitory.'

'That's good news.'

'It's not all,' said Miller. 'Tech have been going through Cooper's records and Thompson thinks he's found something.'

'Go on.'

'Well, it seems like someone has been paying Cooper a regular amount of money every month.'

'Like a salary?'

'Could be. Thompson accessed his bank records and Cooper has been receiving a transfer into his account on the same day every month for the last ten years.'

'Ten years?'

'I know. And it's not from a company, but from a private account.'

'Do we have the details?'

'Yes. The name on the account is an Evan Larsson. There doesn't seem to be much on him yet, but Thompson is trying to find out who he is. We do have an address in Central London linked to the account.'

'Right. So, there's maybe a second person at the schoolhouse with Cooper and a possible connection to someone who's been financing him, and maybe the Collective, for a decade?'

'It seems that way,' confirmed Miller.

'Right. Take a couple of officers and go and bring in this Evan Larsson.'

'Do you want me to try to find out a bit more about him first?'

'No, Thompson can work on that while you go and get him. Whatever we find, he's still got questions to answer. It may be his prints in the bedroom near the murder scene, and anyway there's a connection to the murder victim. He should be able to tell us more about the Collective and what it actually is.'

'OK, I'll sort out a car and go and get him,' said Miller. He made several calls and arranged to meet a team in the garage beneath the station.

As Miller was leaving the office, Brody spoke again, his face creased with concern. 'Be careful. We have no idea who we're dealing with.'

'Will do.'

* * *

Pope arrived at the office soon after Miller had left. After she had made a coffee and sat down, Brody came over and sat in the chair next to her.

'I'm really sorry about what I said yesterday, Bec. It was thoughtless. I was just worried about you taking Alice Lowrie home when we don't have the full facts yet.'

She smiled. Brody could always be relied upon to do the right thing. 'It's OK. We were both pretty tense. I just couldn't think of what else to do with her. A cell didn't seem right.'

'I shouldn't have mentioned the Tina Waterson case in that way. I know how much it means to you.'

'Yeah, well, you might have been right. I'm not a hundred per cent sure it was the right thing myself, but it's done now. I can't say it wasn't in the back of my mind. Anyway, I've got bigger problems to sort out.'

'Why? What happened?' asked Brody.

'Needless to say, the day I decide to take Alice Lowrie home, Alex and the girls reappear.'

'What? That's great, though, isn't it?'

'It is. But the timing could have been better. Alex wanted to surprise me and didn't let me know he was on his way over. So when they suddenly turned up I had a guest. In Alex's house. He wasn't best pleased.'

'Did you explain?'

'I did. I left out the part about her probably stabbing Nicholas Cooper, though. So now I need to find somewhere for her to go ASAP.'

'Where is she now?'

'She's still at mine. I've got two officers outside and I promised Alex that I'd arrange for her to go somewhere else. He wasn't impressed. I'm hoping to sort something out this morning.'

'How did the girls react?'

'As you might imagine. After what happened to Chloe last year, I wasn't high on anyone's favourites list when I explained that Lowrie had been attacked at the hospital and I had her there for safekeeping.'

'I can imagine.'

'I need to sort that out, then Darke is coming in. I spoke to him again last night to update him on Alice Lowrie, and he offered to ask a colleague of his who's apparently a leading authority on cults to come in and speak with us first thing. Hopefully they'll be able to shed some light on all this Collective stuff.'

'Some interesting news overnight,' said Brody. 'Thompson looked at Nicholas Cooper's bank account and it seems that he's been receiving regular payments from the same individual every month since he arrived in the UK.'

'Hasn't he been here for ten years?' asked Pope.

'Yeah. For all that time he has been getting money from someone called Evan Larsson. No record we can find, but we have an address. Miller has gone to pick him up, so we can talk to him after we meet Darke's cults expert.'

Pope was stunned. 'That's great. Is there any connection with the people Cooper was hanging out with in Paris?'

'Not yet, if you're thinking about the terrorism angle. But Thompson is working on it. Hopefully he'll find something useful before Larsson gets here.'

Pope felt that familiar rush of adrenaline you only get from a potential big lead in a case. But this was mixed with unease at the fact that she had left Alice Lowrie at home with Alex and the girls. She vowed to make arrangements to rectify that situation, but just then her phone rang and the duty sergeant informed her that Tobias Darke was in reception with a guest.

'Send them up.' Her other problem would have to wait.

* * *

Tobias Darke, as ever, was in a jovial mood. He strode into the office, followed by a tall, slim, striking woman in her mid- to late thirties, dressed in a dark suit and with long red hair.

'Bec, James, how are you both?' He hugged them both, then introduced his companion.

'Bec Pope, James Brody, this is Elizabeth Hartford, professor of applied psychology at Edinburgh University.'

'Hello, nice to meet you,' said Hartford, shaking hands with both of them. She had a light Scottish accent, the geographical lilt polished but not completely eradicated.

'Thanks for coming. You're a long way from home,' said Pope.

'I was down in London giving a guest lecture at UCL, so the timing worked out well.'

'Elizabeth shares my speciality in criminal psychology, but it just so happens that she also teaches a course on the psychology of cults and is one of the foremost academic experts in the country,' said Darke.

Hartford smiled, said nothing. *No false modesty here*, thought Pope.

They sat down around the conference table. Hartford was neat and contained, proper.

'I've filled Elizabeth in on your young woman and told her as much as I know and my impressions from the preliminary assessment. Anything else we need to know?' asked Darke.

'Yes, a couple of things. It seems that this group lived in a communal arrangement down in Kent, in an old schoolhouse. There seemed to be a dormitory with eight beds, a communal cooking and eating area, an office and a sort of study-cum-bedroom with a double bed. We've identified the dead man we found as Nicholas Cooper, an American who moved here by way of a few years in Paris. Alice Lowrie has admitted to killing him. We suspect that there might have been a history of abuse and eventually Lowrie cracked and couldn't take it anymore. We'd welcome your thoughts on the likelihood of that scenario.'

Hartford wasn't writing anything down, but maintained an intense eye contact that suggested she didn't need to. Pope guessed that she would remember every detail. She radiated intelligence and professionalism.

Pope continued. 'The other aspect to this is that there seems to have been at least one other person involved. A guy called Evan Larsson. It appears that he has been paying Cooper a substantial amount of money each month. We're not sure why or for what. Hopefully we'll be talking to him later today. What we're worried about is that Cooper had some links to some members of a terrorist group who were involved in the Bataclan attack in Paris in 2015. We need to know if all this is linked, or if the cult, if that's what it is, is a separate entity and those links are purely coincidental.'

'That's quite a bit of new information since we last spoke,' said Darke.

'Yes, sorry, Tobias. We only found out some of this this morning,' said Pope.

'No problem,' said Hartford. 'What is it that you're hoping I can tell you?'

'It would be useful to know a bit about the situation with cults in the UK, how and why people are recruited and something about what kind of person becomes a cult leader. We still don't have that information, although Nicholas Cooper and Evan Larsson are clearly persons of interest in that sense.'

'OK. That's fine. I'll tell you what I can.'

Pope noticed that Brody had his pen and notepad at the ready. He seemed to be hanging on Hartford's every word.

'Firstly, cults are far more numerous than you might expect in this country. Estimates are around five hundred to a thousand in the UK alone. There are reckoned to be more than ten thousand in the States, although I'd take that number with a large pinch of salt.'

Pope was surprised at the number. Brody was taking notes. She was sure he knew quite a bit about cults already. It fitted his love of conspiracy theories quite nicely.

'The thing to remember about cults is that the people who join them are often fairly intelligent and motivated by change.'

'What kind of change?' asked Pope.

'Lack of family love or connection, the quest for something better, either spiritually, socially or intellectually. Dissatisfaction with some aspect of your life is a key driver in susceptibility to recruitment to these kinds of organizations.'

'Isn't everybody dissatisfied with some aspect of their life?' asked Pope.

'Exactly,' said Hartford. 'That's the point. The pool is huge, and these people get very good at finding the right fish. Cults are presented, and often seen, as an alternative to failing social narratives. Prospective members are disillusioned with the status quo, in whatever form, and this can lead to rejection of traditional societal norms. Cults offer an alternative belief system in a process that happens over time. Before you know it, you're in.'

'You make it sound so easy,' said Pope.

'It is. If you find the right person and you're a skilled manipulator it can be scarily easy. There are many accounts of cult survivors who articulate very clearly how quickly they were sucked in. They employ very sophisticated forms of persuasion and indoctrination. By the time they realize what's going on, it's often too late.'

'But surely people see what's going on most of the time? They see it's a cult?'

'No one joins a cult. They join a form of self-help group, to find discipline, acceptance, answers, shared spirituality.

They join to change their lives and they are often desperate to belong to something. In some ways it's similar to how gangs recruit. If something is lacking, or perceived to be lacking, in someone's life, they offer to provide it.'

'So, what then defines it as a cult?' asked Pope.

'Generally, the term "cult" is applied when activities become sexual or violent.'

Hartford put things clearly and succinctly, with an engaging manner. Pope imagined the woman was very popular with her students.

'Could you tell us something about cult leaders? We're hoping to talk to this guy, Evan Larsson, later on today. It would be useful to have some idea of what we're looking for,' said Pope.

'The leaders, of course, are the key. Often cults are absolutely defined by them. Think of Charles Manson or Jim Jones. They tend to become famous above and beyond the organizations they lead.'

Pope knew them both, although she couldn't immediately think of any other names.

'Successful cult leaders are almost always characterized by diligence, commitment, self-belief, charisma, sociopathy and intelligence. Often very clever people. Maintaining control over their subordinates is imperative and they tend to demand total control, deference and obedience in their followers. Often we see what would be defined as narcissistic personality disorder.'

'How does that show itself?' asked Pope.

'Sufferers of NPD tend to display an inflated sense of self-importance, a lack of empathy and a deep need for admiration from others. You can see why a cult is a perfect vehicle for these kinds of people,' said Hartford.

'So how does that translate in the interview room? What do I look out for?'

'Start by looking out for an abundance of personality and confidence. These guys — and it usually is guys, of course — tend to be very charismatic individuals. Being interviewed by a woman might help, as they won't be able to help themselves from flirting and trying to take control. If that isn't there, you've probably got the wrong man.'

Pope wondered if Elizabeth Hartford had had some sort of personal involvement with a cult. She sounded like she was speaking from experience.

'One more question. How do you leave a cult?' asked Pope.

Hartford looked at her and smiled. 'You don't. Most of the time. A few get away, but leaving a cult requires a personal strength that few possess. The writer James Howard Kunstler described cults as where souls lose all hope. He was not exaggerating. And those who physically escape often say that they don't do so mentally. Once you're in a cult, you're in.'

'That's pretty depressing,' said Pope.

'Did you want me to sugar-coat it, DCI Pope?' She smiled again. She had an incredibly engaging smile.

'No. I'm just thinking about the woman we have who seems to have escaped. It seems like she went to extraordinary lengths to get away.'

'Then she's very lucky,' said Hartford. 'I hope she's OK.'

'So do I,' replied Pope. 'What are your plans today?'

'I was planning to have lunch with Tobias, then do some research work at the university later. Why?'

'I was thinking about what you said about how someone might interact with women. I wondered if you might like to sit in with me and Brody when we interview Evan Larsson and give us your take on him? I haven't met him, so I have no idea what he's like.'

Hartford looked at Darke. 'What do you think, Tobias?' It was the first time Pope had seen her display anything less than absolute confidence.

'Sounds like an excellent idea,' beamed Darke. 'A good opportunity for some genuine fieldwork. Who knows, he might be an interesting character?'

She turned back to Pope. 'OK, DCI Pope. I'll be glad to join you.'

Pope and Brody thanked them both and directed them to the staff canteen. Pope said she would contact them as soon as Evan Larsson was brought in, which should be soon.

After they had left the office, Pope made a coffee.

'What do you think?' she asked Brody.

'She's quite something,' said Brody.

'I meant about the cults.' Pope chose not to tease Brody about his current likeness to a love-struck teenager.

'Everything she said fits well with our current hypothesis,' said Brody. 'The schoolhouse could easily be the base. They kept themselves to themselves and there seems to be one, maybe more, men involved who could be in charge. If it's so difficult to escape, that would explain the extreme lengths that Alice Lowrie went to.'

'Yes. If we assume that Nicholas Cooper was the leader, it would make sense. But what I don't get is how this Evan Larsson fits in. Where is he in all of this and why was he paying a monthly allowance to Cooper? What does he get out of it?'

'Hopefully we can ask him later.'

CHAPTER TWENTY-ONE

Evan Larsson lived in a second-floor apartment on Dean Street, right in the heart of Soho, less than a mile from the nearest Tube station. Miller took two officers with him. One of them drove the squad car while Miller navigated the brief journey.

When they arrived at the address, Miller saw that it was a tall, well-kept building, probably Victorian. There was a smart, expensive-looking bar on the ground floor, a design company in the basement and two residential apartments on the first and second floors. They parked and the three officers got out of the car. One stayed with the vehicle, while Miller rang the bell for Larsson's apartment. After a brief wait, it was answered. The voice was confident, open.

'How can I help you?'

'Is that Evan Larsson?' asked Miller.

'It is. What can I do for you?'

'Mr Larsson. My name is Sergeant Adam Miller from the Metropolitan Police. Can I come in and have a chat?'

'What is it relating to?'

'I'd prefer to talk in person.'

A pause. 'Push the door and come on up. Second floor.'

A buzzer sounded and Miller pushed the door open. The communal stairway was well kept and clean, empty of clutter. Not at all like the flats Miller had lived in — still lived in, in fact. The two police officers walked up the stairs, a door opening as they arrived at the second floor.

'Nice to meet you,' said the man who was standing in the doorway. He was dressed in running gear, a sports bottle in one hand. He shook Miller's hand with the other, firm and confident.

'Evan Larsson?'

'In the flesh. Come in.'

They entered the hallway and Larsson left the door open behind them. Miller appraised him as he led them into a sparsely furnished living room. What furniture there was looked expensive, high-end. Larsson was taller than Miller, he estimated six-one or -two. He had shoulder-length blond hair, swept back. If Miller googled "Nordic athlete", he'd expect to find a picture of Evan Larsson. The man radiated health and vitality.

'Excuse the appearance, Sergeant Miller, I've just got back from a run.' Miller didn't look that composed at the best of times, let alone after exercise. 'What can I do for you today?' He sounded so relaxed, Miller began to wonder if they had the wrong Evan Larsson.

'We'd like you to come to the station to answer some questions.'

'That sounds rather formal. What do you want to ask me about?' His English accent was excellent, with only a trace of his Scandinavian roots.

'It's about Nicholas Cooper,' said Miller. He watched Larsson carefully for any signs or change in attitude, but saw nothing.

'Nicholas. Yes, I know Nicholas. Why, has something happened to him?'

'I'd rather discuss it at the station if you don't mind.'

'How very mysterious. You'll need to give me a few minutes to get changed. Make yourself at home.' He indicated the sofa with his hand and disappeared into what Miller assumed was the bedroom, closing the door behind him. Miller walked over and looked out of the window. The combination of height and location offered a fabulous view of Central London. Miller wondered how much that view cost. A lot more than his.

At about the point that Miller's patience was beginning to wane, Larsson emerged from the bedroom. He had taken a shower and was now dressed in a casual but expensive shirt and trousers, and white sneakers.

'Ready when you are.'

Miller nodded and the two officers led the way down the stairs and out into Dean Street. He opened the door for Larsson, who thanked him, and closed it behind him. Cool as the proverbial cucumber. They drove in silence to the station. Miller texted Pope and Brody to tell them that he was on the way.

* * *

'Just got a message from Miller. He says he'll be here with Larsson in five. No problems, apparently,' said Brody.

'Good. Let's get downstairs. Can you go and get Elizabeth Hartford and bring her to the interview room? I'll make sure it's ready.'

'How do you want to play it?'

'I'll lead. You and Hartford in there with me, see what you think. We'll put Miller and Darke behind the one-way mirror. I'll decide how to play it once we've met him. It may be that he has a perfectly reasonable explanation for everything.'

'Is that what you think?' asked Brody.

'No. But let's see.'

Pope checked her email and saw a message from Thompson with the title "Evan Larsson". She read it on the way down to Interview Room One. Thompson outlined what he had been able to find out about Larsson, which didn't appear to be very much. Aged forty-two, born in Norway. He had studied at the University of Oslo, taking a degree in

165

psychology and philosophy, followed by a Master's degree in philosophy. He had then lived in Paris for some time before relocating to London. Since arriving in the UK, Thompson had found nothing so far. Pope was struck with how similar his path had been to that of Nicholas Cooper. That surely gave them a connection.

She arrived at the interview room and placed three chairs on one side of the table and one on the other side. She looked around and settled herself for the interview. Her territory, her interview. Pope rolled her shoulders. She was ready.

Just then the door opened and Brody walked in, followed by Elizabeth Hartford. She had put on fresh lipstick and smiled at Pope as she came in.

Pope indicated the chairs. 'If you want to sit on the left there, Brody can sit on the right and I'll sit in the centre.'

Hartford nodded. 'What do you want me to do?'

'Just observe and try to get a sense of who he is. Essentially, I want to know if he tells us the truth, but if it looks like he's involved, I want to know what kind of man we're dealing with. From a psychological perspective.'

'OK.' Hartford sat down. 'I'll do my best.'

Brody sat down and got out his notebook and a pen.

The door opened and Miller ushered in Evan Larsson. He entered the room and stopped, taking in his surroundings and the people present. His eyes went first to Pope, who was nearest, then to Brody, and finally to Hartford. His gaze lingered on her for a little longer than the others as their eyes met. Miller indicated Pope.

'This is DCI Pope. She'll be leading the interview,' said Miller.

'Interview? I thought this was an informal discussion, DCI Pope,' said Larsson, smiling, holding out his hand to hers. She shook his hand — a strong, assured grip.

'It is,' said Pope. 'We call all these meetings interviews if they're held at the station. Have a seat, Mr Larsson. We appreciate you coming in at such short notice, and so early in the day.'

'Evan, please. And not an issue. I wake up early every day for my run.'

'Thanks, Sergeant Miller,' said Pope.

Larsson sat down and looked again at Hartford. Pope imagined she got that a lot.

'This is DI Brody and this is Professor Hartford,' said Pope.

Larsson nodded at Brody, then turned again to Hartford. 'And what is your role here, Professor Hartford?'

Pope answered quickly. 'Professor Hartford is training to work with the police, so she is just observing the interview to see how we do things.'

Larsson smiled. 'Is that right? Well, I hope you find it enlightening.' Hartford smiled and nodded.

Pope had the distinct impression that he had immediately seen through her lie and cursed herself for not thinking of something better to explain Hartford's presence. She felt on the back foot already, and the interview hadn't even started.

Just then, the door opened and a man entered in haste. He was impeccably groomed and wore a well-cut grey suit with a faint chalk stripe and highly polished black brogues. Pope thought he looked around mid-fifties. A solicitor.

As he walked in he smiled at Larsson. 'Which of you is DCI Pope?' he asked, confident and assured.

'I'm DCI Pope.'

He held out his hand. 'Michael Allerton. I'm Mr Larsson's solicitor.' She shook his hand, another overly firm grip. What was it with these men and their desire to show how firmly they could shake your hand?

He looked around and pulled up a chair, sitting down next to Larsson. He opened his briefcase and retrieved a legal pad and a burgundy Montblanc pen. Expensive and designed to intimidate, to connote success.

'I trust you haven't started without me?'

'No, we were just about to get going.' Pope wondered how the solicitor knew that Larsson was here. Presumably

Larsson had contacted him on the way to the station. She introduced the other two to him.

'Right. Mr Larsson, I want to ask you a few questions regarding an incident we're investigating. Your name has come up in connection with this and we need to clarify a few things. Are you happy to proceed?'

'Of course, DCI Pope. I'm always happy to assist the police force if I can be of help. Perhaps you could fill in a few details for me? I'm somewhat at a disadvantage as Sergeant Miller wouldn't tell me anything about the reason I'm here.'

Allerton was watching like a hawk. Pope would have to tread carefully.

'Mr Larsson, do you know a man by the name of Nicholas Cooper?'

Larsson paused, looked at his solicitor. Allerton nodded cautiously.

'Yes, I know Nicholas Cooper.'

'And in what capacity do you know Mr Cooper?'

Larsson was considered in his responses. He thought before he spoke. 'Nicholas and I are friends and we share some business interests.'

'Where did you meet Mr Cooper?' asked Pope.

'We met in Paris some years ago. I was studying at the Sorbonne. We had some mutual acquaintances. We became friends.'

'When was this? That you were in Paris?'

Larsson made a show of thinking back, but Pope had the impression that he knew the answer immediately. She wasn't sure what to make of that. She glanced at Hartford, who was watching him carefully.

'I left around ten years ago, I think. Give or take. How time flies.'

'And what was Mr Cooper doing in Paris at that time? While you were a student?'

'He was writing, as I remember. He had ambitions to become published.'

'And you both moved to the UK. Was that about the same time?'

'Yes. We were both becoming a little bored of the Paris scene and we both, independently, felt that we needed a change of environment. I had always intended to visit London at some point in my travels, and Nicholas thought that the UK might suit him.'

'Suit him in what way?'

'Well, Nicholas thought that the British might be a better market for his work. He was trying to publish his philosophical writings, but Paris is full of philosophers. You can hardly walk along the Left Bank without bumping into one.'

'So, you were both philosophers?'

'Well, we were both trying to think of the best way to live, so yes, I suppose so.'

'What do you mean by "the best way to live"?' asked Pope.

'Philosophy is essentially the study of who we are, why we are here and how we should live our lives. Nicholas and I were both interested in the latter of those areas and we agreed on a great many ideals.'

'On how we should live our lives?' clarified Pope.

'Yes. Most people live by the rules imposed on them by others. By parents, teachers, governments, the media. Some of us look beyond that and try to organize our lives by our own ideals, rather than those decided by others.'

Pope had alarm bells ringing. It sounded very much like a sales pitch for a cult. She decided to head in that direction.

'Have you heard of a group called the Collective, Mr Larsson?'

He looked at Allerton again, who nodded.

'Yes, I know something about it.'

'And what do you know about it?'

'I know that it's Nicholas's project. His attempt to put into practice the ideas he's been thinking and writing about for a number of years.'

'Ideas that you share?'

'Yes, to an extent.'

'And how would you describe the Collective? As a group?'

Larsson paused again. 'The Collective, as far as I know, is a group of like-minded people who are trying to live life according to their own rules. They don't agree with everything our society dictates and they are trying to follow a truer path. A path that more accurately reflects how they feel about the world.'

'And it appears that you were financing this group. Is that right?'

'Financing?' asked Larsson.

Pope checked a sheet of paper in the folder in front of her. 'Yes. You were paying Nicholas Cooper every month. Presumably this was to finance the Collective?'

Larsson seemed surprised that Pope knew this, but quickly regained his composure.

'Yes. I was supportive of what Nicholas and the group were trying to achieve. They had some worthy charitable activities of which I approved, and I was interested in their philosophy and how they wanted to live.'

'What do you do for a living, Mr Larsson?'

'I write, mainly. But if you're asking where my income comes from, that is from my parents' estate. They died many years ago and I'm fortunate that they left me enough so that I wouldn't have to get a regular job if I didn't want to.'

'Nicholas Cooper's parents both died when he was fairly young too, didn't they?'

'They did. Maybe it was that which drew us together.' Larsson smiled.

'Maybe,' said Pope. 'Would you say that you and Mr Cooper were kindred spirits?' She was beginning to feel that the relationship between Larsson and Cooper might be at the heart of this.

'Kindred spirits? What a quaint expression.' Larsson smiled again, then looked again at Hartford and back to Pope. 'We got on well, we were friends. And we agreed that the control of societal expectations by government was not a good fit for us. Or indeed for anyone who is really thinking for themselves.'

'So you founded the Collective to try to put this into practice?'

Allerton interrupted. 'DCI Pope, my client has already explained that this group you speak of, the Collective, is Nicholas Cooper's project. His involvement is limited to financial support.'

'That's true,' said Larsson. 'You really need to be talking to Nicholas about all this.'

Pope wanted to hold back the information about Cooper's death for a while longer. She knew that Allerton would pull the plug as soon as he knew it.

'How often did you visit the Collective, at their base in Lenham?'

'I have visited on a few occasions. Nicholas wanted to demonstrate that my money was being put to good use. And I'm sure he wanted to try to ensure that it continues. Which it does.'

'So, how often do you visit?' asked Pope.

'I've probably been, let me think, maybe three or four times. It's a lovely place. A pleasant change from London.'

Pope decided to take a chance. She made a show of looking at a piece of paper in the folder on the table in front of her. 'We have a statement here that says you were a regular visitor to the property in Lenham. That you were, in fact, there frequently.'

Larsson was surprised and glanced at Allerton.

'That's not true,' he said. 'Who have you been talking to who says otherwise? As I told you, I've visited a handful of times, no more.'

'Detective Chief Inspector, could you tell us what the nature of the case is that you are investigating? My client has come to the station, in what seems a rather formal setting, in all good faith. This is beginning to sound like an interrogation.'

'It's not an interrogation at all, Mr Allerton. But we're investigating an incident and we know Mr Larsson is connected to one of the people involved, Nicholas Cooper. He has confirmed that himself. We're just trying to get a picture here of the extent of Mr Larsson's involvement with Mr Cooper.'

'I repeat: what is the nature of the incident you are investigating?'

'I will get to that, I assure you. If you can just answer a couple more questions, I think you'll understand why I'm approaching this the way I am.' Pope was being disingenuous and hoped Allerton wouldn't see through her.

Larsson spoke. 'It's OK, Michael. Let's take DCI Pope at her word. I have nothing to hide.' He stared at Pope with surprising intensity. She knew she didn't have much time left before this interview would be over, so she took out a photograph from the folder and placed it face up on the table, orientated towards Larsson. His eyes passed over it.

'Do you recognize this woman?' asked Pope.

Another pause. 'No, DCI Pope. I don't think so.' He took another look at the picture.

'Take a good look, Mr Larsson. Are you sure you don't recognize her?'

'No. I don't recall ever seeing her before.' He returned his gaze to Pope.

'Do you know the name Alice Lowrie?'

Larsson looked to be thinking, searching his memory. 'No, I can't say that I do. Sorry, DCI Pope. Who is she?'

Pope studied him for a moment. 'Alice Lowrie was one of the women at the Collective. Most of the people there seem to have been women.'

'You'd have to talk to Nicholas about that. The participants in his group are entirely his domain.'

Pope wasn't sure. Larsson was very convincing. Too convincing. He didn't seem to be worried by any of this. Most people would be rattled by now. She wanted to confer with Hartford but knew if she left the room, that could well be the end of the interview. And there was one more thing she wanted to do before Evan Larsson walked out.

'We can't talk to Nicholas Cooper about this. I'm sorry to have to tell you that Mr Cooper was found dead yesterday.'

'Oh my God.' Larsson put his hand up to his mouth. He looked to be genuinely shocked. Pope watched as Allerton did the maths.

'DCI Pope—' Allerton began. She cut him off.

'Nicholas Cooper was stabbed at the property in Lenham. He had been dead for several days when we found him. Do you know anything about this?'

'Of course I don't!' said Larsson. 'Do you not think I would have told you if I knew something like that?'

'That would depend on whether you had anything to do with it, I suppose,' she said.

'OK, DCI Pope. This interview is over. We're leaving.' Pope ignored him while she still could.

'Are you sure that your association with the Collective was as hands-off as you suggest? You weren't a more regular participant in whatever was going on there?'

Allerton stood up. 'We're done here, DCI Pope. Come on, Evan, we're leaving. Now.' He pointed at Pope. 'Any other questions can be directed to me. Mr Larsson won't be answering anything else without a warrant.' He put a business card on the table and Pope placed it on top of the photograph.

Larsson stood up and lifted his jacket from the back of the chair. He glanced down at the picture. 'Is this Alice Lowrie? The picture looks like it was taken in a hospital bed. I do hope she's OK.'

Pope noticed a change in his tone. Before he had been relaxed and seemingly cooperative. Suddenly she saw a different side of him. More assertive, almost threatening. Was this a veiled threat against their witness? He was in control again, but in a different way.

'She's fine, Mr Larsson. Don't you worry about that.'

'So glad to hear it.' He turned to Hartford. 'Ms Hartford. Did you get what you needed?'

She seemed wrong-footed, unsure. 'Yes. Yes, I did. It was very interesting. Thank you.'

He smiled. 'Hopefully we'll meet again.' She smiled back, but without his confidence. Pope noted the predatory look in his eyes as he spoke. She immediately regretted inviting Elizabeth Hartford in for the interview.

Larsson smiled at Pope. 'I'm sure I'll see you again, DCI Pope.'

'I'm certain of it.'

'Well, I'll look forward to that.' He seemed to appraise her from top to toe, his eyes moving over her body. He smiled again.

'DI Brody, can you see Mr Larsson and Mr Allerton out, please?'

Brody nodded and opened the door, leading the two men out.

Pope sat down next to Hartford. 'So, what did you think?'

Hartford faltered. 'It was strange. He was fine for most of the interview, but he really shifted right at the end there.'

Pope nodded her agreement.

'It was almost like two different men. For the most part he was easy-going and relaxed. Had answers to all your questions. But then a sudden change. A form of controlled aggression.'

'Do you think he was telling the truth?'

'Up to that point, I'd say he seemed to come across as very honest. But after that . . . the interview, taken as a whole . . . the confidence, the sudden shift. I think you definitely have a problem with him.'

Pope considered this. 'Are you around for a bit? Would you come to our team meeting and brief the others?'

'Yes,' said Hartford. 'No problem. And you see what I mean about the reaction to women.'

'Yes,' said Pope. 'I noticed that too.'

CHAPTER TWENTY-TWO

Pope sat at the head of the conference table in their shared office. Also present were Brody, Miller, Thompson, Fletcher, Tobias Darke and Elizabeth Hartford. All except Fletcher had a bottle of water in front of them and all looked expectantly at Pope. The slowly rotating fan was working hard to offer a slight breeze, a small respite from the high temperature in the office.

Pope took a moment to gather both her thoughts and the collection of papers from the folder in front of her. Since the interview that morning, it had been a long day of catching up on paperwork, and they'd also had to wait for Hartford to return from her research commitments at the university.

'Right. Thanks everybody. We need to discuss the interview and work out what we think about Evan Larsson. We also need to decide next steps. Everyone OK to get going?'

Pope saw all the participants nod and she began. 'Right, I've asked Dr Darke and Professor Hartford to join us for the meeting this evening. Elizabeth was in the interview and Tobias was watching with Miller. I thought it would be useful to get their perspective on Evan Larsson at this point. It's clear, we think, that Nicholas Cooper was a major player, if not *the* major player, in the Collective. He was found on the premises and Alice Lowrie identified him as a lead figure. However, as he is dead, our attention has turned to Evan Larsson. Larsson, as we know, is financially connected to Cooper and deposited a regular, monthly sum of money into Cooper's bank account. He also confirms that they were friends and knew each other from their time together in Paris. He claims that his only involvement in the Collective was financial support, as he and Cooper shared a number of philosophical beliefs that seem to be at the core of the group. These appear to be around the concept of self-determinism and an unwillingness to conform to the traditional norms of society. We don't know much beyond that at this stage. I'm hoping Thompson and Miller will be able to offer a bit more information.' Pope looked at both men, who nodded affirmatively. 'But first, I want to get an assessment from Professor Hartford and Dr Darke.' She handed over to Hartford.

'OK, first of all it's important to understand that this is not an exact science. The kind of people I deal with, the kinds of people I study, are duplicitous and disingenuous by nature, so it can often take some time to really uncover their true selves. They hide their true personality and only let it show at certain times. Being interviewed by someone in authority is often not one of those times.'

'Understood,' said Pope. 'But what did you think?'

'Evan Larsson appears to display all the characteristics that one might associate with narcissistic personality disorder. If I was working with him professionally, I would need much more time with him to ascertain this diagnosis with any certainty. But, for your purposes, he certainly seems like someone who would find it impossible to have a completely hands-off approach to this group, the Collective, as he suggests.'

'Why do you think that?' asked Fletcher.

'Your interviewee was charismatic and confident, dripping in self-belief. And, crucially, he believed he was in control for much of the interview. He was surprised that we knew he had been depositing regular amounts into Cooper's bank account, but he soon regained his composure. And his response to me and to DCI Pope, the two women in the room, was telling.'

Fletcher frowned. 'In what way?'

'He was flirtatious. In and of itself that might not be unusual. But in this context, in a police interview, the subject of which he didn't know until the end, it is highly unusual.'

'Your expertise is with cults, is that right?' asked Fletcher.

'Yes, and with the psychological profiles of their leaders.'

'So, in your professional opinion, does Evan Larsson fit the profile for a typical cult leader?'

'Based on that interview, I would say yes — to the extent to which any cult leader can be said to be typical, of course,' Hartford added. 'But bear in mind what I just said: this type of personality is often difficult to pin down, so this is very much an initial feeling about him.'

'Thank you, Professor Hartford,' said Pope. 'Tobias, do you have anything to add to that?'

'Not really,' said Darke. 'I think Elizabeth is absolutely right. He was so calm, so in control, that a personality disorder is a very logical explanation. Under that amount of pressure, most people wouldn't be nearly so calm. I would like to talk to him at some point. To probe a little deeper. Do you think that might be possible?'

'It depends where the investigation leads. He may just be the financier of the group, with no other connection besides a misguided philanthropy. But if he proves to be involved further and we have him back in, I'll let you know.'

Darke nodded his approval.

'Thank you both for coming today and offering your thoughts. Professor Hartford, your time is much appreciated,' said Pope.

Hartford and Darke said their goodbyes, and Darke led the psychologist out of the office.

'Right. Miller, what have you got?' She knew Miller was far more confident speaking to groups than Thompson, who was always happiest behind a computer screen.

Miller lifted his iPad and brought it to life. 'The strangest thing is the similarity between the stories of Evan Larsson and Nicholas Cooper. Both lost their parents when they were young, both headed to Paris, both then moved to the UK and, of course, both have connections to the Collective. Given these connections, it seems highly likely that Larsson may well have had more connections to the group than he is admitting to.'

'What else do we know about him?' asked Pope.

Miller checked his notes on the iPad. 'Thompson filled you in on most of what we know. Everything seems reasonably normal up to when he left Norway. In Paris he seems to have kept pretty much under the radar for most of the time. But something happened when he was studying at the Sorbonne.'

'The university in Paris?' asked Fletcher.

'Yes. He was enrolled there, studying for a PhD in philosophy. But he only stayed for the first year and a half. He seems to have left very suddenly. I called them early this morning, but they won't give out any information over the phone. They wouldn't even confirm that he had been a student there, although records confirm that he was.'

'So, why did he leave the course?'

'That's the question. What is clear is that very soon afterwards he and Nicholas Cooper left Paris and arrived in London. Since then, Larsson has kept a consistently low profile. His bank accounts show no apparent links to anyone else, except Cooper, and no records of any paid employment. He transfers a regular amount from one account to his current account every month.'

'Larsson's more involved than he's letting on. I think Hartford's right. He's too controlling to be a sleeping partner in something like this,' said Pope.

'Do you think he could have killed Cooper? Is Alice Lowrie lying?' asked Fletcher.

'I don't know about that. I think Alice Lowrie probably killed Cooper. But I think Larsson is central. Brody?'

'I agree. He was far too relaxed in that interview. He knows more than he's admitting.'

'So, are we saying that Larsson is now a major person of interest in this case?' asked Fletcher.

'Yes, we are. He's our key focus until we get anything else,' said Pope.

'How do you want to proceed?'

'I want to go to the Sorbonne and find out what really happened in Paris.'

Fletcher looked surprised. 'You want to go all the way to Paris? Why not call them?'

'Miller has already tried that and they weren't forthcoming. Add in the language barrier and I think face to face will work much better. You know how important it is to talk to a witness in person.'

'We don't even know the extent of his involvement yet,' said Fletcher.

'Which is exactly what we need to find out. It's only just over two hours on the train. Brody and I can go first thing and be back in the afternoon. He's our main lead aside from Alice Lowrie. It's worth it. Besides, if it was Brighton you'd have no problem, and it takes almost the same amount of time to get there.'

Fletcher looked at Pope. Considered. 'OK. But I want an update as soon as you've spoken to them there.'

'Good. Miller, can you book two tickets on the first train tomorrow morning to Gare du Nord for me and Brody. Send the tickets to our phones. Also, get in touch with the university first thing and tell them we're coming and that we'll need to speak to Larsson's professors or personal tutors, or whatever they have there. Someone who knows about him.'

'Will do.'

'Thompson. I want you to continue digging into Larsson. Anything and everything.' She turned to Fletcher. 'Can you organize a car outside Larsson's place in Soho? I want to know where he goes and who he sees until we can find out a bit more about him.'

Fletcher nodded.

Pope turned to Brody. 'How's your French?'

* * *

Pope hadn't realized the time. She finished up in the office and was on her way to the underground garage before she looked at her watch. *After eleven. Shit.* She'd left Alex and the girls with Alice Lowrie all day. She had planned to get back much earlier but the break with Evan Larsson had changed all that. With the interview that morning, the subsequent work she'd had to do, the wait for Hartford to return and the team briefing, the time had run away. The morning seemed like a very long time ago. She stopped on the stairs and texted an apology to Alex, asked how things were at home. She hadn't received a reply by the time she reached her car.

How things were "at home" seemed like a strange concept for her. At home had been on her own in what was technically Alex's house for nearly the last year. Suddenly he was back, Hannah and Chloe in tow, and the dynamic had shifted dramatically. Her response had been to disappear for the whole day, leaving a murder suspect in the house and a police guard outside. It wasn't the fresh start she had repeatedly gone over in her mind. Pope rested her head against the back of the driver's seat and closed her eyes. She was exhausted. Drained. She opened her eyes. Rest wasn't an option. She shook herself awake and started the car.

The drive home was quiet and in theory she should have had time to reflect, to plan, think about how she was going to fix the current situation. But she was so tired that her mind was numb, blank and incapable of focusing on what she wanted it to. She gave up the battle and concentrated on driving home.

When she turned into her street, the first thing she saw was the marked police car sitting right outside her house. What must Alex think about that? She pulled up behind it and got out.

A constable stepped out of the vehicle when he saw her approaching. 'Evening, ma'am.'

'Everything all right?'

'Fine. Nice and quiet. No one in or out, except Chloe, who came in about an hour ago.'

Pope looked at her watch. Almost midnight. She sighed. 'What time is shift change?'

'Six.'

'OK. Thanks. Make sure you keep warm.'

'Will do. Goodnight, ma'am.'

Pope found her keys and let herself in quietly. She listened, but heard nothing, as if the house itself were asleep. Walking into the kitchen, Pope saw the familiar signs that she wasn't living alone anymore. Plates and glasses left out, Hannah's coat on the back of a chair, Alex's wine glass by the sink, the remains of the red evident. She felt a familiar pang of guilt. She should have been at home sharing a glass of wine with him and helping out with dinner.

She was just about to pour herself a drink — God knows she needed one — when she felt the buzz of her phone receiving an email. She checked and saw that Miller had sent through the tickets for the Eurostar tomorrow morning. She clicked on the email and saw that the attached ticket was for 5.40 a.m. She regretted asking Miller to book the first train. She looked at the wine bottle and decided that sleep was more important, somewhat against her inclination. She locked the front door and walked silently upstairs. The door to the spare bedroom was firmly closed, and she decided against checking on Lowrie. Alex would have called her if there had been a problem.

Alex was fast asleep. As she got ready for bed and slid gently in beside him, Pope considered waking him. But something stopped her. Had she lost her confidence with Alex? Had she lost her ability to read him, to predict how he would react? The last thing she wanted to do was to have to deal with his anger if she got it wrong. She opted instead to let him sleep. She would get four hours at best.

She'd be gone before he woke.

CHAPTER TWENTY-THREE

It was still dark when the car arrived to collect Pope. That meant the heat hadn't started to take hold, and Pope was grateful at least for that. The driver texted her that he was outside, and she said she'd be five minutes. She'd managed about three hours' sleep and had even woken up once in that time. Her head had been too full to get to sleep immediately, despite her overwhelming tiredness. Between thoughts of Alice Lowrie, Evan Larsson, Tina Waterson and Alex and the girls, sleep was a long time coming. She'd managed a shower this morning, but had no time for a coffee. Perhaps the coffee on the train would be drinkable. As she left, she checked on Lowrie. She opened the door quietly and saw that she was fast asleep. She went back to her bedroom and left a note for Alex: *Had to go in early. Won't be late tonight. Will sort somewhere else for our guest by tonight at latest. X*. She left it on his bedside table and slipped silently out, wondering again whether she should have woken him.

The car whisked her along the Old Kent Road and over Blackfriars Bridge. As they crossed Fleet Street she got a message from Brody letting her know that he was at the station and where he was waiting for her. She saw the market traders heading to Smithfield Market and looked at her watch. 5.15 a.m. Too early.

She found Brody quickly at St Pancras. The station was empty but for a few hardy souls.

'How's Lowrie?' he asked.

'Fine. Asleep when I got back last night, asleep when I left this morning.'

'And Alex?'

'See above.'

'Ah. Some work to do there, then.'

'Yeah. It's great that he's back but I need the time to sort things out with him. Now is not that time.'

'When is it ever?' asked Brody.

Pope sighed. 'What platform?'

'Over here,' said Brody, indicating the international part of the terminal. 'Come on.'

Brody led the way and they both scanned their tickets and went through security and passport checks. Everyone was weary, going through the motions as if in a dream. Pope hoped she'd get a chance to catch up with some sleep on the journey.

They moved along the platform, Brody checking his ticket to find the right car. Pope left it to him. Eventually, after walking endlessly beside the long train, they found car C and boarded. About half the carriage was full, bleary-eyed executives staring ghost-like in front of them, wondering why they had chosen a job that made them board international public transport at dawn on a Friday morning. Brody found their seat and, chivalry personified, he stood aside to let Pope take the one next to the window. She settled in, noting how narrow and uncomfortable the seats were. She looked at her watch. Ten minutes to spare.

'As soon as we get going, I'll go and find some coffee,' said Brody.

'That'd be great.'

They both realized that there was unlikely to be any productive discussion before a caffeine injection, so both sat with their own thoughts. Pope looked absently out of the window, watching the passengers who had cut it fine rushing to board the train. Then they were moving. The train was mercifully quiet as it cut through South London, then it sped up slightly as it moved towards the Kent countryside. Pope watched the suburbs give way to the green fields. She wasn't really thinking about anything.

'I was surprised at how many cults there are in the UK and US,' said Brody.

Pope nodded absent-mindedly.

'I was reading that there are a number of cults that have grown up around the belief in UFOs and extraterrestrials.'

Of course Brody had spent his evening reading up on cults. 'Don't go down that rabbit hole.'

'No, it's true. Where governments obviously hide information from their citizens, some groups try to combat that misinformation and search for the truth.'

Pope looked sceptically at Brody.

'Not all cults are necessarily negative.'

'Are you joining QAnon now?' asked Pope.

Brody rolled his eyes. 'I can see you're not in the mood to discuss this now. I'll hunt down some coffee. Do you want anything to eat?' he asked, getting up from his seat.

Pope looked at her watch again. 'No, just coffee for the moment, thanks.'

Brody looked both ways to work out the direction of the buffet carriage, then walked away. Pope closed her eyes, hoping in vain to find her missing sleep. But she was too awake now and a multitude of problems swarmed into her head demanding solutions. At the moment, she didn't have any. She opened her eyes again and watched the countryside go by. It was easier not to think.

Brody returned with the coffee and the first sip was the jolt Pope needed. She felt the caffeine course through her and then she was ready to face the day.

'So, what are we expecting at the Sorbonne?' asked Brody.

'Larsson is clearly involved somehow. With Cooper, with the Collective, possibly with Alice Lowrie. But we don't know much about him. My instinct tells me he's more involved than he's letting on and I'm hoping we might find out more about him from those who knew him at the university.'

'Yes, there aren't any other obvious contacts flagged in his background.'

'Exactly. That's why I wanted to see his tutors face to face. It's the only lead that we have with Larsson so far. I want to know about his time in Paris and why he left the Sorbonne.'

'It's a shame we haven't been able to talk to Alice Lowrie about Larsson yet,' said Brody.

'We'll be able to ask her about him when we get back later today. I'll get her to look at a photo and see if she recognizes him. I don't believe that he's only been to the property in Lenham a few times.'

'No, he doesn't seem to be the hands-off type, as Hartford said.'

There was a natural pause in the conversation and Brody took the opportunity to change the conversation.

'What are you going to do about Alice?' he asked.

'In what sense?'

'Well, you can't have her at your place for much longer. Have you thought what you're going to do with her?'

'Not really. You're right, she needs to go somewhere. It's not fair on Alex and the girls to have her there. I've told him I'll sort somewhere by tonight. I don't think she's a risk, but having her at ours isn't a long-term solution. I'll talk to Fletcher when we get back and we can figure something out for her.'

'How long do you think we'll be in Paris?'

'Not long, I hope. No romantic walks along the Champs-Élysées, I'm afraid.'

Brody smiled.

'I want to get in and out quick. We need to get back and talk to Alice Lowrie and I need to put in an appearance at home. Otherwise there's a good chance Alex might leave again before we've even started.'

Brody was serious again. 'I'm sure he'll understand. It's a pretty serious case we're in the middle of.'

'Alex is like most people who live with police officers. They're understanding until they're not. That time has already come once before, and I need to make sure it doesn't come again. If it hasn't already,' she added.

Out of the window the landscape was changing. Green space gave way to concrete sidings and rows of overhead electrical wires, and Pope knew they were nearing the entrance to the tunnel. Then it was suddenly dark. The train had slowed down considerably and Pope knew that they would be crawling for about twenty minutes. It felt frustrating to be going so sluggishly after the relatively swift progress so far.

'Have we heard anything from Miller about who to contact when we get there?' asked Pope.

Brody checked his phone. 'No reception.' He showed her the screen as if to offer proof.

Pope looked at her phone and saw that she, too, had lost all reception.

'To be honest, it's probably too early to contact them yet anyway. Hopefully he'll have had some luck by the time we get to Gare du Nord,' said Brody.

There was nothing to do but wait.

* * *

Adam Miller picked up his coffee, took a sip and watched the couple walking by along Dean Street. They were younger than him, but not by much, and were on the way back from a run. He watched them enter the communal front door of an apartment and wondered what they did for a living that allowed them to own a place on this hip, expensive street in Soho. Maybe they rented, he told himself. That didn't make him feel any better. He still rented. Although they hadn't been together for long, it was going well and his girlfriend was very keen for them to buy somewhere, but on his police officer's salary and her nurse's, that was still a while away. This line of thinking wasn't doing him any good. He checked the time on his phone. Just past seven. He tried the number for the Sorbonne general switchboard again. It would be eight o'clock there. Still no answer. He'd try again in half an hour.

He had bagged a spot just back from the large window at the front of the De Luca café. It was a couple of doors down and across the road from Evan Larsson's second-floor apartment. He'd relieved the previous officer at six thirty, just as the café was opening. While the constable had spent his shift standing on the street in the cool night air, Miller had been the first customer to order a coffee and had his pick of the tables. He had a good view of the front door of the apartment but couldn't be seen from the windows of the second floor. He checked his phone again. Nothing from Pope or Brody. His orders were to watch the apartment and to stick to Larsson if he left the building. Miller hoped Larsson wouldn't go for a run this morning. He wasn't sure how he would handle that. Maybe he didn't go every day. And after his interrogation yesterday, maybe he would have other things to attend to. Miller could only hope. He sipped his coffee and returned to wondering about the employment and income of those walking along Dean Street at this early hour.

* * *

Several hundred miles south, Pope and Brody were speeding through the French countryside. Pope didn't know why the train travelled so much faster on the French side than the English side, but the difference was obvious. She was on her second cup of coffee, had eaten a croissant and was starting to feel human again. She checked her phone and saw that it had picked up a French carrier and showed good reception. She sent a message to Miller asking if he had managed to contact the Sorbonne, then a message to Fletcher updating them on their progress, such as it was. She also told him that she needed to organize somewhere for Alice Lowrie to stay and asked him to get someone on it. Miller replied instantly — no luck so far, but he would try again and let her know as soon as he had anything. No response from Fletcher. She tapped Alex's number, but then couldn't think of what to write, so cancelled the message and put her phone away.

'Should be there in about an hour,' said Brody, distracting her from her sense of failure in communicating with Alex.

'Good. Miller is still trying to get in touch with the university, but if he has no luck we'll just head there and find someone who can talk to us.'

'It's only about three miles from the station, so shouldn't take us long in a taxi.'

'Can you actually speak much French?' asked Pope. She realized that her holiday French would only get them so far and suddenly began to worry that communication would be a problem.

'*Un peu*,' replied Brody.

'Seriously. How well do you speak it?'

'I was being serious. A little. I can order beer and wine and a bit of food. Understand a bit. Not much more.'

'Great. Hopefully the staff at the Sorbonne will speak English. Or at least we should be able to find someone who can translate for us,' said Pope.

'The French are generally much better at speaking English than we are at speaking French. We'll be fine, I'm sure.'

Pope nodded. Her phone vibrated and she saw a message from Miller. He had got through to the Sorbonne and had managed to speak to the pastoral manager there. She was willing to speak to them when they arrived and also said she would try to organize for Larsson's personal tutor to be available to talk to them. He gave them the names to ask for. Pope thanked Miller and relayed the information to Brody.

'That's good news. Hopefully they'll have something useful about Larsson. Any news on him?' asked Brody.

'Not yet. Miller's watching his place at the moment but no sign of him so far.'

Pope saw that outside the train the green of Normandy was giving way to the outskirts of Paris. Pope had always favoured the city. She wasn't particularly gregarious or sociable, but she preferred to be around people. She loved to visit the country, but she would always live in a city. As the suburbs of Paris began to thicken, she began to feel more at home. Then they pulled gently into the Gare du Nord and the train came to a halt.

Brody was up and out of his seat as soon as the train stopped, and after passport control they exited and found themselves on the pavement amid a sunny Parisian morning. It wasn't quite as hot as London, which was a welcome relief.

Rush hour was in full flow, taxis, cars and scooters everywhere, bikes flying past. There were few cities that could make London's traffic appear relatively calm. Paris was certainly one of them. Pope was instantly refreshed as she felt the exhilaration of arriving in a new city, even if it was for a quick work trip. She breathed in the Paris air and took in the view.

Brody spotted a taxi rank and walked towards it. He was attempting to talk to a driver when several locals loudly explained that there was a queue and indicated the end of it, gesticulating wildly. They joined at the end.

'A good start to embracing the local culture,' said Pope.

'Yeah. Who knew we'd get schooled on queuing in Paris?'

Soon they were at the front and a taxi pulled up. The driver got out and Brody asked him to take them to the Sorbonne. Pope wondered if her French was actually better than Brody's, but decided to let him take the strain for the moment. It didn't seem to be doing any harm. The driver moved extremely fast in and out of the traffic, dodging motorbikes and pedestrians, coming within centimetres of oncoming traffic.

Pope raised her eyebrows at Brody.

'It's a cliché for a reason,' he said.

'You're not kidding. It's like being in a video game.'

'Welcome to the speed-driving capital of the western world,' said Brody.

After about half an hour of their theme park ride, the cab pulled up outside an imposing, sandstone-coloured building that covered an entire Paris block. The doors were navy blue and each one was guarded by a suited doorman, like a high-end hotel. The first impressions were of age, accumulated wisdom and decorum.

Brody paid the taxi driver and the two of them got out and smoothed down their clothes. Pope took in the expanse of the building.

'Not your usual university.' She was impressed by the scale and style.

'One of the most famous in the world. I guess it has to dress to impress.'

'I guess so.' Pope looked around for what might be the main entrance. There were several candidates. 'What about there?' She indicated the double doors in the middle of the block.

'Let's give it a try,' said Brody.

Pope led them towards the entrance. The doorman moved forward a step as they arrived, said something very quickly that Pope didn't even begin to understand. She turned to Brody, who shook his head.

'Do you speak English?' she asked.

'A little, madame. What do you need?'

Used to dealing with sightseers. Pope checked the message on her phone from Miller. 'We have an appointment with Sophie Vallence and Marc Pridot. London Metropolitan Police.' She held up her warrant card. The doorman seemed distinctly unimpressed. *Why wouldn't he be?* thought Pope.

He nodded, turned away from them and said something into his walkie-talkie. A reply came back. 'First floor. Madame Vallence will see you at the reception.'

'*Merci beaucoup,*' said Pope, attempting to make an effort. The doorman nodded courteously.

They entered the building through the large doors and Pope was immediately struck by the calm and quiet of the place. That and the sheer beauty of the architecture. It connoted academic prestige and the value of learning, but also, like many such universities, wealth and privilege. The few students who were making their way past them as they walked to the main staircase looked like they were not short of money. A far cry from her own student days in Sussex, where relative poverty was the norm.

When they reached the top of the stairs they followed the signs to reception. At the wide reception desk a middle-aged woman with a smart haircut and a grey suit was typing into a computer. Just as Pope was about to say something to attract her attention — although she was pretty certain the woman knew full well that they were waiting — she heard a voice from behind them.

'Madame Pope, Monsieur Brody?' The greeting came from a blonde-haired woman in her early forties. She was so stereotypically Parisian in appearance, Pope almost laughed. Slim, dressed in black trousers and a black silk blouse, with impeccable hair and make-up. Of course, her English was excellent.

'Yes. Madame Vallence?'

'Yes, good morning. Nice to meet you. I'm Sophie Vallence. I'm the pastoral manager for postgraduate students at the Sorbonne.' She shook first Pope's hand, then Brody's. 'Come with me, we can talk in my office.'

'It's a beautiful building,' said Pope, as they walked along the wood-panelled corridor away from the reception.

'Yes, isn't it? It's a lovely environment to work in.'

They turned a corner and their guide pressed the card she kept on a lanyard around her neck against a security pad, opening the door to her office. She indicated for them to sit down in chairs arranged around a coffee table.

'Would you like a coffee?' she asked. 'I'm afraid I don't have any tea.'

Pope smiled. She wasn't the only one working on stereotypes. 'Coffee is great, thanks.'

'Yes, coffee, please,' said Brody.

Sophie Vallence poured two cups and handed them to Pope and Brody. She didn't offer milk. Pope sipped what was one of best-tasting coffees she had had in a long time.

'I'll call Marc. He should be able to answer your questions about Evan Larsson.'

'Did you know him? Larsson?' asked Pope.

'I did. But only towards the end of his time here. I have overall management of the postgraduate students' welfare here, but Marc was Evan's personal tutor and supervised his work, so he knew him much better.' She picked up the phone, dialled a number and had a brief conversation.

'He's coming,' she said when she had put down the phone. Almost immediately there was a knock at the door and a man stepped into the office. Marc Pridot was older than Sophie Vallence, Pope guessed mid-fifties. He wore black Levi's and a dark blue shirt smartly tucked in. He had his hair cut very short, almost certainly to disguise the effect of the male-pattern baldness encroaching with middle age, and wore a pair of round, wire-framed glasses. He held a folder stuffed with a great many pieces of paper. Pope wondered if it was Larsson's file. He shook both of their hands, then took a seat opposite.

'Madame Pope, Monsieur Brody, this is Professor Marc Pridot,' said Vallence.

'Nice to meet you,' said Pope.

Pridot nodded politely.

'Marc was Evan Larsson's personal tutor. At the Sorbonne, that means he was the first point of contact for any pastoral matters, and he also supervised Larsson's academic work. Of all the staff here, Marc would have known Evan best, I think.'

'Why do you want to know about Evan Larsson?' asked Pridot. 'The message I got doesn't tell the circumstances, but I think it is serious for you to travel from London.'

The professor's English was almost as confident as Vallence's, though the accent less clear. She wondered if all staff at the Sorbonne spoke excellent English.

'He has come up in one of our investigations. We don't yet know the nature of his involvement, but we think he may be connected to a serious crime. It would be very helpful for us if you could tell us anything about him and why he left the university before completing his studies.' Pope found herself speaking a little slower than she normally would.

192

Pridot nodded and seemed to understand the seriousness of the enquiry. He opened the folder he held and checked the first page. He saw Pope and Brody looking at the rather tattered card folder.

'Most of our records are digital now. But when I started teaching it was paper. I prefer that, so I keep paper copies of my records on students. It is better for me.'

'What can you tell us?' said Pope.

'Evan Larsson was here for about eighteen months. He came from the University of Oslo with a Master's degree and he enrolled on a postgraduate programme. He was studying for a doctorate in philosophy. His early study had been in philosophy and psychology, but, as with his Master's, he chose to specialize in philosophy only for his doctorate.'

'Why was that, do you think?' asked Brody.

'Evan had some strong ideas about ethics and morality and he wanted to explore these in more depth. He was developing his own philosophical ideas and so this seemed the right path for him.'

'And was it?' asked Pope. 'I mean, was he a good student?'

Pridot thought for a moment. 'Evan is very intelligent. He has a very good mind and can apply that mind to anything he chooses. The problem is that he finds it difficult to accept criticism. He is used to being right, to being the most clever person in the room. He does not react well when his ideas are challenged.'

'Is that what happened?' asked Pope.

'Yes,' replied Pridot.

'What were the ideas that caused the problems?'

'To understand Evan's thinking, you really need to know a little about Nietzsche. But he was most interested in Nietzsche's idea of the *Ubermensch*. Are you familiar with the concept?'

Brody answered. 'The superman? That idea that some men are above others and can act in the way they want, rather than fitting in with society?'

'Yes, that is right,' confirmed Pridot. 'It is often translated in English as "Overman". In essence, Nietzsche argued that the *Ubermensch* does not have to fit to the, er—' Pridot struggled to find the word — 'to the idea of the common man, of the common ideals. He is able to rise above the idea of good and evil and establish a higher set of values. When in a group, the Overmen devise their own rules and morality for the situation.'

'And how are these rules constructed?' asked Brody.

'Nietzsche developed the idea of perspectivism. This is the rejection of objective reality, replaced by a new sense of reality, of knowledge, that can be constantly reassessed depending on context and perspective.'

'And this was what Larsson argued?'

'Yes. He was very interested in this and began to focus on it as the main basis of his work.'

'Was that a problem?' asked Pope.

'Not in itself. But he became so obsessed with it that he was unable to accept any criticism, unable to discuss rationally the enormous problems with Nietzsche's theories.'

'What problems?'

Pridot smiled at Pope, as if it were obvious. 'Many evil men have used this idea to rewrite a moral code and set of ethics to justify their own actions. Mussolini, certainly. Hitler, probably. Many killers have referenced Nietzsche over the years. He is vital in the arguments of many fascist groups and individuals, many right-wing thinkers and philosophers, psychiatrists and psychologists.'

'Mr Pridot, do you think Evan Larsson would act upon these ideas? I mean, was he advocating all this theoretically, or might he be the kind of man to put it into practice?'

'I can't answer that. I'm not a psychologist. But I saw Evan get very angry when challenged on the value of his thinking. From what I have read of psychology, the closest I could think of was, I don't know the English, I'm afraid. In French, *un narcissique*.'

'A narcissist,' said Pope. 'Almost identical.'

Pope looked at Brody. They were thinking the same.

'Yes, yes, that's it. The most difficult circumstance was that Evan began to argue for what he called "alternative philosophical religions". He advocated groups where people would practise the ethics and rules decided by the Overman. In France, we would call these *cultes*.'

'In England too,' said Pope. 'We think Larsson might be involved with a group like that. Did he ever talk about this kind of thing?'

'Yes. He proposed the idea. But only in theory. I never got the idea that he was going to really do it.'

'Would it surprise you if he did? If he got involved with setting up a cult?' asked Pope.

Pridot gave this a bit of thought. 'He was very passionate about his ideas.'

'One more question, Mr Pridot. Why did Larsson leave the university? Did he choose to leave? Or did you ask him to?'

'He was asked to leave.'

'Can you tell us why?'

Pridot looked at his colleague.

'I can answer that,' Vallence said. 'Evan Larsson got in a fight with another student.'

'Do you know the circumstances?' asked Pope.

'Yes. He was in the cafeteria here, on the ground floor. He was arguing with another philosophy student. I don't know the exact nature of the argument, but it became very intense and, according to witnesses, Evan simply attacked him.'

'Attacked?'

'Yes. He started punching the other man, who fell to the floor. At that point he began to kick him while he was lying on the floor. It took three security guards to pull him off and make him stop.'

'What happened to the other student?' asked Pope.

'He was in hospital for two or three days. Permanent damage to one of his eyes, a broken rib. There was a lot of blood.'

'So he was asked to leave?'

'We have a no-tolerance policy for violence on the campus. It is made very clear to the students when they enrol. He left immediately.'

'Madame Vallence, Monsieur Pridot, you have both been very helpful. I feel like we have a much clearer picture of Evan Larsson. Thank you for seeing us and for giving up your time today.'

'You are welcome. We are happy to help. I hope you manage to solve your case,' said Vallence.

'I'm sure we will.'

'Monsieur Pridot.' Pope shook his hand, followed by Brody.

They said their goodbyes and Pope said they would see themselves out. They walked along the corridor and Pope checked her phone. No messages. She sent a text to Miller saying that they were done at the university and were heading to the station.

'Let's get back and see what else we can find on Larsson. After that, he's jumped to the head of my persons-of-interest list,' said Pope.

Brody hailed a taxi. 'Absolutely,' he said.

* * *

Miller was on his fourth cup of coffee. He felt a moral obligation to keep buying drinks, to pay for the table and chair he was taking up. The late morning trade was in full swing and, although most customers didn't want to sit down, he still felt obliged. He was just beginning to wonder how long he might realistically keep consuming caffeine, when he saw the door of Larsson's block open. Sure enough, Evan Larsson stepped out into the bright late morning. He was dressed casually, jeans and a shirt, with a small rucksack over his right shoulder. He stood in his doorway and seemed to be taking in the air. Then he turned left and started a brisk walk in the direction of Oxford Street. Miller, relieved of his responsibility to drink more coffee, left his cup on the table and exited the café. He stayed on the other side of the street to Larsson and held well back in order that Larsson wouldn't see him. Larsson didn't look back, which Miller took as a sign that he was blissfully unaware that he was being followed. At the end of the road Larsson turned right into Carlisle Street and skirted around the edge of Soho Square. From there he took a number of backstreets, confident of his knowledge of the area. After around ten minutes of walking Miller recognized Great Portland Street underground station and knew that Larsson was heading for Regent's Park. He radioed in and told dispatch that Larsson was on the move and that he would be back in touch when he had a confirmed destination.

Larsson continued straight into the park and Miller followed at a suitable distance, but then lost sight as he changed direction and moved to the right, around a clump of trees and large bushes. Miller sped up, but when he reached the point where Larsson had disappeared from view, he saw no sign of the man. Miller looked left to right, but saw no one. His heart beat a little faster and he cursed under his breath.

As Sergeant Adam Miller stood still, working out where Evan Larsson could have gone, and assessing which way he should walk in order to best find him, he had absolutely no idea that Larsson had doubled back, moved around the group of trees that had shielded his change of direction and was now some way behind him, watching the police officer try to decide which way to go.

CHAPTER TWENTY-FOUR

Pope and Brody arrived back at the Gare du Nord a few minutes after a train to London had just left. Pope cursed as Brody went to the ticket office to book them on the next available service.

'Must be the quickest day trip to Paris ever,' he said. 'We're on the 12.05.'

Pope looked at the time on the digital departures board overhead. Just under an hour to wait. 'Shall we get a coffee?'

They found a table at the nicest-looking café they could find just outside the station. The coffee was, predictably, very good, and was served with a small chocolate square next to the cup.

'I have to say, the more I find out about Larsson the more my alarm bells start ringing,' said Brody.

'He certainly comes across as someone who fits the profile Elizabeth Hartford described. Controlling, narcissistic, doesn't like to be challenged. I mean, it's not exactly hard evidence, but it does cast our interview with him in a different light.'

'That's what I was thinking. From Pridot's description of him, he really doesn't seem like the type to take a back seat.'

'No, he doesn't. And he ticks all the boxes Hartford talked about when she described the typical psychological profile of a cult leader. When we looked around the place in Lenham, we were only thinking about Nicholas Cooper. But I think we need to go back and consider it through the lens of Evan Larsson. He has to be much more involved than he's letting on.'

Brody took a sip of coffee. 'How do you think he might be involved?'

'I'm beginning to suspect he might be the main guy.'

'Do you think so?'

'I don't know. But I wonder if the regular amount that Larsson paid to Cooper was less philanthropic support and more like a salary. I think Larsson might have been the leader of the Collective, with Cooper a . . . I don't know. Maybe a manager, if that makes sense?'

'Not sure how we'll prove that if the only connection we can find is financial.'

'The first step is to see if Alice Lowrie recognizes Larsson. Then we need to hope that Miller and Thompson can find something interesting to connect him in a more concrete way. Something tells me that another interview isn't going to get us very far. Not until we have something to confront him with.'

Brody paused. 'Do you think he might have had something to do with the Tina Waterson murder?'

Pope took a beat. 'Good question. I don't know. They disappeared at around the same time. But it could be coincidence. We need to talk to him about that, but not yet.' She stared into her coffee cup. 'Let's focus on understanding his connection to the Collective first, and then we can see where that takes us.' Pope had learned that dwelling on the Tina Waterson case was counterproductive.

Brody seemed to read her. He looked at his watch. 'Come on, let's get to the train.'

They paid, and Pope made a last attempt to speak a few words of French to the waiter as they left. He smiled curtly and nodded, in the way that people often did when you were destroying their language but for commendable reasons. She felt embarrassed, and wished she hadn't made the effort.

Outside, the sun was shining and the streets around the Gare du Nord were bustling. Pope felt the strong urge to turn round and walk into the heart of Paris. To walk with no real aim other than to lose herself in the narrow side streets of this beautiful city. To be David Geffen in Joni Mitchell's "Free Man in Paris". She felt the desire to shed all responsibility and disappear into the anonymity of a city that was not her own. Not today.

Brody led her into the station and through passport control again — more rigorous this time — then through security. Once on the train Pope was overcome with the need for sleep. She had been up since before five and had lots to do when she returned to London. This might be the only couple of hours she got to rest for some time. The train pulled away and trundled along smoothly as she watched the suburbs of Paris thin out, then they were once again cutting swiftly through the northern French countryside. She glanced at Brody, who was busy on his phone. Pope leaned against the window and eased back into her chair, closing her eyes. She was asleep within a couple of minutes.

* * *

Where the hell is he? Miller admonished himself for losing sight of Larsson. He knew he couldn't be far away. The man had been just in front, but the tree cover had been just what he needed to get out of Miller's line of sight. He wasn't sure if Larsson had realized that he was being followed and had deliberately evaded his pursuer, or if he had simply changed direction and Miller had lost sight. Either was possible. He took out his phone and dialled Pope, all the while scanning the area. Straight to voicemail. Then he tried Brody, with the same result. He quickly texted Pope: *Lost Larsson in Regent's Park. Still looking.*

Miller moved forward, unaware that the figure he sought was quietly walking up behind him, under cover of a number of large oak trees.

* * *

Brody checked his phone as they entered the tunnel leading them from France to England. No missed calls or messages. Pope was still sleeping. He was pleased with that. He knew that she suffered from insomnia, and he knew that it would be worse at the moment with the nature of this case and Pope's perceived connection with Alice Lowrie. He hoped that his boss would give enough attention to her relationship with Alex in among all this, but he doubted it. Still, for now, an hour or so of sleep was probably just what she needed. He picked up the copy of *Le Monde* that was lying on the empty seat across the aisle and started the masochistic task of seeing how much he could understand of the French newspaper.

* * *

Miller stopped and looked around. He had walked ahead, but was still beneath fairly dense tree foliage. No sign of Larsson. In fact, he couldn't see anyone. This was the quietest part of the park. He wondered if Larsson knew this, if he had been spotted early on and this was all part of a plan to escape the attentions of the Metropolitan Police. If so, it added weight to the suspicions against Larsson. It was right or left. He mentally tossed a coin, wondering what his colleagues' reactions would be to his losing Larsson. He had to find him.

He decided to head left. Miller didn't hear the man walking up to him until he was right behind him. The grass allowed for a silent approach. By the time he realized what had happened, it was too late. He made to spin around, but suddenly felt a sharp, cold sensation in his lower back, then another one and another, lightning quick. Then Miller couldn't speak, then he couldn't take a breath, and then he was down on one knee, the pain radiating from his lung. He knew he had been stabbed in the kidney and in the lung, he didn't know where else. He tried to balance, but fell over on to the grass, under the shade of the cool oak trees overhead. He could see the light dappled above, a blue sky, largely obscured by the heavy foliage of the trees. Then a shadow. He looked slightly to his side and saw Evan Larsson standing over his body, looking down at him, his expression absolutely blank. Miller tried to speak, but was unable to make any sound. He watched Evan Larsson walk away, saw that he didn't look back, not even once.

* * *

Pope woke as the Eurostar was ten minutes from St Pancras station. She stretched, yawned and checked her phone. She sat immediately upright when she read a message.

'Miller says he's lost Larsson in Regent's Park.' She checked the time. 'That was an hour ago. Shit.'

'He must have sent it while we were in the tunnel.'

She dialled his number. No answer. She took a moment to grasp the situation. 'If he was tailing Larsson, how would he lose him? Unless Larsson gave him the slip? And why hasn't he updated us in the last hour?'

'Why don't you call Fletcher and get him to send a couple of cars over there?'

'I will.' Pope made the call and Fletcher confirmed that he hadn't heard anything from Miller since late morning. He said he would send a patrol car to the park and would arrange to have Pope and Brody picked up from St Pancras. Pope had a bad feeling. It made the final ten minutes of the journey unbearable.

* * *

Adam Miller looked up at the canopy of trees above him. Then he slowly moved his head to the left. He could hear distant voices, and an intermittent thud of, what was it, maybe a football being kicked not too far away? He tried to call out, but couldn't make a sound. Why was that? When he tried to breathe, he found it difficult and painful and heard a gurgling sound every time he took a breath. He knew that wasn't good. Thoughts of his girlfriend swayed through his mind, but kept intersecting with images of Pope. He had failed both of them. He had to let Pope know who had stabbed him. He had to tell them it was Evan Larsson. Somehow.

* * *

Pope saw the car waiting for them as soon as they hurriedly exited the station. It was right there on the forecourt and she and Brody jumped in quickly.

'Let's go.'

The officer driving pulled away quickly. 'Won't take long, ma'am. Straight down the Euston Road.'

'Have you heard anything?' she asked.

'Not yet. We can't reach him, but they've tracked his phone. Units are heading there now.'

Pope sat back in the chair and closed her eyes. 'Shit.'

'Miller will be fine. He knows how to handle himself,' said Brody.

'So why hasn't he been in contact?'

Brody had no answer for this.

The officer was right. They pulled up towards the park in just a few minutes, the blue lights cutting a swathe through the afternoon traffic. Then Pope saw the flash from an ambulance.

'There.' She pointed.

The car swerved and headed for the ambulance. The moment they arrived Pope could see a commotion. Three paramedics and a number of police officers were wheeling a stretcher trolley into the open vehicle. She and Brody leaped out. Pope got there first, just as Miller was being lifted into the vehicle.

'Adam!'

Miller was looking at her, but didn't attempt to say anything. He smiled a little, held out his hand. Pope took it and held it in both of hers.

'You're going to be fine.' Pope avoided eye contact with the paramedics in the ambulance.

'We need to work on him. Mind out of the way, give us some space.' Pope was reluctant to move, to let go of Miller's hand, but the medic moved her away. As she stepped back, Brody put his arm around her shoulder. The two of them stood there, watching helplessly as people they didn't know held Adam Miller's life in their hands. One of the police officers who had been helping with the stretcher came over to them.

'Did you find him?' asked Pope.

'Yes, ma'am.' He looked down at the ground, then back up. 'He's been stabbed in the back several times. It looked pretty bad.'

'Anyone else on the scene?'

'No. We're about to start canvassing the area. We found him in quite a secluded part of the park, so I don't know how successful they'll be. But someone might have seen something.'

'OK. Keep us posted.'

The officer walked back to his colleagues just as one of the medics came out of the ambulance and towards Pope. 'We've stabilized him, stopped the blood loss, and we'll get him to the hospital now. He wants to see you. I think he wants to tell you something. Please be quick, we need to get moving.'

Pope climbed the steps into the ambulance. Brody followed, but waited just by the entrance to the vehicle. One of the paramedics was sorting out the hanging of a drip attached to Miller's arm. An electronic monitoring unit was attached to electrodes on his chest. Bandages were wrapped around his torso. The floor was covered in screwed-up wads of gauze and cotton wool, each turned red, soaked in Miller's blood. She leaned in close to him. He was trying to speak to her, the effort all-consuming for him. She leaned closer, her ear near to his mouth.

'What is it, Adam?'

He paused, closed his eyes, summoning up the energy to speak.

'You need to rest. We can talk at the hospital.'

Miller frowned and shook his head; it was barely perceptible. He spoke inaudibly.

'Don't, Adam.'

'Larsson.' The single word.

'Did Larsson do this to you? Was it Larsson?'

He nodded, closed his eyes again. Then he was trying to say something else.

'I'm sorry,' he said.

Pope opened her mouth to protest, to refute his apology, but suddenly he stiffened and the monitor started making alarm sounds.

'Out of the way. Get out of the ambulance!' The medic outside pushed past to get to her patient. Pope almost fell out, once again into Brody's outstretched arm. This time Pope wouldn't let herself be held. Couldn't. She moved a step away, eyes fixed on her officer and the medics working on him.

But the machine continued the alarm, then it was a flat, continuous beep. Pope closed her eyes. '*No*,' she said under her breath. She couldn't lose Miller, couldn't take another blow, not now. Pope and Brody stood still, now both fixed on the scene unfolding in front of them.

It seemed like a very long time, in the way that those things do. The clock seems to stop and the emotion, the shock is so powerful that there is no feeling, no words. The numbness surrounds you as if wrapping you in a bubble and there is nothing to do but wait, in silence, for an outcome over which you have no control. If you are used to being in control, it is unbearable.

It was suddenly deathly quiet. Pope held her breath. Then one of the medics stepped out of the ambulance, looked straight into Pope's eyes and shook her head. 'I'm sorry. The wounds were too severe, too deep.' She started to explain, but Pope couldn't really hear it. She pushed past the woman and stepped up into the ambulance.

'Bec. Bec, don't,' she heard Brody calling behind her. But she needed to see Miller. She stood by his body. His dead body. For a moment the numbness protected her again, kept her mind from really registering. Then it vanished, receded to where it had come from. And she sat down on the small seat next to her sergeant, and she wept. She wept for the life of Adam Miller.

CHAPTER TWENTY-FIVE

Pope stared into the coffee cup that Brody had just put in front of her. The steaming liquid was still circulating from being stirred, and it provided a small distraction. She had spent the car journey from Regent's Park back to the police station blankly staring out of the window, and then she had retired to the bathroom and stared at herself in the mirror for what seemed like hours. Staring seemed to be the only thing she was currently capable of doing.

When she had walked into the office, everybody already knew. The devastation had been obvious as soon as she opened the door, so there was nothing to say. She knew it would be her job to rally the troops, to get everyone back on track in hunting down Miller's murderer. But at the moment, she was paralyzed. All she could think about was that she had directed Miller to follow Evan Larsson while she and Brody had taken the train to Paris. She had placed him in danger, on his own. She had underestimated how dangerous Larsson was and Miller had paid the price for her miscalculation. The worst thing, however, was Miller's final word to Pope: *Sorry*. She was devastated that he died thinking that he had not done his job properly, had disappointed her. Miller had been one of the most promising officers she had worked with. He was young, intelligent and conscientious. He also had seemingly boundless energy and an old-fashioned sense of duty that was much more common in older officers. She couldn't actually think of a single time that Miller had let her down. Not once. The fact that his final breath was an apology to her was something that Pope would have to live with for a very long time.

Pope looked around. The room was silent. No one knew what to say. Miller had been such an integral part of Pope's investigative team that it was impossible to think of working without him. Pope realized she needed to say something. Just then, Fletcher came in and headed straight to Pope's desk.

'I'm so sorry, Bec.' Fletcher talked quietly, just to her. 'Miller was a good man and an excellent police officer. We'll get who did this.'

Pope looked at Fletcher and nodded. She gathered her strength and stood up, moved to the centre of the room.

'This is an unbearable loss for our team.' She looked around the office, every face turned towards her. 'Adam Miller was a great officer and a warm, intelligent and supportive colleague. We all relied on him at different times, and we were never let down. That's quite some achievement.' There were nods and words of agreement. 'Without doubt, this leaves a huge hole in the team and in many of us personally. We all need to grieve, both individually and collectively. There will be time for that, and we will honour Miller's life and contribution to all of us in due course. But before we do that, we need to find the man who killed our colleague, our friend.' Pope's tone had moved from melancholy to resolute. 'Miller told us, right before he died, that it was Evan Larsson who stabbed him.' She flinched, remembering hearing the words in the ambulance. Pope steeled herself. 'Our first priority is to find Larsson. It's what Miller was working on, it's what he would have wanted us to do and it's our job to hunt down this killer. If anyone needs time, please come and have a word with me. It's completely understandable. But I want this team, every one of us, focused on finding our man.

Once we've done that, our attention will turn to remembering Adam Miller.' Again, most people nodded, muttered agreement.

Pope turned to Fletcher. 'Thanks, Bec,' he said.

'Is there an APB on Larsson?' she asked.

'Yes. I've just put it out. Everyone's searching for him.'

'Good. And we'll need a car on his apartment. No solos. I want minimum two officers at all points until we find him.'

'I've already sent two unmarked to his place. No sign so far.'

'I doubt he'll go back there anytime soon. But maybe IT can track him using credit cards or his phone. I'll talk to Thompson.'

'Good. But also take some time for yourself, Bec. You've been through a lot.'

'I'm fine.'

Fletcher looked at her for a moment, then nodded and turned. He closed the door gently behind him.

Brody came over to Pope. 'That was good. Exactly what people needed to hear, I think.'

'I hope so. How the hell we get through this, I don't know. But having a focus for the moment might help.'

'Are you OK?' he asked.

'Define "OK". I'll be OK when we find Larsson. Come on, let's go and talk to Thompson, see what he might be able to do for us.'

The two of them headed down to the tech office and explained to Thompson and his colleagues what was needed: a location for Evan Larsson, and quick. Thompson was predictably subdued. He and Miller had been friends outside work, Pope knew. But he was also professional and she knew she could rely on him. Compartmentalizing feelings was a key skill in police work. Twenty years on, Pope was still working on it.

Back in the office, Pope was considering her next course of action when her phone rang. She looked at the caller ID and saw that it was Alex. She had completely neglected him, although she felt some justification. She didn't want to have to have this conversation and she didn't want to have to tell Alex about Miller, but she felt that she had to talk to him. She couldn't ignore the call, although she felt a very strong urge to do exactly that.

The phone call was difficult. First, Alex was clearly put out that Pope hadn't made it back before he went to sleep last night. And unimpressed that she had had to leave so early this morning. Pope tried to explain, but the old excuses of a difficult case, limited resources and the weight of responsibility of a DCI just seemed to retread the old arguments, compounding the problem. Then, she had to explain what had happened to Miller this afternoon. Alex was dismayed that one of her officers had met with such violence. She ended up trying to console him, which, she considered, was possibly the wrong way around. She simply didn't have the reserves to soothe his fears, albeit about her safety, so she cut the topic off, telling him they would discuss it when she came home, which would be soon. Finally, Alex expressed serious reservations about Alice Lowrie. He told Pope that she was becoming increasingly agitated at being in the house, and kept asking for her. She had argued with Chloe, the latter stomping out of the front door to an undisclosed location. Alex wasn't sure that her staying in his house was sustainable any longer and Pope promised to get her moved.

She knew that above all she needed to get home. These problems, while not serious compared to what she was dealing with, seemed huge to Alex and she had to respect that. Too much time living on her own had dulled her senses when it came to family compromise and he needed her attention. And, she knew, deserved it. All their problems were of her making. So she had the responsibility of making them right. Another responsibility.

Pope saw that it was early evening. 'I need to get back and talk to Alice.' She told Brody. 'I'll show her a photo of Larsson and see what she says.'

'Do you want me to come with you?' he offered.

'No. There's a unit outside if I need them.' She paused. 'I also need to do some bridge-building with Alex and the girls. I've managed to get everything wrong since they've been back.'

Brody smiled. 'I have no doubt your diplomacy skills will do the job admirably.' He put his arms around her and gave her a hug. It was absolutely the right thing after the day they'd had, the loss they'd suffered. 'I'm going to stay for a while. I'll be in touch if we get anything.'

Pope left her office and called into Fletcher's on her way out. He was typing something into his phone and put it down when she entered.

'I'm off home to talk to Alice Lowrie. Did you manage to find anywhere for her?'

'Yes. There's a women's refuge for vulnerable witnesses in New Cross. I haven't used it before, but it's very secure. Comes recommended by a colleague.' He didn't go into any more details.

'Do you think a refuge is the right place? Sounds more like a secure unit,' said Pope.

'Not much choice at short notice, I'm afraid. She'll be fine there. It's very safe and we can keep an eye on her until we know a bit more. We can't just send her anywhere, given the circumstances.'

'OK,' said Pope. 'If you send me the details, and send a car to my place in a couple of hours, I'll explain it all to her and make sure she's ready.'

'Will do.'

Pope left and headed to the car park. The events of the day were weighing heavily on her and she breathed an audible sigh of relief she got in and closed the car door. She needed to get out of here now. She could feel palpitations coming on, something from which she periodically suffered. As she pulled out on to the road, she vividly remembered the last time this had happened. Last year. The Cameraman case. Then the ensuing publicity and attempts to destroy her privacy by the media. She'd felt extreme stress at that time, and now, as she drove home through the Friday-evening revellers in Central London, she was starting to feel it again. The emotional fallout from that case had been extreme and, if she was being honest with herself, she had only recently begun to feel at peace again. It was ironic, but when Alex finally left her alone in the house, it was actually just what she had needed. She couldn't tell him that, of course. But it had allowed her to grieve and to manage a set of particularly difficult and conflicting emotions that she couldn't have managed if there had been other emotional demands on her. She was able to lose herself in her work during the days, and in John Coltrane and red wine in the evenings. The nights, as so often the case, were the problems. But she had more or less managed to get things back where they should be and move on.

Until today. What had happened to Miller had brought grief all of its own, but had also allowed other wounds to reopen, exposing the old anguish beneath. Pope realized that, certainly for her, grief was never really dealt with. It simply waited, sometimes hidden from view, for an opportunity to return, often when you least expected it, and definitely when you were least able to deal with it. This was one of those times. She knew deep down that she didn't really deal with emotional issues, she simply found ways to block them, evade them and, as a last resort, run from them. But up until today she had convinced herself that she was doing a good job.

Pope knew that she was still in shock. The full emotional impact of what had happened was, worryingly, still to come. But she also realized that she had to clear her head and get herself to a point where she could deal with Alex, with Hannah and Chloe, and manage Alice Lowrie. At least that was in hand. Now she had the small matter of finding and arresting Evan Larsson. She considered where she was and how long it would take her to get home. She had about thirty minutes to sort herself out.

* * *

Alex watched the young woman sitting on the sofa. She was gently rocking back and forth, with her arms wrapped around her. A case study in insecurity and alienation. He had tried to talk to her at various points during the day, attempted to make her feel at home and a little more relaxed, but she had been impossible to get through to. Pope had told him that she had lost her memory, but she seemed to have lost her social skills and powers of conversation too. Then he immediately felt bad for being so judgemental. He didn't know what she'd been through and so it was probably no surprise that she was finding being here in a strange house difficult.

The argument with Chloe had been predictable. She had found it uncomfortable to be around this awkward, seemingly hostile stranger and the end result had been her storming out of the house. Presumably she had fled to Tyler's — her usual refuge at points of conflict. Hannah had avoided being around her, which was fairly easy as the woman had spent most of the day upstairs in her room with the door closed. Bec had promised that she would be gone by this evening. He looked at his watch. Not long to go to keep that promise.

Now she was downstairs because Alex had finally decided that she needed to eat something. All he had to do was open up the lines of communication and he was sure he could manage to relax her a little bit. Although judging by her body language on the sofa, that might be easier said than done.

Just then he heard a key in the lock. He knew the officers outside would stop anyone other than Bec or Chloe. Sure enough, he heard the front door close and moments later Chloe walked in.

'Hi, Dad.' As if nothing had happened. Alex decided to play along for the sake of peace.

'Hi, Chloe. How was Tyler?'

She shot him a look. 'Fine. What's for dinner?'

'I'm just working that out.'

'It's a bit late, isn't it?'

Alex bit his tongue. 'I'm trying to work out what our guest might fancy to eat.'

At that point Hannah came down the stairs.

'Hannah,' said Alex, 'any thoughts for tea? What would you like?'

'I thought you were asking our "guest",' said Chloe.

Alex turned to see Lowrie get up from the sofa and head towards the door.

'Where are you going, Alice? Don't you want to stay for something to eat?' She didn't reply, or look at him, so Alex moved a step forward to place himself in her eyeline.

She reacted instantly, shouted, 'Get away from me!'

Alex froze. 'What is it?'

With a quick movement, she straightened her arm and a long knife slid out from her shirt sleeve and into her hand. She held it up towards Alex. 'I said get away from me.'

Hannah rushed to Chloe, who screamed. She had been through so much last year; she wouldn't be able to deal with this. The two sisters backed against the wall, got as far away as they could.

Alex glanced at the knife block on the kitchen worktop, saw that the largest knife was missing.

Lowrie skirted warily around Alex and out of the room, never taking her eyes off him, the knife between them. Alex's heart was racing, thundering in his chest, but he tried to appear calm for his daughters' sake. Then she was gone. Alex went to his daughters, put his arm around them and gave them a hug.

'Hold on.' He walked tentatively out of the doorway. He saw that the back door to the garden was open, saw Lowrie running down towards the fence, then over it, then he couldn't see her anymore. He ran to the door and closed it, fixing both locks. He turned, put his back against the door, trying to control the panic in his racing heart.

'Dad, what's happening?' Hannah called from the kitchen.

'It's fine.' He rushed back to his daughters and Hannah threw her arms around him, eyes fixed on the doorway in case Lowrie came back. Chloe stood backed against the wall, eyes equally searching.

'She's gone. I've locked the door. She can't get back in.'

'What the hell is wrong with her?' screamed Chloe. 'She had a knife!'

Alex reached out and brought Chloe into the hug with them. He held them both close. 'She's been through a lot. She was probably scared.'

Chloe looked at Alex with ferocious scepticism. 'Seriously?'

'She's gone now. She won't be back. Not in this house.' He was resolute, speaking more to Pope than anyone else.

'I need to talk to the officers out front. Stay here.' Both girls looked terrified. 'OK, come to the front door. I'll be able to see you from there.' The girls nodded and followed him out of the kitchen. Alex walked to the back door and checked the handle again. Both girls followed him with their eyes. He walked back and opened the front door.

He turned. 'Stay here. I'll be a minute.' Chloe and Hannah huddled in the doorframe, eyes switching between the back door and their father. Alex walked quickly to the police car waiting outside the house.

One of the officers saw him coming and got out.

'Everything OK?' he asked.

'She's gone. Run off.'

The officer's eyes widened. 'What do you mean?'

'She had a knife. From the kitchen . . . I don't know why. She threatened me with it, then ran out of the back door.'

'Christ.' The officer signalled to his colleague, and the pair ran towards the front door.

'I'm sorry. There was nothing I could do.' Alex called after them, but they weren't listening.

Chloe and Hannah moved quickly out of the way when they saw the two officers running towards them. They disappeared into the house.

* * *

As Pope pulled up behind the police car outside her home, she saw two police officers running into the house. Alex was standing out front, by the gate. The hard work and effort to calm herself on the way here was instantly undone. Her heart rate jumped and adrenaline ramped it up further. She turned off the engine and got out of the car.

'Alex . . . ?'

'Bec. Jesus. I . . . I . . .'

She walked quickly to him, placed her hand on his arm, her eyes darting to the front door, seeing Chloe and Hannah looking frightened in the doorway.

'Alex, what is it? What's happened?'

'She's gone. The girl's gone.'

'What do you mean? Alice?'

'Yes. She had a knife. The girls were terrified. So was I,' he added.

'Are you OK?' Pope looked again at the girls.

'I am.' He, too, looked at his daughters. 'I don't think they are.' He shot a look at Pope. She understood. *You've endangered our family. Again.*

'Where did she go, Alex?'

'Out the back. I've locked the door.'

'Let me go and make sure it's safe, then we can get everyone back inside.'

Alex beckoned Hannah and Chloe, who came and stood with him while Pope went inside. She found the two officers in the back garden, shining torches over the back fence.

'Anything?'

'No, ma'am. Not yet.'

'Have you secured inside?'

'Yes, we've checked, she's not there.'

Pope joined them and peered over the fence. There was a collection of trees and bushes, a wild area at the back of their home that separated them from the houses behind and afforded a degree of privacy. It was one of the things Pope liked about the house, but it was also an easy escape route and not the most secure of arrangements. There were several directions Alice Lowrie could have gone. She scanned the area.

'You two go around to that side. Check the area and start to canvass the houses there.' She indicated the houses behind her own. 'I'll get you some more people and sort an APB.'

The two officers nodded and hurried back to the house. Pope called Fletcher. She explained what had happened and asked him to send a couple more cars to help in the search of the immediate area and the house-to-house enquiries. She also asked for an APB to be put out on Lowrie. Fletcher said he would need to see her in his office first thing in the morning. She ended the call. That was a meeting to look forward to. Lowrie was here because of Pope and she was now missing as a result. She would have to take full responsibility for that, knowing full well that Fletcher, and Brody, had warned her against taking Lowrie to her house for exactly that reason.

Pope took a deep breath and turned back to the house. Now she had to talk to Alex and accept yet more blame. It was turning out to be a horrific day. She wasn't sure if she could deal with it, but hoped that Alex might give her a break. They both knew she had screwed up.

Alex and the girls were by the front door, waiting for her OK to enter the house.

'It's fine to come back in. She's long gone.'

All three of them were eyeing her suspiciously. They'd been back forty-eight hours, and it was fair to say it hadn't gone as smoothly as Pope would have hoped. She ushered them in and closed the front door. They all went into the main room, which was open-plan and combined the kitchen and living room.

'What happened?' asked Pope.

'She went crazy!' shouted Chloe. 'That's what happened. She had a knife.'

Chloe was getting hysterical. Pope realized that the trauma she had suffered last year was still lying close to the surface, just waiting to be reactivated. Lowrie had done just that. She should have moved the woman as soon as Alex and the girls had returned home.

'It's OK, Chloe. She's gone now. We'll find her, but she won't be back here. I'm sorry I put you all in this position. I'll make sure it doesn't happen again.'

'That's what you always say,' said Chloe, her inhibitions masked by a surge in adrenaline. 'And it's always a lie.'

'Chloe, that's enough,' said Alex.

'Really? Is it? We should never have come back. It's exactly the same. She doesn't care about us. She cares more about that woman.'

'Chloe, cut it out. This isn't the time.' Alex's tone was firmer now.

'Isn't the time? It's exactly the time!' shouted Chloe.

Hannah looked embarrassed. Pope tried a conciliatory look at her.

'I said cut it out, Chloe. Bec lost a colleague today.'

'Expect that was her fault too, was it?'

'Chloe! Enough! Leave the room!' Alex raised his voice and Chloe shot Pope a look full of scorn as she walked out of the door.

'Sorry, Bec. You didn't deserve that.'

'Yeah, I did.' She sighed wearily.

'I'll go up and talk to her.' Hannah had grown up since Pope had last seen her. She walked over to Pope and gave her a hug, smiling as she looked at her. Then she followed her sister. It was the nicest thing that had happened to Pope all day. By a very wide margin.

She and Alex looked at each other, standing up and leaning against opposite work surfaces.

'Jesus. What a mess,' said Pope, looking up to the ceiling and closing her eyes. There was silence. Neither knew what to say.

'How are you doing?' asked Alex. It was not what Pope was expecting.

She opened her eyes. 'I've had better days.'

'What happened with Miller?' His voice was kind, soothing.

'He was following a guy we weren't sure about. Turns out we were right to have our suspicions.'

'Who's the guy?'

'He's a connection to Alice's case. I'm not sure how exactly, but now it's sort of irrelevant. Now it's murder.' She flinched when she said the word.

'Christ. You must feel terrible.'

'It was me who set up the tail on him. Me who suggested Miller follow him this morning.'

'That's not on you, Bec. You were just doing your job. You can't take the blame for that.'

'I know. But if I had only insisted on there being two officers.'

'Did you know he was that dangerous?'

'No idea. We didn't know much of anything about him at that point.'

'Well, then.' Alex paused. 'I know it doesn't make it any better.'

'No. But thanks for trying.'

Fighting back tears, Pope looked at the floor then up at Alex. 'I'm so sorry, Alex. I didn't mean for any of this to happen.'

He didn't say anything, but the temperature changed. Pope had to fill the silence. The onus was on her.

'I should never have brought her back here. It was stupid. I never would have done if I'd known you and the girls were coming back.'

'You promised things would be different, Bec.' His tone had changed quickly.

'They will be. This was a mistake. It will never happen again.'

'I wish I could believe that.'

'Alex, I can't do this now. Not today, not after what's happened. Let me sort this out, then we'll sit down and talk properly. What about a weekend away? Sort things out.'

219

He looked at her sceptically. 'When was the last time we went away for a weekend together?'

She wanted to point out that he had walked out last year, so weekends away were not really an option, but she chose not to.

'I know. It will be my way of showing you that things are going to change.'

'Are you here for the evening now?' he asked.

'Yes, I'm here.' She really ought to be out looking for Evan Larsson and Alice Lowrie. But she had to leave that to others for tonight. She was emotionally hollowed out and she knew that what reserves she could muster would have to be used to soothe Alex. All she really wanted to do was go to sleep.

'Let's get some food sorted. I bet you haven't eaten all day.'

Pope remembered the croissant on the Eurostar early this morning. It was a lifetime away. 'No,' she said, 'I haven't. I'm going to have a shower, then I'll come down and help you with dinner.'

Alex nodded his agreement. Pope walked wearily up the stairs. She could hear Chloe and Hannah talking quietly behind Chloe's closed bedroom door and considered putting her head round, but thought better of it. Chloe needed longer to calm down and Pope couldn't face another argument. She saw that the door to the spare bedroom was open and walked in. The bed was made neatly, the pyjamas folded on top. Of course, Alice Lowrie had left in a hurry, and other than the clothes Pope had given her to wear, she hadn't taken anything with her — the second time she had done that in the last few days. Pope wondered where she was, what had spooked her. She suspected that, given her aversion to men, Alex might have been the problem. But she wouldn't suggest that to him.

As the water poured over her, Pope tried to lose herself. She always imagined that she could wash away the evil she encountered during the day, the cascading water taking it all away. It never seemed to work.

After she had finished and got dressed, she texted Brody to tell him what had happened and told him she would be in early in the morning. His reply told her to take care of herself and rest, which she fully intended to do. Downstairs Alex and Hannah were cooking. There was no sign of Chloe. The conversation was easier than it had been earlier and Pope was almost ready to believe that things could get back to normal. Certainly, both of them were making an effort and Hannah actually seemed glad to be home. They talked about Hannah's school and her grandparents and her sports clubs. She acted as sous chef to her father. Pope's main role seemed to be laying the table and pouring the wine. As the first slug of red went down, she felt herself relax a little and was suddenly very grateful for the calming, normalizing experience of her family. Yet again, she felt on the verge of tears, so she set about laying the table to distract herself.

Chloe ate more or less in silence once she slunk downstairs, although she did answer a few of Pope's questions in a slightly less hostile tone than previously. As soon as they had finished she excused herself and then started upstairs. But Pope heard her pause, then come back down and into the room. She walked up to Pope, then leaned down and gave her a hug. Pope didn't know what to do, but hugged her back.

'I'm sorry about your colleague,' said Chloe. 'And I can see why you wanted to help that girl.' She let go.

'Thanks, Chloe. And I'm so sorry about what happened.'

Chloe gave a half-smile and left the room. It was the second hug Pope had got in the last hour and it meant the world.

Pope heard footsteps up the stairs and Chloe's bedroom door close. Hannah stayed for a while then also went upstairs. Pope and Alex sat across from each other at the dining table, sipping their wine and coming to terms with being back in each other's company.

'It's good to have you back,' said Pope. 'Really good.'

'Yeah. It feels right for us to be here. I'm sorry that we had to leave.'

Pope reached out and put her hand on his. 'I know. It's fine. You don't have to explain.'

'But we do need to make things different. For all our sakes.' The warning was unspoken, but very clear.

'I know. And we will. I will. It's my responsibility and I know what needs to happen.'

'Do you feel any better after a shower and something to eat?'

'Yes. Now I need some sleep.'

'How have you been sleeping?'

She rolled her eyes. 'Work in progress.'

Alex smiled and squeezed her hand. 'Shall we go to bed?'

Pope nodded gratefully. 'Yes, please.'

They made love, falling back easily into each other's rhythms. Afterwards, Alex fell asleep quickly, as he invariably did, leaving Pope staring at the ceiling, the digital clock by the bed, anything to try to lull herself to sleep. But the intrusive thoughts kept coming. Often her thoughts turned to Tina Waterson at this time of night, the great unsolved case. But tonight her mind was elsewhere. Evan Larsson was in her head, forcing her to think of him when she should be sleeping. She replayed the interview, the only time they had met, looking for ideas, for clues to where he might be. Then she thought of Alice Lowrie and again wondered where she had gone. If she could remember nothing, how could she find anywhere she knew?

But tonight, her thoughts settled on Adam Miller. She imagined what might have happened with Larsson. She couldn't stop herself. She imagined them fighting, Larsson plunging the blade into Miller's back during the struggle. Or had he taken Miller unawares, a cowardly and evil act? She thought of the police officer that Miller had been, and the life that he should have had, rising through the ranks of the Metropolitan Police, maybe getting married, having children. Sleep wouldn't come but, eventually, the tears did. And Bec Pope cried for a long time, as Alex slept soundlessly beside her.

CHAPTER TWENTY-SIX

It had now developed into a predictable pattern. Rarely was there any deviation. Pope would try desperately to get to sleep, often utterly exhausted by long, emotionally draining days, but would lie awake until the early hours playing the same motifs in her head. Yesterday had been an even worse day and, paradoxically, despite her need for sleep, it had taken her hours to drift off. She didn't even know what time it was as she had given up looking at the clock by then. Too depressing. And now she was awake and it felt like only a few hours later. Six thirty. The days of lying in were long gone. Now her circadian rhythm had settled into a new cycle, and she seemed incapable of altering them. She wondered whether a sleep clinic would be able to do anything for her. Or maybe she needed medication. Like so many other things on her mind, a problem for another day. This time she did wake Alex, after a shower and a cup of coffee, to say goodbye. He kissed her and it all felt like some form of normality. She allowed herself to enjoy that feeling for a moment, before the realities of her current situation elbowed their way back into her consciousness.

In the car on the way to work, she listened to Miles Davis. She thought *Kind of Blue* was too much of a cliché for her current state, so opted for *Porgy and Bess*. The arrangements by Gil Evans suited Davis's playing and the material sublimely, and it lifted her enough to think through the day ahead.

First, she needed to get the team back on track. They would be devastated, and it would have sunk in overnight. Despite her own feelings, she had to make sure they were able to focus. Pope felt guilty for thinking this, felt guilty about Miller. But she had to do it. There would be time later to deal with their feelings.

The two priorities were finding Evan Larsson and Alice Lowrie. She flinched. She was responsible for losing both of them. It was a mess and she needed to be the one to clear it up. She considered who was the priority — Larsson was the obvious choice. He had murdered a police officer and was suspected of other crimes related to the Collective. He had to be apprehended as soon as possible. But Lowrie might hold the key to finding him, and there was still the matter of who was responsible for the death of Nicholas Cooper. Pope decided to split the team. There were already APBs out on both of them, so the other work could be divided. By the time she arrived at the station she had formulated a plan and had got her head in the place it needed to be. More or less.

Pope arrived before most of her team. Brody had checked in on her with a text message that morning, saying he was on his way in. No sign of Thompson yet. She needed to talk to him, but he had been the closest to Adam Miller, so he would need time.

Her phone rang, and she saw it was Fletcher. She didn't answer, but went straight to his office instead, preparing herself for the imminent admonishment. She knocked on his office door.

'Come in.'

She opened the door. Fletcher was immaculate in his uniform, as ever.

'Sit down, DCI Pope.'

Pope took a seat and braced herself.

'How are you doing?'

'I'm OK. I think it's hit everyone hard.'

'Yes, I'm sure it has. Well, if you need any support, just let me know.' He had covered the empathy section of the conversation. Box ticked. 'No news on Alice Lowrie.'

Pope wasn't sure if this was a question. 'Not yet. We're working on it.'

'Everyone is looking for her. And Larsson.'

Pope nodded. She knew this.

'Why was Miller on his own when he was following Larsson?'

Pope felt like she'd been punched. 'Because we don't have unlimited resources and because we didn't think he was an immediate threat.'

Fletcher seemed to grasp her implicit criticism of his staffing levels, but his voice remained even. 'He should have been with another officer.'

'In retrospect, yes. But there was nothing in our investigation of Larsson up to that point that suggested he posed a danger to the officer following him.'

Fletcher stared at her. Said nothing.

'But I accept full responsibility.' Pope knew that this had been Miller's choice and that he could have taken another officer with him if he had chosen to. But, ultimately, it was her team and therefore her call. She certainly felt that weight.

'There will be a full review of the handling of the case when it is completed.' Pope had expected this. 'But for now, we focus on finding our two suspects.'

'Yes, sir.'

'We will also need to review the arrangements regarding Alice Lowrie. She won't be going back to your house.'

'No, of course not.'

'I should remind you that I cautioned against that course of action right from the start. I warned you of the possible dangers.'

'I'm aware of that.'

'But you thought that was the correct decision.' He was ensuring that they were on the same page regarding her culpability. And his lack of it. He didn't want any repercussions if the Alice Lowrie situation got any worse. One thing about Fletcher, he was adept at covering his back.

'I did. I thought it was best to have her stay where I could keep an eye on her. That was a mistake.'

'It wasn't just me, DCI Pope. DI Brody agreed with me. He also warned you.'

'I remember. As I said, I take full responsibility. I'll find her.'

'I hope so. And when you do, I want her arrested and charged with the murder of Nicholas Cooper.'

'Sir, with respect—'

'This is not up for discussion, DCI Pope.' Fletcher raised his voice now. 'It is a direct order. Find Alice Lowrie, bring her here and formally arrest her. This is what we should have done in the first place.'

Pope chose not to argue. In truth, she couldn't really disagree with anything Fletcher had said. She was not convinced that it was the right thing to do, but now was clearly not the time to debate that part of the case.

'Understood, sir.' Polite but terse. She needed to get out of here. She'd had enough of being kicked when she was down.

'That's all. Keep me updated on any progress.'

Pope nodded, got up and left the office. She couldn't be angry with Fletcher this time. But she was irritated nonetheless.

She went to the bathroom and composed herself. A dressing-down from Fletcher was something Pope had experienced a number of times and she had learned to ignore it because most of the time he was wrong. But on this occasion, she had no reply. Although his increasingly pompous tone and his obvious motive of clarifying the blame annoyed her, there were things she should have done differently. And the consequences had been disastrous.

In particular, Pope knew now that she had been blinded by Alice Lowrie. As Brody had said, she had connected her too closely to Tina Waterson and seen her through that lens, rather than as a possible murder suspect. That had been a grave error of judgement. But she was clear now. She would find both Evan Larsson and Alice Lowrie and deal with them accordingly. And this time, there would be no mistakes.

When she arrived back at her desk, the mood in the office was sombre. The first thing she did was find Stephen Thompson in the tech office. He was hard at work at his computer, his two colleagues the same. She walked to him and put her hand on his shoulder. He looked up from the screen.

'Are you OK? I know you and Adam were close.'

'I'm fine, thanks, ma'am.'

'Do you need to take some time? No one would blame you if you needed it.'

'I'd rather be here working if it's all the same to you. The best thing I can be doing now is finding Adam's—' he couldn't say the word — 'is finding Evan Larsson.'

Pope smiled and squeezed his shoulder. She was relieved. She needed him. 'I know. I think we all feel like that. We'll find him.' As she turned, Thompson cleared his throat.

'I, er, I went to see Rachel last night.' Pope looked blank. 'Adam's girlfriend.' Pope should have known that.

'How was she?'

'She was a mess. She thought he was about to propose to her any day.'

Pope didn't know what to say. She felt it, but didn't know how to say anything that would make this better.

'We'll find Larsson and we'll make him pay. I think that's the only thing we can focus on at the moment.'

Thompson nodded. He tried to smile, but it came out as something else.

'Let me know if you get anything.' Their relationship worked better on a professional level. For both of them.

'I will,' he replied, before turning his head back to his computer screen. Thompson lost himself again in the world of online technology.

227

As she climbed the stairs back to her office Pope could have kicked herself for not knowing the name of Miller's girlfriend. They had never met and he had not really spoken about her. At least not to Pope. But still. Another reason to feel guilty. There were too many of those at the moment.

At her desk again, Pope asked Brody to come over.

He sat down, placing his coffee on the desk. 'So, you had an eventful evening, then?'

'Just what I was hoping for after a quiet day.'

Brody smiled. 'What happened?'

'Just to let you know, before you say it, I've already had the "I told you so" speech from Fletcher. He made it very clear that both you and he warned me what a bad idea it was to have Alice at home. So, I certainly don't need a rerun of that, OK?'

'Got it.'

'I arrived home just after it happened but, as far as I can tell, I think she might have got spooked by Alex. Certainly, being in a house full of strangers wouldn't have helped. She ran.'

'I heard something about a knife.'

'She took a kitchen knife with her.'

'Oh. So, what's the plan?' said Brody.

'There's an APB out on her and Larsson. That's a good start. She should be pretty easy to spot and I can't imagine she has many places to go, particularly given her amnesia.'

'Either that, or she has a plan and knows exactly where she's going.'

'OK, that's also a possibility. But either way, everyone's looking for her. Can you contact the police in Maidstone and fill them in? Get them over to the Lenham property as soon as possible. I don't think she'd go back there, or Larsson for that matter, but we need a presence there.'

Brody nodded.

'Thompson's team are working on getting hold of the CCTV footage around my house and the route Larsson would have taken to Regent's Park. They're also doing a deeper dive into Larsson now we know what we know about him. Hopefully that will give us some contacts or places he might go. But I think he must have known Alice if he was involved in the Collective. She'd been there for some years and it's inconceivable that they hadn't run into each other. If he was more than simply a financier, the question remains where he and Cooper stand in relation to each other. We thought Cooper was the boss, but I think it's Larsson. I think Cooper was his day-to-day manager, but Larsson was the main man. With all that entails.'

'Meaning what?' asked Brody.

'I think Larsson used the Collective to make his philosophy real. I think he ran it like his own personal ideological experiment. And, I'm afraid, I think both he and Cooper took sexual advantage of the young girls there. It would explain everything about how Alice presents. It's a great shame I didn't get a chance to show Larsson's photograph to her. That might have confirmed my suspicions.'

'You might still get the chance.'

'Maybe. I'm just hoping that it's not going to be too late.'

'You mean because we won't be able to find them?'

'Let me ask you a question.'

Brody sat up a little straighter in the chair. 'Right.'

'Let's say you were right all along and Alice is faking her memory loss.'

'OK,' said Brody.

'And let's say that you had killed Nicholas Cooper because he had been sexually abusing you for years. You finally snap, grab a knife from the kitchen and stab him.'

'OK. So far I would actually say that.'

'I know. If we're right, and Evan Larsson was also involved, what's the one thing you would be looking to do if you were Alice Lowrie?'

Brody nodded his understanding. 'I'd go after Evan Larsson.'

'And why would you go after him?' asked Pope.

'To do the same to him as I had to Cooper. To punish him. To kill him.'

'We can't let that happen,' said Pope. 'As much for Alice as for Larsson.'

CHAPTER TWENTY-SEVEN

Stephen Thompson had not gone home last night. Driven by the death of his friend and colleague, he was determined to find the man who killed him. He knew he wasn't responsible for what had happened, but he also knew that he was going to do everything within his power to find the man who was: Evan Larsson. He had spent the night using every technical trick he could to track him down. Suddenly, he was getting close.

After hours of searching CCTV footage and using facial recognition software, Thompson had finally got a hit. He had created an alert for Larsson's digital image and eventually he had been flagged moving back towards Soho, presumably on his way back from Regent's Park. The use of facial recognition in the Met Police was still in its infancy and was fraught with legal complexities and challenges. But Thompson didn't care. Not today. Not if it would find Evan Larsson. He would deal with any problems after Larsson had been apprehended.

The first time he was flagged was crossing New Cavendish Street as he walked down Harley Street. He had avoided the main roads, but CCTV was endemic in Central London. Then he was caught again as he approached

Cavendish Square. He could be seen walking east around the square, then he disappeared. As he didn't then appear on the next camera, some twenty yards along the same street, Thompson realized that the most likely explanation was that he had entered a property between those two points. He brought up a plan of Cavendish Square and pinpointed the parameters. The space there was occupied mainly by a hotel, the Cavendish Townhouse. Thompson looked it up. Exclusive, high-end, expensive. A pool, a doorman, butler service if required. It would suit Larsson perfectly. He printed off some screenshots, noted down the address and dashed out of his office.

* * *

Pope was on the phone to Trish Waterson. That was a call she really didn't want to make, but she had to find out if Lowrie had, by any chance, turned up at the Watersons' house. Apparently, she had not. It was one of the shortest calls she had made in a long time. For that much, at least, Pope was grateful. Just as she was putting down the phone, Thompson came rushing into the office.

'I've got something.'

Both Pope and Brody came to attention and Brody joined the other two at Pope's desk as Thompson explained.

'I think I may have found where he went — Larsson.' He was mildly breathless from racing up the stairs.

Thompson showed them a screenshot of Larsson.

'Where is this?' asked Pope.

'Harley Street, yesterday afternoon.' Thompson then put the next photograph in Pope's hands. 'This is him at Cavendish Square, soon afterwards.'

Again, Pope scanned the photo. 'Where does he go after this?'

'That's the last image I can find. But he seems to disappear from the cameras right by a hotel called the Cavendish Townhouse.'

'I know it,' said Brody. 'Expensive and pretty exclusive, from what I remember.'

'Perfect for Larsson,' said Pope.

'That's the first thing I thought,' agreed Thompson. 'I called them up. The receptionist checked and said they didn't have an Evan Larsson as a member. But she wouldn't play ball when I described Larsson and asked if he was staying there under a different name.'

'I'm sure,' said Pope. She looked at the photograph again. 'So, this was yesterday afternoon?'

'Just after one.'

'Great work, Thompson. Brody, let's go and see what we can find at the Cavendish Townhouse.' She turned to Thompson. 'Can you let Fletcher know where we've gone? I don't want to waste any time.'

Brody drove while Pope called the hotel and demanded that the manager be there to meet them when they arrived. Reluctantly, the receptionist said she would try to arrange it.

When they pulled up, Brody parked a little way away from the front entrance. Pope saw that the hotel was set across several typical London townhouses and rose four storeys. It looked elegant and discreet. The kind of place you stayed at if you had money but didn't want to be noticed. The opposite clientele to the Ritz or the Savoy. They walked to the door, which was opened from the inside by a doorman dressed impeccably. In the thickly carpeted hallway, they were greeted by a young woman who looked as elegant as the facade of the hotel, and was as smartly dressed as the doorman. She had a confident and welcoming smile.

'Morning, sir, madam. How can I help you?' Her accent was cut-glass, with not a trace of a regional accent.

'I called ahead. DCI Pope, this is DI Brody.' They both showed their warrant cards. 'I need to speak to the manager.'

Displaying no signs of being put out, she nodded courteously and picked up the phone. After a brief conversation, she replaced the receiver.

'Mr Hanson will be out in a moment.'

True to her word, a door behind her opened and a tall man with an expensive suit and an equally expensive haircut walked out.

'DCI Pope, I'm Richard Hanson, manager here at the Cavendish. How can I help?'

'We believe a man might have been here yesterday and we need to confirm if that is indeed the case and if he might still be here.'

Hanson smiled politely. 'DCI Pope, at the Cavendish we pride ourselves on our discretion. I'm afraid that without a warrant I am unable to disclose the private details of our guests. I'm sure you understand.'

'Normally, I would. And I can go and get a warrant and be back later. But if I do that, I'll get a warrant for the whole hotel and that means I'll need to return with a great many officers, insist that all your guests come down to the police station to answer questions and search every single room. Your choice, Mr Hanson.'

Hanson looked a little uncomfortable. 'DCI Pope, I really don't respond well to threats and I think you're being a little heavy-handed in—'

'Mr Hanson. I'd rather work *with* you, but this man has murdered a police officer. A friend of mine. And believe me, I will find him. I am more than happy to go on national television this evening and tell the whole country that you were unwilling to help me find the man who killed my colleague. You're welcome to join me and tell your side of the story.' She hoped the rather obvious bluff would work.

Hanson stared at her. He thought for a moment, then turned to his receptionist. 'Ms Poole, please can you assist DCI Pope and her colleague in their enquiries? Do let me know if I can help in any other way.' With that he stepped back and waited.

'Thank you, Mr Hanson.' Pope took out her phone and brought up a picture of Larsson. She showed it to the receptionist, who had maintained her composure throughout. 'Do you know this man? We think he entered the hotel yesterday afternoon and may have stayed here last night.'

She took a good look at the image on the screen, then looked over to her manager. He nodded slightly. 'Yes, he is staying with us at the moment.'

Pope looked at Brody. 'Is he here?'

'I don't think so. He left the hotel early this morning.'

'Checked out?'

'No, he didn't check out.'

'When did he arrive?' Pope asked.

She scanned the computer screen and tapped a few keys. 'He checked in yesterday afternoon.'

'And how long is he staying for?'

'It's an open reservation. He hasn't told us how long he'll be here.'

'Do you have a name and address?'

She pushed a different key. 'Yes . . . his name is Nicholas Cooper. An address in Lenham, Kent. The Old Schoolhouse.'

'You're kidding me,' said Brody.

'No, those are the details we have.'

'What time did he go out this morning?' asked Pope.

'I'm not sure exactly, but I think around eight. It was quite soon after I came on shift.'

'We'll need to look at his room.' She glanced towards Richard Hanson. 'Can you take us there?'

'DCI Pope, I really think—'

'Do we need to go through this again? I need to see the room and it needs to be now.'

Pope stood stock-still, looked him squarely in the eye. He was no match for that look.

'OK, follow me. What room, Ms Poole?'

'301.'

Hanson led Pope and Brody into the small lift and the door closed as he punched the button for the third floor. The three of them stood uncomfortably for the ten seconds or so it took before the lift glided smoothly to a halt and the door opened. More plush carpeting led them along a narrow corridor. Pope's adrenaline was spiking and she was hyper-alert as they stopped outside room 301. Hanson knocked on the door, waited. He then repeated his knock. When he got no reply for the second time, he took out a credit-card-sized master key and inserted it into the lock. There was a slight motorized sound as the lock opened and he pushed the door, standing aside so they could enter.

'Wait here,' said Pope, as she and Brody walked in.

The room was smartly furnished. Dark woods, pristine carpet, luxurious fixtures and fittings. A large sash window with a lovely view over Cavendish Square flooded the room with an abundance of natural light. Pope looked around and saw no personal belongings.

'You're sure he hasn't checked out?' she repeated.

'Apparently not,' he said, although he didn't sound sure as he surveyed the room himself.

'So, where's all his stuff?' asked Pope.

The bed had clearly been slept in, and when she looked in the bathroom Pope could see that it had been used.

'If he came here in a hurry, maybe he didn't have time to collect anything,' said Brody. It was left unsaid between them that this would mean Larsson had arrived at the hotel directly from killing Miller in Regent's Park. Pope nodded.

At that moment Brody's phone rang. He answered and stepped out into the corridor. Pope looked around the room more carefully. It looked like a hotel room where the occupant had checked out, but it seemed that Larsson planned on coming back.

'That's all I need from you, Mr Hanson. We'll take it from here.'

'DCI Pope, I really ought to—'

'We'll just be looking around and I need to talk to my colleague. We'll be down soon. I'll take care, I promise. I won't steal the bathrobe.'

Reluctantly, Hanson left the room as Brody walked back in.

'How did you get him to leave?'

'I promised not to steal anything.'

'That was Thompson. Local police are at the place in Lenham. No sign of anyone. No comings or goings whatsoever.'

'We know where Larsson's been. What about Lowrie?' asked Pope.

'Thompson says no sign. They can't find her anywhere.'

'OK. So, Larsson checks in here yesterday afternoon. He obviously can't go home. He has to know we're on to him, has to assume that we know Miller was following him yesterday. So he comes here and spends the night under an assumed name.'

'Calling himself Nicholas Cooper is so arrogant. It's like he can't resist trying to make us look like idiots.'

'It's exactly that. Arrogance, thinking he's cleverer than all of us. That's how Marc Pridot described him. He doesn't think he has to play by the same rules as everyone else.'

'So where is he now?'

'Maybe he's gone to get some supplies. If he can't go home, he'll need to get a change of clothes from somewhere. Something tells me that Evan Larsson is not the type to slug around in day-old clothes in the Cavendish Townhouse,' said Pope.

'If he can't go home and he can't go to the schoolhouse, where's left?'

'My guess is that Larsson has a number of places he could escape to if the going gets rough. Although he's arrogant, he's far from stupid. He thinks we won't catch him, but he'll have a plan just in case. Maybe back to Paris or Norway. Who knows?'

'Do you think we need to put a watch on all the ports and points of exit?'

'Good idea. Can you sort that?'

'Will do.' Brody took out his phone again and dialled.

Pope sat on the chair. She didn't think they needed Forensics, so she wasn't compromising evidence. *Think. Where would Larsson be?*

* * *

237

Evan Larsson walked around Hanover Square keeping his face turned towards the pavement in front of him. He knew there were fewer CCTV cameras on the backstreets he was taking, but it paid to be careful. His hood shielded his face quite effectively, but he was being cautious. He'd picked up some clothes from a couple of shops in Covent Garden, keeping the number he visited to a minimum. He only had one busy road to cross on his way back to the hotel and the sheer volume of people on Oxford Street would afford him the anonymity he needed.

He wasn't concerned about the police. He knew they would be looking for him — looking hard, given the events of the last twenty-four hours. But they wouldn't find him at the hotel and he had absolutely no intention of returning to his flat in Dean Street. He knew how he would get out of London, out of the country. They'd be left scratching their heads.

It was regrettable what had happened to Nicholas and the Collective. But it had been good while it lasted and, as his mother used to say, nothing lasts for ever. He could recreate the Collective anywhere else. And he had just the place in mind. The work and effort hadn't been wasted. It had provided him with a number of opportunities, and he had learned how to put a group together. The next one would be even better, even stronger. He put his hand in his pocket and felt the reassuring, cool steel of the pistol. He wouldn't need it. But just in case.

Larsson crossed Oxford Street quickly, the throng of pedestrians coalescing around him to provide a human shield from prying eyes. He walked on to Holles Street, which became much quieter. As he approached Cavendish Square, he was pretty much the only person walking.

* * *

'I've put the watch out on all airports, ports and train stations. The Eurotunnel, too. We'll see if we get anything.' Brody walked to the window and looked out, then turned and looked at Pope. 'Do you think he'll come back here?'

'I think there's two possibilities. One, he's done a runner and he's already on his way somewhere else.' She looked at her watch. 'Given what Ms Poole downstairs said about the time he left, he could already be on his way with a false identity. It depends how prepared he was for this kind of eventuality. He wouldn't necessarily be inclined to check out if he was in a hurry.'

'And the second possibility is he'll come back to the hotel?' asked Brody.

'Maybe. If he went out for supplies, he may be planning to lie low for a couple of days before leaving. It's fairly anonymous here, particularly if you use a pseudonym. They seem quite discreet.'

'So, what do we do? Wait here? Call for backup?'

Pope considered. 'I'll call and arrange a car to sit on the hotel. We'll wait until they arrive, then we need to get back.' She dialled Fletcher and had the conversation.

* * *

As he approached the hotel, Larsson stopped at the corner of Cavendish Square. He looked carefully at his surroundings but saw nothing to suggest any problems. Why would there be? They would never find him at this small, very private hotel. He had spent the night here some years ago and it had always stayed in his mind as a good place to hide out. It almost seemed to be set up for that. He knew he was being paranoid. No, cautious was a better way of putting it. And cautious was good.

Larsson crossed the square and walked in through the main entrance. Unusually, the attractive young receptionist was not at her desk. A shame, as he enjoyed his brief exchange of pleasantries with her. He could see the door to the manager's office behind the desk was ajar and he heard hushed voices inside. He continued to the lift. The door was already open and he walked in, pushing the button for the third floor. As the door closed and it began to ascend, he retrieved his room key from his jacket pocket. He had it ready as the doors opened again.

* * *

Pope put her phone away. 'Fletcher says he'll have someone here in half an hour.'

'How was he?'

'Not that impressed that we came here without backup and without checking with him first. But he'll get over it.'

'Who's he sending over?' asked Brody.

'Not sure. But he said he'd get them here as soon as possible.'

Suddenly, Pope was alerted to a vague scratching sound at the door, then a quiet, motorized hum. She looked at Brody and stood up out of the chair. They both tensed, watching the door carefully. Pope saw it open and suddenly, standing there was Evan Larsson. The man who had killed their friend and colleague. Larsson strode in then froze as he saw the two police officers standing by the window. Pope could see him weighing up his options, could see how shocked he was. Shocked that someone as clever as him could have been found so soon. He looked quickly behind him, trying to decide whether to run, whether he would be able to get the elevator called, the doors open and then closed again before Pope and Brody got to him. Of course, that would be impossible. They were only yards away from him. But he had no option, unless . . . she realized it too late.

Larsson reached into his pocket and swiftly pulled out his pistol. He pointed it at Pope, moving forward and letting the door close behind him.

They stared at each other for a moment.

'Sit down. Both of you.' Pope and Brody remained standing, staring at the gun. Larsson cocked the pistol. 'Now.'

Both of them slowly sat, Pope on the single chair, Brody on the edge of the bed. Pope knew that sitting down put them at a significant disadvantage. But she also knew that, at this point, Evan Larsson was in absolute control of the situation.

CHAPTER TWENTY-EIGHT

Pope weighed her options. She could attempt to rush at Larsson, take the pistol. It might be possible if she could signal to Brody and they both acted at once. But with Larsson staring at her, that was unlikely. She could try to distract him, allowing Brody the chance to act. Again, she would need to let him know the plan. No, for the moment, she could only try to talk him out of this. With what she knew about Larsson, she wasn't sure how easy that would be.

'You found me. You must be a better officer than I gave you credit for, DCI Pope.' He was standing in front of the door, pistol pointed straight at her. 'How did you manage that?'

Pope decided that engaging with him was the best course of action for the moment. 'It wasn't that hard. CCTV's everywhere these days.'

'Yes, that's true, I suppose. I thought I'd managed to be pretty careful, but there we go.'

'What's your plan, Larsson? What are you going to do now? You realize we have more officers on the way. You won't escape.'

'Well, I could easily kill you both and be out of here before they turn up. How about that?'

Pope didn't doubt that he was capable. He'd killed Miller. But the fact that he hadn't shot them immediately suggested that this wasn't his plan. He liked the sound of his own voice, enjoyed an audience. Perhaps this was too great an opportunity to resist. She needed to keep him talking. Knew that Brody was watching, waiting for the chance to act.

'Why Sergeant Miller? Why did you have to kill him?'

'I knew he was following me straightaway. It was all too easy to lead him away from prying eyes. You really shouldn't have sent a boy to do a man's job, DCI Pope.'

Pope had never wanted to rip a man's throat out as much as she did now. She glanced at Brody, who was staring at Larsson with an expression that suggested he was thinking exactly the same.

'He was a good man,' she said.

He shrugged. What did he care?

'Tell me about the Collective.'

'Ah, the Collective.' He looked over her shoulder and out of the window for a moment, as if remembering something special. Then his eyes returned to hers. 'That was a chance to put some ideas into practice. Very successfully, I might add.'

'What kind of ideas?' asked Pope.

He smiled. Did he know she was trying to keep him talking?

'The kind of ideas that most people refuse to accept, but actually make an awful lot of sense.'

'You mean like the U*bermensch*?'

Larsson started, then composed himself, like she had seen him do during the interview. He didn't like surprises.

'Why do you mention that, DCI Pope?'

'Nietzsche. Your philosophical hero, according to Professor Pridot at the Sorbonne.'

Again, he looked surprised. 'You have done your homework, haven't you? Are you a fan of Nietzsche?'

'I don't know much about him. Except that he is a firm favourite among dictators and well-read serial killers.'

Larsson smiled. 'Simplistic moral judgements do you no credit at all. I'd recommend a closer reading of his oeuvre. It's a very coherent body of work, taken together.'

'Is that right? And that's what you based the Collective on?'

'It was a starting point. We certainly tried to find ways of realising those concepts.'

'How did Nicholas Cooper fit into all this?' asked Pope. Brody was still a silent observer and Larsson seemed fixated on Pope alone.

'Nicholas and I shared a common vision. He managed the day-to-day running of the group and I oversaw the work. It was very much a joint enterprise.'

'But you were there often.'

'I visited when I had the chance, yes.'

'To have sex with the girls?'

'DCI Pope, you have a very judgemental tone. And a very undeveloped sense of moral relativism. Everything that happened at the Collective was by consent. No one was forced to do anything they didn't want to do.'

'Thirteen-year-old girls can't give consent.'

'We lived differently. That was the whole point. Juliet was that age when she slept with Romeo. Things were different then and there is absolutely no reason why they shouldn't be different again. Just because society dictates something at a particular time, doesn't mean it is right.'

'It's the law,' said Pope.

'Not everything that's right is governed by the law.'

'You're talking about abolishing common law and allowing everyone to make up their own minds what they want to do, how they want to act?'

'It's not that simple. But there should be a degree of individual choice in certain things.'

'Things such as statutory rape?'

'Again, I refer you to what I just said.' Larsson was so sure of himself that he wasn't fazed by her goading. Pope could see that she was unlikely to rile him, get him off guard.

She had to keep him talking and hope reinforcements arrived in time.

'If it was so consensual, why did Alice Lowrie stab Cooper?'

'Alice? She was special. A good mind and very open to new ideas. That's the key, you see, to choose people who are open to new ways of thinking. Who see this society for what it is and want something better.'

'She didn't agree with you, though, did she?'

'Alice had a crisis of faith. It happens sometimes. Usually they get over it quite quickly, but Alice . . . As I said, Alice was something special.'

Pope didn't like the way the conversation was turning. The use of the word "special" angered her.

'So why did you attack her in the hospital? It was you, wasn't it?'

Larsson didn't say anything. Had Pope found something he felt guilty about? Unlikely. She changed tack.

'Alice disappeared at the same time as a girl called Tina Waterson. Do you know anything about her?'

'Yes, I remember Tina. Unfortunately, Tina changed her mind about joining us at the last minute. But she had already seen too much. I knew she'd go back home and tell everyone about our group. It was a great shame, I liked Tina. But the good of the group has to come first.'

Pope felt as if the ground was a fire about to swallow her up. She was so furious, so full of rage, she felt ready to lunge at Larsson and take her chances. Brody must have read it, as he reached out and touched her arm. She looked at him and his expression counselled restraint.

Larsson watched her. 'Of course, DCI Pope. You were the investigating officer at the time. I remember the name. With that idiot, Phillips. It must have been infuriating to have an unsolved death, and the disappearances as well. It's a good job DI Brody is here to calm you down.'

'Did you kill her? Did you kill Tina?'

'As I said, she had to keep quiet for the good of the Collective.'

'And Sarah Banks? Belinda Forsyth?'

'They were much more successful. Nicholas did well with them.'

Pope wondered how many other girls had disappeared, recruited to the Collective without her knowledge.

'And where are they now?' she asked.

'Sarah and Belinda? I think they left at the same time as Alice. I have no idea where they are now. Alice has brought that particular group to an end.'

Pope wondered if there were other groups. Or whether Larsson planned further versions of the Collective in the future.

Pope was suddenly aware of Brody in her peripheral vision. He jumped up and ran towards Larsson, but Larsson had obviously been expecting this and was ready. He moved swiftly aside, just enough for Brody to miss as he lunged, and Larsson brought the pistol down on Brody's head. The force of the blow made a sickening thud on his skull and he fell to the floor, unconscious.

Pope leaped up and ran the few steps to Brody. She kneeled down and cradled his head in her hands. She felt for a pulse, found one. She looked up towards Larsson, who was still pointing the gun at her. She wanted to scream at him. But she had to keep calm. He wouldn't care. Elizabeth Hartford had been right. A sociopath. She breathed and thought practically, not vengefully. Not yet.

'Call an ambulance. He's unconscious and could have concussion.'

'No, I don't think we'll do that at the moment. He'll be fine.'

Pope took off her jacket, shaking her head. She placed it carefully under Brody's head.

'He needs an ambulance. He needs to go to a hospital.'

'I'm sure he will. I think it's time I left, DCI Pope. Then you can look after your colleague.'

'Where are you going?'

'It wouldn't be a very successful exit strategy if I told you that, would it? Let's just say I'll be fine, you'll be fine.'

Pope stood up. 'I'll find you, Larsson.'

'Very admirable, DCI Pope. To threaten someone who is pointing a gun at you. Admirable or stupidly reckless. I'm not sure.'

'You don't scare me. I've dealt with more dangerous men than you.'

Larsson smiled. 'You're getting a bit boring now. The empty threats are all well and good, but I have to leave. I doubt we'll meet again.'

Pope was pondering her next move, and realizing that she couldn't immediately think of one, when there was a knock at the door. It was so unexpected that both of them jumped. They turned and looked.

'That'll be the officers I told you were on the way. You're out of options. Put the gun down, Larsson.'

He looked at her, the seed of panic in his eyes. He was frozen, trying to formulate a plan.

Then a voice came from the other side of the door. 'Sir, it's me.'

Larsson's face showed recognition. Pope had no idea. He moved to the door and slowly opened it, looking out to check. Then he moved back and let the visitor enter.

Alice Lowrie stood framed in the doorway, just as she had been when Pope first saw her in the doorway of Charing Cross Police Station less than a week ago.

CHAPTER TWENTY-NINE

Pope saw that Alice Lowrie was wearing the clothes she had given her back at the house and felt an immediate sense of betrayal. Lowrie had run away, although Pope still didn't know why. Still didn't know the whole story. But she was sure that Alice Lowrie turning up here, now, was very far from a good thing.

Larsson looked straight at her. Pope realized she had a chance, but it was too risky. The gun could go off, and now she had to worry about the young woman standing in the doorway as well as herself.

'Alice. Nice to see you. Where have you been?' Larsson's voice still sounded confident, in control. Pope looked down at Brody. It was a nasty head wound and it was still bleeding. She had to get him out of here before it was too late.

Lowrie said nothing. She moved into the room and closed the door. Pope wondered how she had found them, got past the diligent receptionist.

'How did you get up here?' Larsson asked, echoing Pope's thoughts.

Lowrie ignored the question, said nothing. There was a blank, neutral look in her eyes that Pope didn't trust.

'Alice, why did you run? You were safe at the house.' Lowrie turned to Pope, but her expression didn't change.

'Thank you for taking me in. But it was time to go.'

'Where have you been? We've been searching for you.'

'I needed a bit of time.'

'For what?' asked Pope.

'To find Evan here.' She turned her attention to Larsson, and suddenly it was as if Pope weren't in the room.

'I killed Nicholas,' she said. 'I stabbed him.'

Pope's gut clenched. This was an entirely different version of Alice Lowrie.

'Why did you do that, Alice? He looked after you, made sure you were safe. He gave you the opportunity to be yourself.' Larsson smiled.

Lowrie ignored the question. 'Why did you take us there?'

'To the Collective?' asked Larsson.

'Yes.'

'You know why, Alice.'

'Explain it to me.'

'I don't think I need to. We talked all about this in great detail many times. We were exploring other ways to live. Exploring how we wanted to live, rather than how others wanted us to live.'

'How you wanted us to live. We didn't get a chance to decide how we wanted to live.'

'That's not true, Alice. You were all integral to the decision-making. We never forced you to do anything you didn't want to do. We discussed everything.'

'You took advantage of us. Of the girls. You raped us. All of us.'

It was the first time Pope had seen Larsson look angry. 'That's not true, Alice. That is absolutely not true.'

'Yes, it is.'

'You were never forced to do anything. Nobody was.'

'You manipulated us. And we were underage, so it's rape anyway.'

'Only if you accept that what mainstream society dictates is the only way to live.'

Pope was furious with Larsson for what he was saying, but Lowrie seemed to be keeping her cool.

'The problem is you justify everything with that argument. If there are no boundaries, then you can't cross them. But there are boundaries. Moral boundaries.'

Larsson looked at Pope, smiled. 'She's learned well, you must agree. Very articulate, don't you think?' The proud teacher.

'Don't patronize me, Evan. You know what I did to Nicholas.'

Larsson raised his eyebrows. 'Fair enough, Alice. What, actually, is it that you want to achieve today?'

'I want you to explain why you thought it was OK to take teenage girls away from their families for the purpose of having sex with them.'

'You're reducing what we were trying to achieve to a simplistic, crude cliché. You should know better than that.'

'Why don't you enlighten me?'

'I've already explained. And you know full well what we were trying to achieve. This is a waste of time.' Pope could see that Larsson was getting irritated. She needed to redirect the conversation.

'How did you find us here, Alice? How did you know where we were?' she asked.

'It wasn't very hard. I had Nicholas's and Evan's credit card details before I left the Collective. I went to an internet café this morning and checked both accounts. Evan's had been used to pay for the room here.'

Pope was impressed at the ingenuity. 'How did you learn to do that?'

'You'd be surprised what I learned during the years I was there. Isn't that right?' She turned back to Larsson. 'Lots of useful skills.'

'And the amnesia? Was that ever real?'

Lowrie looked sympathetically at her. 'I needed a bit of breathing space to give me the time to find him.'

Pope shook her head. 'And why me? Why come to Charing Cross?'

'I'd researched what happened when I disappeared. I saw that you were the police officer on the case back then. I found out where you were. I knew you would help me. After what happened.'

She'd been played. But after all that Lowrie had been through, she couldn't blame her. The young woman had done what she felt she had to do.

'Alice, you need to get justice for what's happened to you. And the other girls. We're going to take him in and he'll be punished. He'll go to jail for a very long time. For life.' Pope was trying to control two dangerous people in one confined space. She didn't know what Lowrie had planned, but she assumed the woman hadn't come here without a plan.

'The thing is, Evan doesn't really subscribe to the idea of justice handed out by society. He doesn't believe in society at all, really. So I don't think the law is the way to punish him. Not the kind of law you represent.' She was talking to Pope, but looking squarely at Larsson. 'What do you think, Evan? Do you think prison is what you deserve?'

Pope noticed that, as she was talking, Lowrie was edging closer to Larsson. She wasn't sure if he noticed, but she could see it. He still had the gun pointed at Pope.

'I won't be going to prison, Alice. I have other plans that don't, I'm afraid, involve allowing a group of twelve sheep to decide where I spend my time.'

'You don't have any choice,' said Pope. 'You're accountable to the law, even if you don't accept it. That's the concept of the law. It doesn't require your consent.'

'In your eyes, I'm sure that's true, DCI Pope. But the way I look at it is different and that's the whole point.'

Lowrie moved a little closer. 'We were taught to make our own rules, DCI Pope. Taught that the only person who had a right to decide about you, was you. So, Evan and I agree that society shouldn't decide what happens to him. Prison is not the answer.'

Larsson smiled a little, but he clearly understood Lowrie was dangerous. Pope knew he wasn't naive enough to ignore what had happened to Cooper.

'Did you know that both my parents died while I was away?' Lowrie's voice was still calm, but now there was a steel edge.

Larsson's smile disappeared. 'No, I didn't know that, Alice. I'm very sorry to hear it. But you had moved on from them, hadn't you? They were not in your life anymore.'

Pope watched Lowrie carefully. She knew what his words, his callous indifference, would mean to Lowrie, how they would make her feel.

The woman nodded slowly.

Suddenly there was movement to her left and a sound. Brody groaning, moving his hand to his head. Larsson turned to look, his gun instinctively turning with him. It was the chance Lowrie needed. Pope saw her hand reach into the waistband of her jeans, and in one fluid movement, she withdrew a sleek silver blade and lunged straight for Larsson. Before he knew what had happened, Pope saw her own kitchen knife pierce through Larsson's skin and straight into his heart. It was a perfect aim and it went deep. Pope had no time to stop her. By the time she reached Lowrie, the woman was not resisting. She simply watched him as Pope jostled her back, her blank expression unchanging as Larsson gasped for breath, his face a mask of shock. He dropped the gun and clutched his hands to the wound, to his heart. He fell to his knees, tried to hold on to the table with one hand, but failed. He tumbled to the floor, a foot away from Brody. Pope held Lowrie. She didn't have time to go to his aid. Blood gurgled from the side of his mouth as he tried to inhale. Then, slowly, he stopped moving and the life left his eyes.

Pope took out her handcuffs and bound Alice Lowrie's hands together behind her back. Lowrie didn't resist. Pope pushed her down into the chair, her frustration getting the better of her.

'Alice, why did you do that? We would have dealt with him. He would have stood trial. Gone to prison.'

Lowrie's expression remained blank. 'What he did to me, to all of us, for so long.' She looked down at Larsson's body. 'He got what he deserved.'

Pope checked the body for a pulse, but it was too late. She took out her phone and checked on the location of the squad car, then ordered a priority ambulance.

Within minutes, officers arrived on the scene, followed by the hotel manager. Pope asked them to take Lowrie away. She asked the officer in charge to formally arrest her for the murders of Evan Larsson and Nicholas Cooper. She couldn't do it herself. Lowrie didn't even glance back as she was being led out of the room.

Brody was conscious now and Pope was trying to make him comfortable. 'An ambulance is on the way. We'll get your head sorted.'

He was trying to push himself up, but Pope stopped him, made him lie with his head on her jacket and a cushion from the chair underneath.

'No, don't get up. Stay still.'

'What happened?' He sounded groggy.

'It's over. Larsson's dead.'

'You?'

She shook her head. 'Lowrie.'

Brody closed his eyes, didn't reply.

As the paramedics were taking Brody out on a wheeled stretcher, Pope told them she would ride with them. She gave her car keys to one of the officers still there and told him to get her car back to the station after the coroner arrived.

As she was leaving, Pope took a final look at Larsson. He was no longer the charismatic, enigmatic cult leader. Stripped of that artifice, Evan Larsson looked like any other dead body Pope had seen. She left, walking quickly to catch the lift so she could travel down with Brody.

CHAPTER THIRTY

Pope stayed with Brody at the hospital until he was given the all-clear by his doctor. He was conscious when they arrived and made good progress through the rest of the afternoon. She had been by his bedside the whole time, except when the staff were doing their assessment and deciding how to proceed in treating his head wound. Then she had waited in the corridor. Pope thought back to the conversation in the car on the way to see the Watersons and wondered if Brody's new partner would be visiting. That seemed like a lifetime ago.

The train of thought took hold and she took out her phone to call Mick and Trish Waterson. But as soon as she had dialled the number, she cancelled the call and put the phone away. Tina's parents deserved a face-to-face conversation to tell them that she now knew who had killed their daughter eight years ago. Pope deserved it too. She resolved to do it today.

Back in Brody's room, she saw that he was sitting up, looking decidedly more alert than he had been on the way to the hospital. The doctors had explained to Pope that he had a concussion, but all the signs were positive. They would give him some IV medication and keep him in overnight for observation, but he should be allowed to go home the following morning. Pope was relieved. Brody needed to be OK.

'That was quite a whack you took in there,' she said.

His usual broad smile was somewhat tempered. 'Didn't really notice.'

'Sure. How are you feeling?'

'Not too bad. Hell of a headache.' He turned to the IV bag on the stand by his bed. 'But this should sort me out.'

'What have they given you?'

'Painkillers and something else that I can't remember.'

'Good that you're keeping on top of things.'

'I rely on you to keep on top of things. You're the boss, that's your job.'

'Right. Well, I got you out of there, didn't I?'

His tone changed. 'What happened in there? How did Larsson end up dead?'

'I knew Alice was after him, wanted some form of vengeance. But I didn't think she had a weapon. She was confronting him about the Collective and I concentrated on trying to divert her away from that. I told her that we'd get justice for her, but she wasn't interested.'

'Larsson had done his job too well.'

'Exactly. Moral relativism in practice.'

'So, she stabbed him?' asked Brody.

'Yes, straight through the heart. With my kitchen knife.'

'Oh. That was her idea of justice.'

'I think Cooper and Larsson had sexually abused those girls for years. Groomed, manipulated, controlled. Then something snapped in Lowrie. I don't know what. She dealt with Cooper and she was now determined to make Larsson pay.'

'And the amnesia?'

Pope shook her head. 'No. She faked it. She knew that I had investigated her disappearance all that time ago. All she had to do was buy some time and she thought I would join the dots and lead her directly to Larsson. Pretty clever. She probably didn't really need us, but we did the hard work for her.'

'Told you.'

'Very helpful, thanks.' This, at last, brought Brody's smile back. A small price to pay.

'Have you told the Watersons? Or the families of the other two girls?'

'Not yet. I'm going to see Alice, then I'm going to see them.'

'Alice? Why are you going to see her?' Brody seemed surprised.

'I need to see her. I need to make sure she knows what comes next and explain how it will work. She hasn't been living in society, she may have no idea of how the criminal justice system works.'

'You've still got a soft spot for her, haven't you?'

Pope took a moment to clarify her thoughts. What did she feel about Lowrie? 'I know she manipulated us. Me. But that's what she knows. Larsson and Cooper taught her that manipulation is how you get what you want. Living in that community, with those two men, it's the only thing she could do. I can't blame her for that. She took revenge, but she sees it as justice.'

'*Sudden Impact.*'

Pope looked confused. 'What?'

'The fourth *Dirty Harry* film. Eastwood discovers that Sondra Locke has been killing the men who raped her and her sister years ago. He decides that her form of justice is acceptable in the face of a weak system and lets her off.'

'Great. So now you're comparing me to Dirty Harry?'

'There are worse role models,' said Brody.

'Really? Name one.'

Brody looked about to launch into a defence of the ethics of the movie detective, but Pope gave him the look and he decided against it. He really was feeling better.

'I'll stop by later. See how you're doing.' She got up from the chair by Brody's bed.

'You don't need to. I'll be fine.'

'I know, but I will anyway. Make sure you're not irritating the nurses too much.'

'OK. You're the boss.'

'That's the second time you've mentioned that. Keep it in mind.'

'I will.'

She walked to the door.

'Bec.'

She stopped and looked round.

Brody turned serious. 'Thanks. For getting me out of there in one piece.'

'I need a better record with my partners than Dirty Harry.'

As she walked along the corridor she thought of Miller and immediately regretted the comment.

* * *

Alice Lowrie was in one of the cells at Charing Cross Police Station. She was on her own. Pope had insisted on that. As Pope walked down the stairs, she had a strange mix of emotions. Pity, relief, sorrow. And she was annoyed. Annoyed that Lowrie had conned her. The balance of those feelings seemed to change minute to minute. But as she entered the holding area and saw the young woman sitting in the corner of the cell, it was pity that won out.

The officer in charge let her into the cell and stood by the open door as Pope took two steps inside. There was still a fair amount of space between the two women. Lowrie looked up, but Pope couldn't work out her expression.

'Hello, Alice.'

'Hello.' The voice was soft, quiet.

'How are you being treated in here?'

'It's OK.'

'Have you had something to eat?'

'Yes.'

There was a moment of silence. Pope broke it. 'You shouldn't have done it, Alice. Out here, in fact even in there, in the Collective, you don't take things into your own hands.

You don't kill. Even Larsson's warped sense of morality must have taught you that.'

Pope was trying to understand. Trying to make Lowrie understand. But she knew it was unlikely to happen. For either of them.

'You don't know what he did to us.' The rage had gone.

'No, I don't. But nothing justifies murder, Alice.'

'In your opinion.'

'In everybody's opinion.'

'No, not everybody. Evan was right about that. Not in my opinion. They got what they deserved. That's the end of it.'

'But it's not the end of it, is it? Because now you have to face the consequences of what you did.'

Lowrie shrugged. She really didn't seem to care.

Pope moved to business mode. 'You'll be charged with the murders of Nicholas Cooper and Evan Larsson. There are mitigating circumstances and they will be presented to the court. They may or may not take them into account. Your job will be to explain exactly why you did what you did, and what those two men did to you and the other girls at the Collective. Do you understand what I'm saying?'

Lowrie nodded vaguely. She had lost interest. Pope knew she had nothing left. Her parents were dead and her life, such as it was, had evaporated. All she had left now was prison. Pope hurt for Alice Lowrie, but there was nothing else she could do.

'I'll be there at the trial, Alice. And I'll speak on your behalf.'

Lowrie made no acknowledgement of what she had said.

Pope sighed. 'I need to go. I'll see you again soon.'

Lowrie looked up, engaged. 'Did you find the other girls?'

'No, not yet.'

Lowrie smiled to herself. This had made her happy.

'Goodbye, Alice.'

Lowrie didn't respond. Pope left as the cell door was being locked. The scrape of metal on metal echoed and Pope winced at the harsh sound.

* * *

Pope had typed the address for Mick and Trish Waterson in her satnav. The next visit she had to make. As she drove in the late afternoon sunlight she thought about Alex and what they had been through. He was back in her life. For the moment. But as soon as he had returned, she had, once again, turned their lives upside down and put them in danger. She knew that Alice Lowrie had never been a danger to them, but Alex didn't know that. Nor did Chloe and Hannah. She could see that, from their perspective, her actions looked reckless and dangerous. If they were to work as a family, she had to repair the damage she had caused. She had been here before, but this time was different. She was going home now to make them see that. Pope didn't underestimate the task. But there were, at least, the beginnings of a breakthrough with Chloe and that needed to be nurtured.

Tomorrow she would be at Miller's funeral. It was going to be a fairly small affair, but quite a few of his colleagues would be there. Pope was dreading it. She would have to face Miller's parents, his family, his girlfriend, all of whom would no doubt hold her responsible in some way. But it was part of her job and she had to accept it.

Being with Alex, and with the girls, would make tomorrow easier. It would make everything easier. And then she would fight for Alice Lowrie, and continue that fight for every Alice Lowrie and every Tina Waterson. Pope knew that was her future.

THE END

ACKNOWLEDGEMENTS

I'd like to express my gratitude to my editor, Emma at Joffe Books, who keeps a close eye on all my work and offers fabulous ideas when I'm stuck. Also to the rest of the team at Joffe whose excellent attention to detail and professionalism is so appreciated. And to my agent, Bill at the Bill Goodall Agency, who gave me that crucial first opportunity. Neil Lawrence has been an excellent sounding board and writing buddy for years. Rob McInnes is a talented and supportive co-conspirator — one day Blue Skies will rise! Thanks to my advance readers, Jackie, Neil and Nik, for catching the plot holes and general all-round encouragement. Thanks to JJP and BSF for the unwavering support.

THE JOFFE BOOKS STORY

We began in 2014 when Jasper agreed to publish his mum's much-rejected romance novel and it became a bestseller.

Since then we've grown into the largest independent publisher in the UK. We're extremely proud to publish some of the very best writers in the world, including Joy Ellis, Faith Martin, Caro Ramsay, Helen Forrester, Simon Brett and Robert Goddard. Everyone at Joffe Books loves reading and we never forget that it all begins with the magic of an author telling a story.

We are proud to publish talented first-time authors, as well as established writers whose books we love introducing to a new generation of readers.

We won Trade Publisher of the Year at the Independent Publishing Awards in 2023. We have been shortlisted for Independent Publisher of the Year at the British Book Awards for the last four years, and were shortlisted for the Diversity and Inclusivity Award at the 2022 Independent Publishing Awards. In 2023 we were shortlisted for Publisher of the Year at the RNA Industry Awards.

We built this company with your help, and we love to hear from you, so please email us about absolutely anything bookish at feedback@joffebooks.com

If you want to receive free books every Friday and hear about all our new releases, join our mailing list: www.joffebooks.com/contact

And when you tell your friends about us, just remember: it's pronounced Joffe as in coffee or toffee!

Milton Keynes UK
Ingram Content Group UK Ltd.
UKHW010635290424
441924UK00005B/298